D1826440

MELODY OF MURDER

Books by Bv Lawson

Scott Drayco Series

Novels

Played to Death
Requiem for Innocence
Dies Irae
Elegy in Scarlet
The Suicide Sonata
Deadly Dance
Melody of Murder

Scott Drayco Short Story Collections

False Shadows
Hear No Evil

Adam Dutton & Beverly Laborde Series

Steal Away
Hide Away
Burn Away

Melody of Murder

A Scott Drayco Mystery

BV Lawson

Crimetime Press

Published in the United States of America.

For information, contact:

Crimetime Press
6312 Seven Corners Center, Box 257
Falls Church, VA 22044

Trade Paperback ISBN 978-1-951752-10-1
Hardcover ISBN 978-1-951752-11-8
eBook ISBN 978-1-951752-09-5

Harp of Wild and Dreamy Strain

Harp of wild and dreamy strain, when I touch thy strings,
Why sound out of long forgotten things?
Harp, in other, earlier days, I could sing to thee;
And not one of all my lays vexed my memory.

But now, if I awake a note that gave me joy before
Sounds of sorrow from thee float,
Changing evermore.

Yet, still steeped in memory's dyes, come sailing on,
Darkening my summer skies,
Shutting out my sun.

poem by Emily Brontë, music by Lothar Klein

1

Scott Drayco opened his eyes and saw nothing but pitch blackness. Why was it so dark? Why couldn't he move? What the hell was going on?

As his senses came back online, he became aware of a scratchy fabric over his eyes, a rough cord cutting into his wrists, and the roaring of an engine. He forced himself to focus, to take stock of the who, what, where, when, why, and how.

The good news was he was alive, and nothing seemed to be broken. But judging by the engine noise and jarring bumps, he must be in the trunk of a car.

He inched his body around the space as best he could since his hands and legs were bound. It was a pretty tight fit. Whose car was this, and how did he even get here?

He struggled to shake off the brain fog and nausea. After several minutes of pounding his bound fists against the side of the car in hopes the pain would shake him out of his haze, the evening came back to him in bits and pieces.

He was in Georgetown walking down the street to meet a new client for dinner at a restaurant. It was night, it was crowded, someone jostled him . . . and he felt a stinging in his hand. Couldn't be a wasp or bee in late November, could it?

He'd shrugged it off, and then he got a call on his cellphone telling him to go around the next block to meet his client. The "client" had advised him to take a shortcut—an alleyway—to avoid a large group of noisy street partiers.

He'd headed down the alleyway and made it as far as a couple of blocks. Then his legs turned to rubber, and he felt as if he were in a descending elevator plummeting to the ground. The next thing he knew, he was waking up in the trunk of this car.

Definitely not a bee sting, then. More like some kind of drug, maybe propofol?

The scratchy fabric was apparently a blindfold, and Drayco started working on it, rubbing his face against a piece of plastic sticking out from the side of the trunk. The cloth was pretty tight, but he got it to ride up a bit. It was enough to tell him it was still nighttime because no peeks of sunlight streamed through cracks in the trunk latch.

Good thing he had on his jacket since the forecast called for near-freezing temps. Even so, he could feel the cold seeping through his pant legs.

He struggled to get his bearings. Must be an older sedan, fairly large, judging from the roomier space not found in an economy car. As he moved, he could tell from the rough material that the floor had a carpeted surface, not plastic, reinforcing his hypothesis about the older-model car. But it should be modern enough to have a safety release. If he could operate it.

He took some deep breaths to quiet the rising tide of panic as his claustrophobia bubbled up despite his best efforts to shut it down. He'd had to deal with that not too long ago on another case, and he was getting sick and tired of being stuffed into confined spaces.

Breathe in, breathe out. Breathe in, breathe out. He focused on the icy sensation from the cold air and also the sounds around him—in case he got out of this ordeal and needed to retrace his route. It was largely quiet with no traffic noise, so he couldn't still be in Washington, D.C. Must be out in the country somewhere?

He worked on the rope around his wrists to see if he could free himself, but just then, the car began slowing down. Moments later, he heard the crunch of tires on gravel as the car pulled to a stop and the engine cut off.

The banging of car doors soon followed, and then the sound of footsteps. The trunk creaked open, and he was hauled out of the car and onto the ground, where someone cut the rope around his legs so he could walk.

He noticed his blindfold-removal efforts created a gap at the bottom, and he tilted his head up toward the sky—just in time to catch a glimpse of one man's face staring back at him. The man called out to one of his companions, and someone slipped a hood over Drayco's head.

Two men, one on either side of him, grabbed his arms and dragged him toward the building he'd also glimpsed briefly. He got the impression it was nothing out of the ordinary, a simple house-like structure with nondescript siding and plain windows.

As they made their way inside, Drayco heard a buzzing noise not too far away . . . and the faint ringing of bells in the distance. Not a siren or cowbells or church bells. This sounded more like a carillon. Very few of those around, so which one could it be? Were they even still in the Washington metro area? They could have been driving for hours, as far as he knew.

He didn't have time to ponder any of that as his captors guided him down a hallway, pushed him into a room, cut the rope around his wrists, and shut the door behind him. He also heard the distinct sound of a deadbolt lock as it engaged.

When he ripped off the hood and blindfold, he saw he was in a tiny, windowless room that was bare save for one twin bed, a desk, and a chair. The lamp on the desk cast light onto a small tray with a mug perched on it. Not exactly the Ritz, but at least there was heat coming from somewhere, so he wouldn't freeze to death. Still, his feet were cold, and he stomped them on the floor to boost his circulation.

He spied a tiny bathroom, but it had no door. He looked around for security cameras and didn't spot one straight away. If there were any, somebody would get a peep show out of it. He hoped that wasn't the motive behind all of this, but quite honestly, he hadn't a clue why he was here—wherever "here" was.

He patted his pockets. No cellphone, keys, or wallet. Of course.

The patches of mold and mildew on the otherwise bare white walls stood in silent testament to the fact the bleach he was smelling hadn't entirely done its job. But the bleach did cover up *most* of the dankness and smelly neglect of the room.

Studying his prison more closely, he noted the tray and mug weren't the only items on the desk. Out of curiosity, he walked over to take a better look. There was also a pile of papers, and the one on top had a list of instructions.

He read the words on the paper with growing disbelief. He was brought here to solve a puzzle, which was attached, and the rules were simple: solve the puzzle, ring the bell, and he'd be returned home safely and unharmed.

Bell? Surely they didn't mean the carillon he'd heard? He looked around for a bell and spied one hanging over the door with a pull rope. Hopefully, he'd be ringing that damned thing very soon. Then again, the "instructions" hadn't said what would happen if he *didn't* solve the puzzle.

He rubbed his eyes. Perhaps the puzzle itself would give him some of his answers, like who was behind this stunt and why. The brief glimpse of one unfamiliar man's face and the equally unfamiliar building hadn't helped at all.

He caught only fragments of whispered voices when they removed him from the car—along with the carillon bells—but one voice had a familiar color and tone. He just couldn't quite put his finger on it. But maybe it was a sedative hangover at work, and it would come to him later.

The question bugging him the most was that surely there were easier ways to get his help than kidnapping? Couldn't they have merely asked? Even a rogue intelligence group would have found another way.

He got a whiff of an aroma more pleasant than bleach and mildew wafting up from the dark liquid in the mug on the tray. Taking a chance, he dipped a finger into it and tasted it. Black coffee. A plastic spoon sat next to it . . . and a little packet of salt. Okay, now this was getting even weirder. What kidnapper in the world would know he liked salted coffee?

The desk had one drawer, which he pulled out, noting they'd "thoughtfully" given him a writing pad, pencils, pens, and erasers. He flipped over the instructions page and studied the next paper in the pile that he assumed must be the mysterious puzzle.

It comprised a bunch of letters, both English and French—with grave and acute accents and diereses—arranged in small groupings. The puzzle filled up an entire legal-sized page. At first glance, it seemed like a simple substitution cipher where one letter stood for another. But it couldn't be that easy, could it? Why in the world would they have needed his expertise, if so?

The instructions didn't say how long they would give him to solve this code. Hours? Days? Weeks? Did he have an expiration date?

With his adrenaline level still kicked into high gear, he knew he wouldn't get much sleep despite the sedative hangover. He might as well tackle the puzzle first. The sooner he solved it, the sooner he'd get out of here—unless they had no intention of "returning him home safely and unharmed," as the note said.

Still, it wasn't like he had a lot of options at the moment. With a sigh, he sat down in the chair and grabbed a pencil. Time to get to work.

2

Drayco awoke with his heart racing, and it took him a few moments to realize he wasn't in his own bed. Right. He'd been drugged, kidnapped, and dropped off in this smelly, clammy dump.

After working unsuccessfully on the puzzle for several hours, he'd tried to get a few hours of sleep, hoping it would help his thought processes. But the bed felt like it was stuffed with rocks—make that ice cubes—so he hadn't slept much.

At least, he didn't think he had. His internal chronometer was usually pretty good, and under ordinary circumstances he'd guess it was about five-thirty in the morning. But how could he be sure with no windows and no way to tell time?

He hoped the mattress didn't have bedbugs, although he'd checked for signs before lying down, prepared to sleep on the cold tile floor if he had to. He could always use his coat as a blanket.

It was a dreamless sleep, a pity. If he were luckier, his subconscious would have worked overtime while he slept to solve the puzzle, and he'd be done with it. But instead, he had more of his paralyzing hypnopompic nightmares on waking—this time, being trapped in dark, brackish water and running out of oxygen. *Wonder why you'd had that one?* His recent near-drowning case loomed in his memory.

With a sigh, he swung his sock-clad feet onto the hard concrete floor, trying to ignore the pervasive bleach-mildew stench in the room. It was showtime again. That puzzle wouldn't solve itself.

He rubbed a hand through his hair in lieu of a comb. Then he hopped up to splash some water from the toilet tank on his face, since the faucet in the sink didn't work. He found he was wistfully hoping for more salted coffee when he noticed someone had placed a new tray just inside the door during his slumber.

Lukewarm coffee, cold bagel. Better than nothing.

He sat down on the bed to "enjoy" his breakfast, hoping it would be a welcome distraction from the tiny room. The dank space wasn't helping the leftover claustrophobia from the car trunk.

One thing Drayco hadn't heard again were the carillon bells. Either he was in an interior room, which made sense because of the lack of windows, or he'd imagined the bells during his half-drugged state while being dragged out of the car.

Coffee in hand, he picked up the notepad, where he'd sketched out different ways of solving the puzzle, and sat down again at the little desk. The puzzle had to be a substitution cipher, but what about the French characters mixed in with the English letters? Not very characteristic of a typical cipher.

Okay, that skewed the whole basic cipher idea, but surely it couldn't be all that hard. He'd worked on far more complicated codes than this without any problem solving them. But he hadn't been abducted, cold, hungry, thirsty, and sleep-deprived, had he?

After what felt like several hours of fruitless labor, he got up and paced in his little cell. The room was so tiny, he could barely get three strides in one direction. Even if he weren't six-four, he doubted he could have paced more than four steps at a time. But the pacing did nothing for his problem-solving.

If only he had his Steinway, he could pound out some Bach fugues and have this thing solved in a half hour. Bach's counterpoint never failed to spark his imagination. It had served him well during his ill-fated piano career, then his thorniest cases at the FBI, and later in his private practice. It was a miracle of the universe.

Frustrated and angry, he flopped onto the bed and looked up at the ceiling, playing through some Bach in his head, hoping it would suffice. Sure enough, after a few passages from the D major fugue, he had a brainstorm.

This time, he knew he was on the right track, and it *was* a "simple" cipher, except the extra French letters were crucial to fill in the key. He'd already tried several combinations and thought he was close. But with this new idea, he figured out what appeared to be a solution.

Or was it? With dismay, he looked at his handiwork. The results were a string of words for numbers, like "three," "nine," and "two," followed by two Latin words, *caelesti* and *amplexus*, and then another group of numbers starting with "six," "five," and "nine."

He leaned back in the chair, staring at those words and feeling irked at both the situation and himself. He was certain he'd solved the cipher, that it must be the only correct solution, yet he didn't know what in the world the results could mean.

Was this the complete answer to the coded cipher? Or was there something more, some other critical aspect he was overlooking? More importantly, would it placate his captors enough for them to release him?

His stomach made rumbling noises. He was suddenly ravenous. His kidnappers had kept him juiced up on caffeine, but hadn't left him much in the way of food other than the one bagel. So he decided to go ahead and ring the bell. What did he have to lose at this point?

Moments later, he heard steps outside the door, followed by the sound of the deadbolt being clicked open. A man walked in, wearing a hood and mask and not saying anything as he carried in a tray with an opened bottle of soda and a sandwich. Even though Drayco couldn't see the man's face like he had with the guy outside last night, he was pretty sure this was a different captor, because this fellow was taller and heavier.

Drayco said, "I think I solved it, at least part of it. But you're going to have to help me interpret the results." He walked over to the table and picked up the paper he'd been working on, which he waved in the air.

The man didn't reply and put the tray on the floor before turning around to leave. Before he shut the door, Drayco heard music playing in the background. Not carillon bells this time, but a big band arrangement of "Twinkle, Twinkle, Little Star," a version he'd never encountered before. Were they holding a dance party out there?

The silent jailer closed the door. Once again, the lock clicked into place.

That went well. So much for the solve-the-puzzle-and-be-released promise. Or maybe the masked delivery boy was just a lower-level flunky who was reporting the news back to his master.

Drayco examined the newly arrived tray of food. It was one of his favorite types of sandwiches, pastrami on rye. Another coincidence, like the salted coffee? And what about the opened soda—poisoned? Drugged? He could go for days without eating. But he was so thirsty, he wasn't sure he could avoid drinking the soda. He wasn't quite ready to guzzle water from the toilet tank without being able to boil it first.

Well, the coffee wasn't drugged, right? He took a chance and sipped some of the drink, which was thankfully not lukewarm. But after only a few minutes, he had second thoughts and said aloud to the empty room, "Maybe this wasn't such a good idea," as he started to get drowsy again. His vision faded around the edges until everything winked out.

3

Once again, Drayco found himself waking up inside a car. This time, bright sunlight streamed through the windows, and he was alone and buckled into the passenger seat. Not only that, but the car looked familiar—a late model Mercedes sedan with a wood-and-leather steering wheel and beige leather upholstery. And a DVD player above the center console.

Where was he now? Not back in Georgetown, nor at his townhome. He heard a tapping on the window, so he tried the door handle and found it unlocked.

As he inched the door open, he stared at the man standing next to the car. "What are you doing here, Dad?"

Looking around at what appeared to be a vacant lot with overgrown weeds and cracks in the concrete, he added, "And where is here, anyway?"

Brock Drayco looked both worried and relieved at the same time. "Someone stole my car last night. Then today, I got a call letting me know where I could find my stolen car but to come alone. To be honest, I was much more worried about you than the car. I've been trying to get in touch with you for two days."

"Seems like a lot longer."

"Where the hell have you been, son?"

"Wish I knew. I was drugged, kidnapped, and taken to a small room somewhere. I have no idea where or how far because I was unconscious during the drive, both to and from."

"But whatever for? Don't get me wrong, I'm thrilled to have you back safe and sound. But why kidnap you just to release you with no ransom?"

"You're not going to believe it." Drayco swung his legs around to the ground to stretch out a few kinks.

"Try me."

"I was tasked with solving a puzzle."

Brock frowned. "A puzzle? Are you kidding me?" He scanned his son's face. "Okay, you're serious. So what kind of puzzle?"

"A substitution cipher. English and French characters that spell out words for numbers and one Latin phrase."

Brock raised an eyebrow. "It's not that I don't believe you, but that's bizarre, even for you."

Drayco muttered. "Tell me about it."

Brock studied his son more closely and said, "I want you to go to the hospital and get checked out. Just to err on the side of caution. Some of those knockout drugs can be pretty potent. Lots of side effects."

"I'd rather not if it's all the same to you. Besides, I'm fine. Other than being hungry. And thirsty." He'd only had a few sips of that drugged soda.

"If you won't let me take you to the hospital, I'll call my personal physician. Maybe he can squeeze you in with an emergency appointment. If he's still there at this time of day."

That's when Drayco noticed the sun angle. "What time is it?"

"Close to three."

Drayco groaned. "Then I've been gone for two full days. I don't have time for this. What if a client tried to get in touch with me?"

Then he remembered the cellphone, keys, and wallet his captors had taken from him. He patted his pockets. They'd been returned. Not that he was going to touch them without getting them fingerprinted first.

Brock whipped out his own cellphone, and Drayco could tell his father had convinced the doc to see him. Brock slid into the driver's seat, saying, "Good thing I had a taxi drop me off." He pulled out his car keys and cranked up the engine.

When they arrived at the physician's office, it was the end of the workday for them, and Drayco and Brock were the only two people left in the waiting room. As he continued to give his son anxious glances from time to time, Brock said, "I assume you recall the answer to that puzzle you solved."

"Naturally."

"Then they must not have known you have a photographic memory."

"I wouldn't be so sure. My kidnappers knew *some* things about me. They had a cup of black coffee and some salt waiting. And my favorite sandwich."

Brock's eyes widened. "Did you see any of them? Or hear any of them? Or observe anything that would offer a clue to their identities?"

Drayco leaned forward in his chair. "I caught a glimpse of one man, but I didn't recognize him. And I have a vague recollection of one specific voice being familiar, but the man was whispering. I was still under the influence of whatever zombie drugs they gave me."

Drayco spied some scratch paper on one table at the end of the room and grabbed it. Brock pulled a pen out of his pocket that he handed over, and Drayco scribbled down the puzzle, starting with the complete cipher and then his solution.

Brock studied it. "I should never doubt your code-solving skills by now. But I'm pretty amazed you figured this out. What do those numbers and that Latin phrase stand for?"

"That part is hazy. I don't know if what I came up with makes sense to them or not. They didn't say, and I didn't have a chance to ask."

"But why kidnap you for this? They could have simply hired you. Or any other code expert." Brock pounded his fist against his leg in frustration. "Whoever could be behind this insanity?"

"I thought about a rogue intelligence group. Or a freelancing spy. But who knows?"

Brock glanced at the paper again and grumbled. "This would even be too low for your shady uncle, Alistair. I hope whoever it was appreciated your efforts."

Drayco sighed. "That's what's bothering me. I solved the puzzle, and yet I didn't. Unless I'm way off on all of this. It's making me doubt myself."

"*You*? Way off? I don't think so. But you'll figure it all out. Give it a little time after you've had more rest."

A nurse popped her head out and said, "Scott Drayco?" And Drayco headed toward the examination rooms, trailed by his father. After some poking, prodding, and blood drawn for lab work, Dr. McDonnell told Drayco he seemed to be fine and to go home and get some sleep.

Brock drove Drayco to his townhome, following him inside. He kept hanging around so closely that Drayco was getting annoyed. "Dad, I'm fine. You heard the doc. I just need rest. As in, put your feet up and watch TV."

"So do it, already."

Brock waited for Drayco to get settled onto the couch, and then he disappeared into the kitchen for a few minutes. When he reappeared with a bottle of Manhattan Special soda, he handed it over and added, "I called Thai Tanic for some Panang curry and spring rolls. Should be here in fifteen."

"Thanks." Brock had remembered that the restaurant was one of his favorites? That was a surprise.

Brock continued to hover nearby. "One thing's for sure. Whoever's behind this kidnapping scheme planned it well. They kidnapped you with no witnesses. As you know, I have pretty good security measures at my house. Yet they stole my car without triggering cameras or alarms."

"They didn't seem like amateurs to me, either."

"For whatever reason, they treated you with kid gloves. By all known kidnapping standards I'm familiar with."

Brock went to the kitchen to grab another soda for himself and sank down onto a chair next to his son. "I must say your safe return is my best birthday present ever."

Drayco groaned. "Oh no. I forgot it was today. God, I'm so sorry."

Brock grinned. "I think you were otherwise occupied."

"I did get you a present. It's around here somewhere." Drayco was still foggy-brained from the lack of sleep, but he got halfway up to go in search of the gift before Brock reached over and pushed him back down.

"As I said, having you returned safely is the only present I need."

"If you can take a rain check, we'll have a belated celebration later." Drayco noticed the bag of crunchies on the counter in the kitchen and suddenly remembered Cat, the half-feral silver tabby who hung around his townhome.

Brock followed his gaze and said, "Don't worry. I gave her fresh food and water while you were away. She even came inside for a few minutes. Does she do that a lot now?"

"From time to time. Like that spider incident a few months ago."

"Right, right. I remember. The hero kitty saving little Scotty from a spidey."

Drayco winced at the "Scotty" reference, since that's what his mother called him, one of the few people who got away with it. But he was both surprised and grateful his father thought to look out for Cat while he was "away."

He almost laughed at that. Sounded like he'd just gone off for a mini-vacation. Come to think of it, some ocean views and a little sea breeze sounded damned good right about then.

Brock took a few more swigs of his soda. "I know what you're thinking. You're gonna want to pursue this and track down those kidnappers. This time, leave it to the police. They're perfectly capable of handling something like this."

"Would you leave it alone if the shoe was on the other foot?"

Brock nodded. "Doubly so, if I already had a full caseload. Solo vigilante justice rarely pays well."

"Thanks for the reminder."

Drayco's tone must have reflected his sudden irritation because Brock soft-pedaled a bit. "I'm only thinking about your career, son. That wasn't a dig."

Maybe not, but Brock knew as well as Drayco that living and maintaining an office in the District wasn't cheap. And that Drayco's budget was often stretched to the limit. Plus, there was Drayco's "gift" Opera House on the Eastern Shore with all its expensive renovations. Something Drayco didn't have the energy to think about right then.

He hated to just let this kidnapping thing go. But his father was right—when you're your own client, all you get is a massive headache and an empty bank account for your trouble.

4

Brock had stayed late into the evening, smothering Drayco with uncharacteristic concern. Truth be told, Drayco had wanted to be alone to decompress for a while. But it was his father's birthday.

After Brock left, Drayco felt whatever remaining energy he had drain from him. He hadn't even bothered showering, although he really needed one, and just stripped and fell into bed.

Maybe that's why he'd slept late this morning, something he didn't like to do. He toyed with the idea of taking his usual jog along the Tidal Basin, but opted instead to sit down at the piano before eating anything. He felt out of sorts and wasn't sure why.

Nonetheless, he was happy to be reunited with his beloved Steinway. In a sense, the instrument was one of his oldest friends. Not that he'd upgrade anytime soon. From a synesthesia point of view, it was the right tone that made all the difference. Hearing the wrong instrument felt like eating raw fish, which was a sensation hard to describe. But his Steinway, with its pearls of cobalt silkiness, was just right.

Good tone, bad tone aside, his thoughts were a jumble. As in his little "prison," maybe some Bach would bring his mind into focus—but what to play? He still had the carillon bells in mind. The opening movement of the eighth Chorale Cantata used a continuo to create a sound like tolling bells, didn't it?

First things first. The rough handling by his captors hadn't helped his gimpy right arm any, and he had to soak it for a good ten minutes in hot water before the muscles stopped cramping. With any luck, the kidnappers' ropes didn't erase any benefits from his recent therapy. Not that his card shuffling and tennis ball-squeezing were helping all that much.

He sat down at the keyboard to create an impromptu transcription of the Bach chorale. But before long, he'd morphed into a riff on "Twinkle, Twinkle, Little Star," the song he overheard during his captivity.

After a few minutes of that, he stopped and sighed. Since he couldn't get that damned nursery tune and those carillon bells out of his head, he might as well do something about it.

He hopped up to conduct some online research about nearby carillons, tapping on the keyboard with his left hand while squeezing a tennis ball with his right hand. One by one, he called up various videos to see if they matched the synesthesia "signature" of the carillon bells from his kidnapping.

The Washington Cathedral bells didn't. Nor did the Taft Memorial Carillon or the bells at the Netherlands Carillon near the Iwo Jima memorial. That last one would have been a bold choice since it was near the Pentagon. After not having much success with the videos of the carillons in the area, he decided he'd cast his net wider to other parts of Virginia, Maryland, and maybe Pennsylvania.

But later, not now. First, he had to take care of his stomach, which was rumbling so loudly that it threatened to overwhelm the piano. He went to the back door to check on Cat and make sure she had crunchies and water and then grabbed the small box of leftover Thai Tanic for himself and made some coffee.

To his surprise, the act of putting his usual salt in the coffee made him lose his appetite. It reminded him of the smells of his moldy-bleachy prison. The Thai food's pungent lemongrass, lime, and sweet basil should have helped, but his stomach wasn't in the mood for that, either.

He tossed the rest in the trash and rummaged through his cupboard, grabbing a box of microwavable bachelor chow and a few items from the refrigerator. It wasn't much, but it would have to do.

And what better activity to go with breakfast than obituaries? Not that he was in a morbid frame of mind. But he'd developed a habit of reading the obits years ago as part of his study of human behavior. Sometimes, he even knew these people from former cases.

He scrolled through the listings in the *Washington Post* and spied the usual Congress critters, professors, business leaders, and diplomats. But one face that popped up made him spill some of his coffee right onto the floor. The photo was of a heavy-set man with thinning blond hair and a small V-shaped scar on his chin.

The glimpse of the one kidnapper's face Drayco saw underneath his blindfold two nights ago was enough to burn that image into his memory. So much so, he was convinced the man staring back at him from the newspaper was the same guy.

But for him to die not long after Drayco saw the man's face? Could that be a mere coincidence? Drayco scanned the text to learn more about the man, Graham Tibbs, and the circumstances of his death. It got even weirder from there. Tibbs had allegedly perished in a fire—five years ago.

The obituary had a footnote that the police were investigating. Since the cause of Tibbs's "latest" death was a hit-and-run in Arlington, Drayco called up the phone number of a beat cop he knew on the APD force, Sergeant Gus Lorenzo. Drayco was in luck—the man had pulled a weekend shift.

"Drayco, you old dog. What is it this time? A missing heiress? Somebody's private Rembrandt was stolen?"

Drayco knew Gus was only half-kidding with his jibes about wealthy clients, and he let it pass. "This isn't a case. It involves a kidnapping."

"If not your case, then whose?"

"Nobody's right now. I was the one kidnapped. And yes, I'm going to file a report, but it was in the District. So you can breathe easier."

Sergeant Lorenzo whistled. "Seriously? So why are you calling me, then? Not that I don't love the sound of your dulcet tones."

"There was a fellow potentially involved in the kidnapping who was killed by a hit-and-run two nights ago. Name of Graham Tibbs."

Drayco could hear the other man gritting his teeth over the phone. "Ah, that guy. What a mess. Was allegedly burned in a fire and buried. But his prints match an old rap sheet in the database. He also had a sister who lives nearby, and we had her in for a positive ID."

"What did the sister have to say?"

"Nothing. Other than she was in shock. Who wouldn't be?"

"That's the woman listed in the obituary, Aria D'Angelo?"

"That's her. A former singer. Opera, I think. But that's more your line, right? Beethoven and Mozart and all that."

"An opera singer named Aria? I'm guessing it's not her birth name."

"Probably, but you'd know more about that highfalutin music stuff than me. We checked her out. Had to retire due to health issues. Lives up in Montgomery County." Lorenzo paused and then added, "You say this Tibbs guy kidnapped you?"

"Pretty certain."

"Huh. Kinda coincidental he dies right afterward, seeing as how it was a hit-and-run."

"Maybe. Or bad karma."

"Yeah." Lorenzo laughed. "Look, maybe you should have a chat with one of the detectives. You know, if your kidnapping and our hit-and-run case are related." Lorenzo had a mocking tone in his voice. "Halabi loves shooting the breeze with you."

Drayco winced at Halabi's name. "Love" wasn't the term Drayco would use to describe his past relationship with the detective. He replied, "I'll do that. Maybe I'll drop off some doogh for you while I'm at it. You still like that nasty Persian yogurt drink, right?"

"If they could find a way to shoot it directly into your veins, I'd be first in line."

"Your boss know you're an addict?"

"You kidding? He's the one who got me hooked."

Drayco hung up and made a note to buy some doogh the next time he was at Shishkabob Express. After grabbing another cup of coffee, he conducted more research, first on Graham Tibbs. He didn't find a lot of details, not even a social media presence, but Sergeant

Lorenzo was right—Tibbs had a rap sheet from years ago when he was much younger.

He also looked up Aria D'Angelo. Like Sergeant Lorenzo said, she was a top-notch opera singer before she retired. Interesting enough. But it seemed unusual to have an opera singer, even a retired one, with a brother who turns out to be a kidnapper who had a rap sheet. But they always say you can't pick your family.

Graham Tibbs. Mystery man. Dead man-turned-kidnapper-turned-dead man. Why would such a guy be involved in kidnapping Drayco to solve a puzzle? And if that wasn't strange enough, who among Drayco's kidnappers knew him well enough to have salted coffee waiting for him? It certainly wasn't Tibbs.

Someone hearing that bizarre story for the first time could be forgiven for thinking Drayco dreamed it all up. Part of Drayco wished he had, and he half-suspected Brock thought so. At any rate, a face-to-face with Detective Halabi was usually something to be wary of, but this time, Drayco felt like celebrating. It was a tangible step he could take, which was a hell of a lot better than stewing in a pot of his own growing anger and irritation.

5

Drayco's stomach grumbling eventually won out over any nausea, but his cupboards were bare even before his kidnapping. Sadly, the magic grocery fairy hadn't stopped at his townhome since. He made a quick trip to the corner market he'd dubbed "Bodega Light" and grabbed a few items. It wouldn't do to be without coffee, salt, or Manhattan Special sodas.

He'd just got home and unloaded his purchases when the doorbell rang. What now? Drayco opened the door as Mark "Sarg" Sargosian waltzed in, carrying a couple of bags he immediately hauled to the kitchen.

Drayco followed him out of curiosity. "Not that I'm unhappy to see you, but to what do I owe the company of your illustrious personage?"

"You know, most people say things like 'well, hello, there' or 'thanks for dropping by.' Did you have a sarcasm sandwich recently? Anyway, thought you might like some good grub after your kidnapping ordeal."

Drayco frowned. "How did you find out about that?"

"Your father. When you went missing, he called me to see if I'd heard anything."

"And did also he call you to tell you about my return?"

"Naturally."

Drayco shook his head. "He didn't say a word about that to me. But I guess that's what I would have done in his place."

He pointed to Sarg's vest, which had a funky pattern resembling multicolored paint splatters. "Elaine get that for you? It doesn't look like it came from your usual once-every-five-years Macy's run."

"It was on sale. Elaine tells me to dress more cosmopolitan, so I bought this. She wasn't amused."

Drayco grinned. "I'm surprised you're still alive." His former FBI partner's wife was a force to be reckoned with.

"She keeps me around for my cooking." Sarg looked over at a bowl on the counter, left over from Drayco's cobbled-together breakfast attempt earlier. "Gaaah. What the hell is that? Looks like something you caught in your backyard. In a trap."

"I'll have you know boxed macaroni and cheese with ketchup is a sacred family tradition."

"In whose family?"

"Somebody's. I would imagine."

Sarg hoisted the bags onto the counter and pulled out some containers as Drayco went over to take a sniff. "What'd you bring?"

"Real food. Via Maison Sargosian. Beef short rib Bourguignon with creamy polenta and warm Brussels sprout salad. And a little Belgian dark chocolate mousse for dessert."

"Not standard breakfast fare."

"Breakfast? Have you looked at the time, junior?"

Drayco checked his piano-shaped wall clock. It was half-past noon. "Guess I slept longer than I thought. I hadn't noticed how late it was." Which was true, not even during his trip to and from the store. His powers of observation were still on the fritz.

As the full aroma of Sarg's cooking hit Drayco's nostrils, he relaxed. "Guess your culinary skills are why I haven't killed you yet, either."

Drayco scrutinized his dining table, piled high with papers, books, folders, and assorted junk. Then he looked over at Sarg. "Um . . . sorry?"

"You haven't changed much, have you?" Sarg banged around in the kitchen closet until he found a couple of TV trays, and they were soon feasting on Sarg's home-cooked gourmet meal.

After wolfing his portion down in record time, Drayco folded his arms across his chest. "Dad's being a mother hen. You're not going to smother me, too, are you?"

"Who, me? It was just a little kidnapping. You've had worse."

Drayco put his feet up on his ottoman. "Leave it to you to make me feel better."

"Didn't think you'd need it."

"It's not the actual kidnapping per se. Okay, so I've been on edge a bit, but not because of any danger I was in. I'm used to that."

"Then what?"

"It's more of an unsettled feeling I can't shake."

"About what?"

"I think it's that damned puzzle I was asked to solve. Make that *forced* to solve."

"Ah, yes. The puzzle. Your dad hinted at that. I'm still having problems visualizing it."

Drayco grabbed a piece of paper lying on the side table and gave it to him. It was the copy of the puzzle and solution he'd made for Brock in the doctor's waiting room.

Sarg studied it for a few minutes. "So, it's a substitution cipher. But in English and French? And what do these numbers mean? Why are they written out like that?"

"That's the problem. I don't know. Yet."

"Okay, what about the *caelisti amplexus* part? Sounds like Latin."

"*Caelisti* means sky or the celestial, and *amplexus* means embrace."

Sarg frowned. "Sky hug? That doesn't make any sense."

"You're telling me. But that's not the weirdest part."

"You mean the part about that guy who allegedly died five years ago and comes back from the dead just in time to kidnap you and get killed? Or killed again, I suppose."

That's one of the many things Drayco appreciated about his former partner. The man wasn't at all dubious about Drayco's story, something he wasn't sure he could say of the Metropolitan PD in the District.

They hadn't hung up on him when he called to file a preliminary police report after his chat with Sergeant Lorenzo. But he wouldn't be surprised if at least one or two of them thought he'd staged the whole thing since he was found in his father's car at the end of the ordeal. A birthday prank.

Sarg shot him a knowing look. "You're going to try to tackle this, yourself, aren't you?"

"If for no other reason than to prove I didn't make all this up. I also don't take kindly to being drugged and kidnapped."

"Okay, then. All we have to do is figure out why an alleged dead man was in on your kidnapping. And why he suddenly turned up dead afterward. Since you got a good look at him, maybe his colleagues figured he was a liability?"

"*We* have to figure out?"

"I've got a light caseload. This is too much fun for you not to share."

Drayco got up long enough to grab another paper, this time off the piles on top of the table. He handed it over.

"What's this?"

"A rap sheet for our dead man, Graham Tibbs. A little birdie faxed them to me."

Sarg scanned the list. "These were all pretty long ago. Nothing recent."

"Nope. But it proves he wasn't a saint. Sometimes skeletons like to saunter out of the closet at the worst possible time."

"Arson of personal property, burglary, shoplifting. Mostly petty crimes. Don't see kidnapping or forced-puzzle-solving."

"I doubt he was the mastermind. Probably a hired goon."

"Do you have any idea where you were taken? We could get some clues there."

"I only awoke right as we reached our destination. But I did hear carillon bells in the distance."

"Carillon bells? Can't be too many of those around."

"Not really. But the grainy, orange-and-blue squished ovals of the bells I heard don't match the sound of the National Cathedral or Iwo Jima. I've checked some online videos for others, but no joy."

"And you didn't notice anything else unusual that could help?"

"One of the kidnappers likes big band music, judging from an arrangement of 'Twinkle, Twinkle Little Star' I heard playing in the background. I looked it up. It seems to have been recorded by a group called Bob Bordelon's Bayou Band. Hard to find recordings of it nowadays. Some old LPs you can get on eBay."

"And the room you were held in?"

"Any identifying features were removed long ago. The place was pretty rundown. If anyone's currently living there, they aren't Rockefellers."

Sarg tugged on his earlobe. "That's not a lot to go on."

"That's why we have to start with the dead man. Oh, and there was one other odd thing—someone knew I like salted coffee."

Sarg sat up. "That's good, though. Means it has to be someone from your past. A former client, a former foe. That could help narrow it down."

"Possibly. As I told Brock, I also heard a whispered voice that may be familiar, but I was still mostly out of it at the time."

Sarg said, "I thought you were calling him 'Dad' now."

Drayco winced. "Old habits. I'm working on it. Four decades of any habit aren't easy to break."

"You called him Brock when you were a little pup?"

"No, but it's not like I saw him all that often to call him anything."

"Ouch. But yeah, I get it." Sarg paused and added, "I got a call from deputy-turned-law-student, Nelia Tyler."

"What? Why? A case? Research?"

"She was worried about you. She'd heard of the kidnapping via your friend, Benny Baskin esquire. Wanted to make sure you were okay."

Nelia's concern was kinda nice, but Drayco also felt a little angry she hadn't called him herself. He had a pretty good idea why, but it still rankled.

It would be healthier for his blood pressure if he changed the subject. "I think I'll start by interviewing the dead man's sister, Aria D'Angelo, a retired opera singer."

"Opera, oh joy. Your favorite."

"I realized this morning that I'd heard of her. She's retired, now. That is, from singing—she does charity work and is in the society papers all the time. I hope she'll agree to see me."

"Sounds like a good jumping-off point. Speaking of music, how's the recital prep going at the University of Maryland?"

Drayco groaned. "I'm wishing my uncle hadn't set up the damned music scholarship in my name, if that tells you anything. Especially one that didn't involve a performance."

"That well, huh?"

"Most of those university kids know nothing about me. Not my history, not the carjacking injury, zilch. My short-lived career ended seventeen years ago. Hell, that was before some of those college kids were even born."

"Still, I think you got this. Injury or no injury. I can understand why your Uncle Alistair isn't your favorite person right now."

"On the Alistair part, I agree. But I'm not so sure about the 'I've got this' part."

Drayco flexed his fingers and rubbed his arm, which was throbbing. "It's not like I can go out and play the Prokofiev sixth. It's all likely a colossal waste of time and energy, so I should just tell them 'no thanks' and be done with it."

Sarg stared at him for several moments. "I've never known you to back off from a challenge."

"There's a first time for everything."

Sarg got up, patted him on the shoulder, and headed toward the kitchen. After some banging of cabinet doors and the crinkling sound of a container being opened, he returned with two servings of his dark chocolate mousse. "Have some chocolate, sugar, rum, and mascarpone. Good for what ails you."

The dark chocolate was slightly bitter, but bitter makes better, as his father used to say. Drayco was grateful for Sarg's cooking and sympathetic ear and maybe even for Brock's concern. But he was a little freaked out by the "new" softer Brock and not a little irritated that everyone thought he was so fragile.

As he took his time with the mousse, he glanced around his townhome. Maybe it was time to rearrange some things. Wasn't that what normal people did, rearrange furniture whenever they got the blues?

And why not? It was a hell of a lot easier than rearranging your attitude or outlook on life, wasn't it? Or maybe what most people needed to be happy was to clear out the cobwebbed expectations they'd accumulated along with their clothes that no longer fit.

That, and to eat more chocolate mousse.

6

It surprised Drayco when Aria D'Angelo agreed to see him. But he followed her directions to her home, which had a long driveway cut off by a gate from the street. Upon closer inspection, the iron gate had a pattern of musical staff lines with clefs and notes. He input the code she'd given him over the phone, and the gates swung open.

The house itself, a slate-roofed colonial with tall columns, looked big enough to be a small hotel. With the opulence of the place, he expected an assistant to open the door when he rang the doorbell. But from the photos he'd studied on the internet, the woman with the heart-shaped face and amber-brown eyes who greeted him was the retired opera singer.

He got a better look at her when she led him into the main living room that was almost as big as his entire townhome. Those famously rare amber eyes of hers were red-rimmed and watery, and she was sniffling.

D'Angelo parked him on a pink brocade divan across from her. "I still can't believe this. Any of it. My brother wasn't dead all this time—and the first I learn about it is when he became dead for the second time."

When he saw a box of tissues on a far table, he got up long enough to grab the box and handed it over to her. She thanked him, and he waited for her to compose herself.

She put a hand to her throat. "Part of me is half-expecting him to return in another few years. I don't understand what this all means. It's like something out of a preposterous opera plot."

As befitting an opera singer, her speaking voice had rounder tones, like dancing reddish sparks with yellow highlights to Drayco's synesthesia brain. He asked, "When was the last time you saw your brother?"

"About ten years ago, I think. We had drifted apart. Graham was my baby brother, younger by fifteen years. I felt more like a mother to him, but that was a mistake. I was far too overbearing."

"The police said they've talked with you."

"They called me after they tracked down 'the victim' from his fingerprints and an old mug shot. He was arrested years ago for dealing a small amount of drugs, I think. I had to ID Graham's body. It was not . . . easy."

"I understand."

"The police seem to be as baffled by this mystery as I am."

"They're investigating, and I'm sure they'll do their best."

She stared out the window for a moment. "After the fire, there wasn't much recognizable left to identify. Not that it mattered since it wasn't really Graham. This time . . . " She wiped her eyes. "I had to see him. The police wanted me to, but I *had* to. To make sure."

"They'll do an autopsy if they haven't already."

"I don't know why, since they say it was clearly a hit-and-run. Besides, I got the impression they're not interested in drawing things out. I think the mystery behind it all intrigues them. But it's not like they don't have any other new cases to worry about, is it?"

"An autopsy is standard procedure."

She deflated a little against the upward curve of the divan. "I understand. It's just . . . I'm incredibly saddened by the whole thing. The senselessness of it all."

He nodded. "Tragedy rarely makes sense. From any angle."

She uttered a harsh laugh. "When the police first told me what happened, I realized I'd been out enjoying myself with a friend at my favorite bistro. My brother was dying while I was eating lobster bisque."

"I'm curious how the newspaper got the obituary so soon?"

"That's no mystery. I recycled the old one since nothing had changed. Well, as far as I know. Except to add the bit about him supposedly dying five years ago. Really, how do you prepare for such an obituary? I felt I needed to do something. But I suppose it wasn't necessary?"

She looked at him as if for approval or an opinion, so he reassured her, "I'm sure it's fine. The notice didn't mention a funeral."

"The body will be cremated." She again put a hand to her throat as she added, "A fiery end, after all. But no funeral or memorial. Perhaps we'll sprinkle his ashes on what is allegedly his real grave. There's already a tombstone."

"Did the police mention an exhumation of the body in the grave?"

"No, but that's up to them. I'm fine with whatever they need to do."

"Were there any suspicions five years ago about his death? From anyone?"

"Not really. I mean, since everyone thought he died in a fire at his old place of business. The police only had one tooth to work with—for dental records—with the skeleton they found. But Graham's former business owner, Leon Sable, was confident Graham was in the building at the time of the fire. Apparently, Graham said he'd be working late. Who else could it have been?"

Drayco managed to get a copy of Graham Tibbs's police report thanks to his "little birdie," so he'd learned about the tooth. "That tooth was an unusual one, with a platinum filling and a gold crown. Was Graham allergic to nickel?"

"Yes, he was."

"But he also had a partial plate?"

"Why yes, he did. At least, that's what the police told me. And I think it was Sable who told them. Graham . . . he didn't always open up to me. I'm sorry to say I knew little about his recent health."

Drayco was disappointed by that. It was rare for only one tooth to be found. So where were the rest of his teeth and the partial plate? It was also surprising to him the police hadn't had more suspicions about it at the time.

He spied a shelf of photos from Aria's various operatic roles and pointed at them. "It's an honor to be in the same room as opera royalty." She perked up at that, which is what he'd intended. He got up to inspect the photos and picked the closest one. "Looks like this is from Mozart's *Magic Flute*."

"That's me singing the famous Queen of the Night aria, 'Der Hölle Rache kocht in meinem Herzen, Tod und Verzweiflung flammet um mich her.' In the old days, I would have sung that for you."

"I'm sorry you had to retire so young."

She put a hand to her throat, a gesture that appeared to be a habit since this was the third time. But opera singers would be a little throat-obsessed, wouldn't they? When she replied, he understood. "It was laryngeal papillomatosis. But forty-seven isn't all that young for an opera singer to retire. Still, I wish I'd had the chance to tackle a few more golden roles."

She looked over at the photo with a wistful expression. "That photo was my last Queen of the Night. Hard to believe it's been thirteen years."

Drayco smiled. "If you were still singing professionally, I could have you headline my opera house."

She stared at him. "You have an opera house? Did I misunderstand? I thought you were looking into my brother's death?"

"I'm a crime consultant by trade, yes. But a client bequeathed me an opera house over on the Eastern Shore of Virginia."

Her eyes lit up. "Oh, how marvelous!" And she gave him a coy smile. "I don't suppose you've decided who you're going to name it after."

He shook his head. "Not yet. However, the venue is probably a lot smaller than you're accustomed to."

"Oh, I wouldn't say that. Still, if you can't think of anyone . . . "

Drayco looked around the room at the performance photos and opera props that filled the shelves. Additional pictures and also framed printed programs hung on the walls. "You should open a museum somewhere."

"Oh, I don't know if there'd be that much interest." But her eyes had a gleam to them.

"I'm curious about your name. If it really is Aria, then you were born for the trade."

She laughed. "The whole name thing came about because I didn't like my birth surname of Tibbs for a stage name. Too boring. I wanted something worthy of an opera singer. I figured the D'Angelo part would endear me to La Scala audiences. As for Aria . . . let's say it came to me in a flash of inspiration."

"Graham was your only sibling?"

Her smile faded. "Yes, quite a bit younger, as I mentioned. We had a fractious relationship at times. Some might say he was even cruel toward me. But perhaps I deserved that."

She stood up, retrieved the sole photo on a chest in one corner of the room, and handed it to him. "That's me and Graham when I was nineteen, and he was four."

"You both look happy here."

"We were happy for a time. We were orphaned when Graham was six. I began traveling around so much for performances and couldn't take him with me most of the time. So he was passed off on my husband before my husband's death and then other family members. That's why I partly blame myself for his problems."

"Were those problems the reason for your recent estrangement?"

"Yes, not that Graham's brush with the law was out of the blue. We had this one uncle, also now deceased. I always suspected the man was into all kinds of trouble. I never asked him because I didn't want to know. But, perhaps it's in the genes, and Graham couldn't help it."

She tilted her head. "Are you helping the police with the investigation?"

"I have personal reasons for looking into the matter. Graham and some other men kidnapped me four days ago."

Her eyes widened. "Kidnapped you? Graham? Whatever for?"

"I know it sounds bizarre, but it was to solve a puzzle. I'm not sure what it was about, though such things are often tied to money somehow."

"Did you figure out this puzzle?"

"I think I decoded the message, yes. I have no idea what it means, but I aim to find out."

She sat still for several moments, chewing on her lip. Finally, she said, "Then I also want you to figure out what that code means because it must be at the bottom of this whole business. Including my brother's death. In fact, I want to hire you."

"I usually charge on an hourly and per diem basis."

"I'm not a billionaire, but I've done all right thanks to some smart contracts I signed. I live below my means because I want to save money for my projects and charities."

Drayco wasn't sure this mansion qualified as living below one's means. But the rich often had different standards of what that meant.

She chuckled. "It was my shady uncle who advised me on those contracts I mentioned. I get royalties from sales of recordings and videos. Another reason I don't want to speak ill of Uncle Hadwyn."

"Hadwyn? That's an unusual name."

"His full name is Hadwyn Hofberg."

"I've heard of him."

"I'm sure you have in your line of work. And I know what you're thinking. He got some horrible press, but he was quite good to me."

Drayco nodded in sympathy. That's another thing he had in common with Aria besides music, a shady uncle. "Do you have names of any friends or associates of Graham's who I might speak with?"

As he pulled out a notepad, she replied, "His childhood friend, Ezra Layton. They stayed close, up until Graham's first death. Really, I'm not sure what else to call that fire thing. Not death, but disappearance, perhaps? Ezra has looked out for me since Graham's . . . disappearance. I just don't see how he could be involved in Graham's demise."

"You mentioned his former business partner, too."

"Yes, Leon Sable. I believe he has some sort of hardware store now. I don't know him, really."

She reached over to a side table and fingered a glass figurine with another crystal shape inside. He pointed it out. "That's unusual. Looks kind of like an octahedron within a globe."

"Ezra gave it to me. He is such a dear boy, so thoughtful. In fact, he called this morning to check up on me and see how I was handling this madness. He is as shocked and devastated as I am. But he's a survivor like I am."

She held up the glass figurine. "It's a lovely piece, and I'm very fond of it. But it's not a collectible, is it?" She frowned. "Too bad it's not covered in gold or precious gems. I could sell that and raise more money for my projects."

"Be careful what you wish for. These things often have a way of coming back to bite you in the end." The jewel-encrusted case and rare Chopin manuscript found at Drayco's opera house were *still* tied up in litigation.

"You're right, of course. But I do so want to leave some sort of legacy behind, other than my singing. Scholarships, endowments, maybe even music schools named after me. Despite my opera success, sometimes I feel like a failure."

"A lot of artists deal with 'imposter syndrome.'"

Her face grew pensive. "I suppose. Well, I put myself out there and gave it my best. It's funny—that reminds me of one of Graham's favorite quotes. That necessity is the mother of taking chances."

"It certainly can be." He thanked her for her time, adding, "If I think of anything else, I'll give you a call."

As he stood up to leave, she asked, "Do you have a card?"

When he handed one over, she added, "I'll have my accountant call you." She walked him to the door and peered outside. "Oh, my, is that your car? It looks like an antique. And such a lovely shade of blue."

"A 1960s Starfire."

"Marvelous. Makes me wish I'd learned how to drive. I never seemed to have the time. But there are always chauffeurs or taxis."

Drayco waved to her as he headed outside. When he climbed into his car and made his way down the twisting drive, the gate opened for him automatically this time.

Aria was an interesting woman, but her perceived career failings in music hit a little closer to home than he wanted to admit. Then again, she'd had her chance at a music career, even a shortened one, hadn't she?

As he took one look back at the mansion, he bit back a small smile. Take that, Brock. Not only was Drayco going to look into his kidnapping case, he now had a client to pay for it.

7

As the mid-afternoon sun began its all-too-early dip towards sunset, Drayco pulled up in front of his father's yellow half-Tudor, half-colonial home. The "Frankenhouse," as Drayco referred to it. He was relieved to see Brock's Mercedes still parked outside. No more car-nappings.

He glanced over at the wrapped present on the passenger seat, wondering if he should drop it off now as he'd planned or wait for more of a celebration. But his father was also on a thorny case at present. If they waited, it could take weeks or even months until they found the time.

As he sat outside, his thoughts turned to his mother, Maura. His recent thoughts about her brother, Drayco's Uncle Alistair, had brought her to mind again. Alistair was one of the few people on the planet who knew if Maura was alive or not. If so, where was she? Was she okay? Or was Drayco kidding himself in some kind of fantasy delusion?

He grabbed the present and headed inside, where he found Brock in the den staring at a computer screen. Drayco smelled a cake baking. Cake? Maybe a belated one for Brock's birthday? Drayco felt a little guilty that he hadn't even thought about stopping by a bakery.

He asked, "Is this a bad time?"

Brock almost jumped out of his seat. "You didn't tell me you were coming over. What's up?"

Hoover, Brock's aging German Shepherd, hauled himself off the floor with a deep stretch and ambled over. Drayco bent over to give the pup an ear scratch and then handed the wrapped present to Brock. The offering made his dad grin at the long object swaddled crudely in red-and-purple paper with a golf ball pattern.

"Either this is the new putter I've been wanting, or you bought me an enormous didgeridoo."

"Happy belated birthday, Brock."

His father grimaced. "We're back to that, are we? Brock instead of 'Dad'?"

"Sorry. Old habits and all." Drayco sighed. "But I guess it's never been easy between us, has it?"

Brock took off his reading glasses. "Eh, I blame myself. My fanatical devotion to my career at the expense of family. But I also blame your mother when she went AWOL. You and your sister were only five, for God's sake."

"I know I should hate her for that."

"We can understand her reasons now, thanks to that recent murder case of yours. Makes it a little easier to handle. But only a little."

It was Drayco's turn to be startled, this time by the sound of a female voice calling out, "Brock, dear? Where do you keep the *ouvre-boîte*? Sorry, I mean the can-opener."

A woman with platinum blond hair and hazel eyes with glints of green walked into the room and stopped short when she saw Drayco. After staring at him for a moment, she said in slightly accented English, "The resemblance is very strong. This must be Scott. And I'm Joyelle. Joyelle Babineaux."

She held out her hand, although all Drayco could do at first was stand there with his jaw hanging open. But he pulled himself together to shake the offered hand. "Your name and the accent. Are you French?"

"I was born in France, but I've lived here in America for half my life. I have a house over in McLean with a studio attached."

"Studio?"

"I'm an artist and sculptor. I work mostly with metals."

Brock butted in to say proudly, "She has an exhibition coming up at the Gerlitz Gallery."

Joyelle seemed to sense Drayco's awkwardness and added, "I'd love for you to come to the opening reception. It's December fifteenth."

Drayco stammered out, "That would be great," which sounded lukewarm even to him.

He stood there tongue-tied and not sure why. Okay, so maybe he was a little upset Brock had a serious woman in his life again. Well, *possibly* serious. But when someone calls you "Dear," it usually means something more than a casual acquaintance.

Brock looked at Drayco's expression and said, "Scott was an earnest boy from the get-go. Hardly ever cried and was curious about every little thing." Brock chuckled. "To a fault. He got into trouble a lot. Had to be saved from disaster several times."

Joyelle smiled. "I was very sorry to hear about your carjacking incident, but Brock tells me you're quite the pianist. I understand your uncle has a scholarship and concert set up for you?"

Drayco gritted his teeth. Why did everyone want to remind him about that? He replied, "My Uncle Alistair set it up in my mother's memory, but he couldn't attach her name to it. Not with her background."

Joyelle bit her lip. "Still, it must be exciting, *n'est-ce pas?*"

"Exciting isn't the word I'd use. But I'll muddle through it."

Joyelle looked over at Brock in confusion. Brock shook his head at her as if to say, "I'll tell you later."

She took a deep breath. "Well, a kidnapping is certainly exciting. And a man who was supposed to be dead was involved somehow? You and your father lead interesting lives. *Très fascinant.*"

"The alleged dead man—who is now most definitely dead this time—had a youthful rap sheet of petty crimes but seemed to have gone straight, as far as I can tell."

"Petty crimes? You mean misdemeanors, no? Shoplifting, simple assault, disorderly conduct, petit larceny?"

"Ah, yes. For the most part. And a little bit of arson."

"Oh, but that is quite interesting, *mai non?* Since the man possibly died in an arson."

Either Brock was filling her in on all the minute details, or she was an avid reader of the news. "Somebody died in that fire, but that's for the police to determine. However, I did have a chat with the twice-dead-man's sister. Turns out, she's a retired opera singer."

"Opera? As in Bizet's *Carmen*? I love *Carmen*."

"She's more of a coloratura than a mezzo. Sorry."

Brock spoke up. "Did you learn anything helpful?"

"Not a lot. Got a few names of her brother's friends and associates. Oh, and she hired me."

"Hmph. At least you'll get paid for your trouble."

Somehow Drayco could have predicted Brock would latch onto that. "She also said she blames herself. They were orphans, and she was gone much of his young life traveling the world."

Brock shot him a sharp look. Drayco knew as soon as he said it that Brock might take his words as criticism about his own absences from his son's childhood. This girlfriend surprise must be making Drayco more off-center than he thought.

Joyelle looked thoughtful. "People don't usually just vanish like that. Not in this country. Unless they are running from something. Or someone. Perhaps he spent time overseas. Have you checked with Interpol, Ameripol, or Europol? Or Homeland Security?"

Drayco's suspicion meter pegged out in the "danger" zone. She was far more acquainted with law enforcement than your run-of-the-mill artist. He asked, "Was one of your parents an agent?"

For a moment, he detected a flicker of uneasiness in her eyes. "An FBI agent? No, nothing like that."

She bent down to kiss Brock on the cheek. "I have a client, myself. She's coming over in an hour to look at a sculpture I'm making for her garden. I'll call you later, dear."

She waved at Drayco as she headed out into the hallway. "It was so nice to meet you, Scott. And I hope I'll see you at the opening night of my exhibition."

After she'd left, Drayco stared at his father. "How long has this been going on?"

"Been going on? That makes it sound kinda sleazy. Joyelle and I have been seeing each other for a few months."

"And I have to find this out by accident? Were you trying to hide her from me?"

"Of course not. You've been preoccupied. And got yourself kidnapped, to boot."

His father's choice of words rubbed Drayco the wrong way. As if Drayco were negligent somehow and allowed the kidnapping to happen.

Brock stood up and left the room, returning a couple of minutes later with two cups of steaming hot coffee. The one he handed over even had salt. A peace offering of sorts. Drayco slid into the leather club chair next to the gas fireplace, grateful for the warmth from both fireplace and coffee.

Brock said, "You haven't mentioned the kidnapping much the past day or so."

"We've talked about it a few times, as I recall."

"Only the mechanics of it. I was wondering how you're handling it, how are you feeling?"

"Now, you sound like that therapist."

"Dr. Kinder? Have you been to see him?"

"Not in a while. Not since the case with Mom."

"Yes, well ... " Brock's voice trailed off. "Maybe you should schedule another appointment."

"I'm fine. Honest. The person I really need to chat with is Detective John Halabi."

"Ah, Arlington's finest. That hit-and-run was in his jurisdiction, wasn't it? I have to say, I'm as gobsmacked as anybody that this captor of yours was involved in a faked death five years ago."

Drayco nodded. "Another bizarre oddity about this case."

"The man's been off the grid, but somehow gets involved with your kidnapping. Then immediately after, he's killed in a hit-and-run? Seems a bit too convenient, timing-wise."

"That's my thinking, too. You can bet I aim to find out what's going on."

"Now that you have a paying client to help with expenses, that should be easier."

Despite his best efforts to remain cool-headed, Drayco's hackles went up again. Was Brock insinuating his son wasn't successful enough to be financially stable?

But Brock didn't have to worry about bills as much, did he? He had his private consulting business on top of generous retirement benefits from the FBI. Drayco, on the other hand, had left after only ten years and struggled more as a result.

He really needed to stop being so sensitive where his father was concerned. Brock was just well-intentioned and not trying to be judgmental, right? Drayco was correct about one thing, though—as he'd told Brock, it had never been easy between them. Maybe that's why his father's comment that "you got yourself kidnapped" had rankled more than it should. Or perhaps it was because that's precisely what Drayco was thinking, himself—that he'd screwed up, let his guard down. Situational awareness in the toilet.

Drayco's belated birthday visit to Brock hadn't gone exactly to plan with this "surprise" girlfriend. Family ties weren't always without their knots, but even knotted ropes could fasten down an anchor when needed. And if family couldn't be your anchor in life, then who could?

8

Drayco dropped off a box of bottled doogh at Sergeant Lorenzo's cubicle before seeking out Detective Halabi in his corner office. It was, as always, a bipolar office halfway between neat and cluttered. The papers on the tan-speckled laminate desk formed perfect rectangular monuments. But books on a corner shelf teetered at skewed angles, with more crammed into charcoal plastic bins on the floor.

The man sitting behind the desk waved him in and pointed at the chair in front. Drayco slid into the industrial black-vinyl chair, which was as ass-numbing as the last time he'd sat there. He asked, "Do you own five different navy blue suits and purple paisley ties and switch them out every day?"

Halabi grunted. "A fashion critic, I see. That's rich, coming from someone who's fashionably late." He looked at his watch.

"Motorcade of some dignitary somebody or other got in the way."

That made Halabi grunt even harder. "Lucky MPD gets to take part in most of those. The motorcycle cops don't seem to mind too much since it gives 'em a chance to ride."

"I don't know. One of them told me once they were mere glorified cop props."

"Yeah. A lot of it's pure theater. Speaking of theatrical, I haven't seen you much since your mother's case. That was clever. Unorthodox, but clever."

Drayco would be sure to write that down in his diary. If he were one to keep a diary. A teensy glimmer of praise from the gruff detective.

Halabi added, "Since we're on the topic of all things theater, I snagged a copy of that report you submitted to the MPD."

Drayco grimaced. "I got the feeling your colleagues in the District suspected I was making up my kidnapping story."

"If it was anyone else coming to me with a story about being kidnapped to solve some puzzle, I'd laugh them out of the office. But since it's you, it's much more believable."

"Meaning you're not entirely convinced of my 'story'?"

"Meaning that as a professional detective, I have to keep an open mind. As you yourself know."

"Of course."

"Do you have any proof the recent hit-and-run victim was one of your kidnappers?"

"I only got a brief glimpse of his face."

"A glimpse? And just of this one man? None of the others?"

Drayco knew how it would all sound to a cop, one reason the D.C police hadn't totally taken him seriously. "I managed to work my blindfold up a fraction, but not much."

"Hmm." Halabi readjusted his position in the black leather chair, making the casters squeak. "I'm very interested in how our hit-and-run case ties into your kidnapping."

"That's why I'm here. Hoping you can help me find those answers."

"I checked in with Feds about this. Could be other states or even other countries involved. A man faking his death, disappearing for five years, being off the grid in the meantime . . . "

"Exactly. What were the circumstances of the hit-and-run? Any witnesses?"

"The only 'witness,' " Halabi used his hands to make dramatic air quotes, "was a drunk since it was late on a Saturday night. The victim, Graham Tibbs, was visiting a puzzle and games store in Clarendon. It's open until midnight, which is unusual, but I guess they know their nerdy clientele. Anyway, he was hit walking across the street after leaving the store. Hadn't bought anything."

"Did the puzzle store's staff say why he was there?"

"Not really. The owner, Johnny Burdell, said he looked around and left, pretty much."

"Going back to the fire five years ago. I saw the original police report, and the identification of that body found in the burned building was made by one single tooth. Kind of unusual, isn't it?"

"Unusual ID or unusual tooth?"

"Both."

"I didn't work that particular case. The detective who did left the department for a California gig, but I read that same report you did." Halabi gave Drayco a slight scowl. He didn't ask how Drayco got his hands on the copy, but he wasn't happy about it. "Platinum and gold aren't a common combo in teeth."

When he saw Drayco open his mouth to retort, Halabi hastened to add, "As for Tibbs's alleged partial dentures, the report said there was no sign."

"No sign? Any forensic dentist will tell you even acrylic dentures can survive high temperatures if still in the mouth. Which means they were likely removed. Weren't there some suspicions at the time?"

"Look, I'll be the first to admit it was odd, bizarre, kooky, take your pick. But not unprecedented."

"The ME's report also showed the body seemed to have no other injuries. But it was inconclusive whether or not he was alive or dead when the fire happened."

"Probably got surprised by a thief. Tibbs's business partner said they'd had a burglary within the past two months. Unfortunately, they hadn't got around to installing security cameras."

"No signs of arson? Accelerants?"

"According to the report, that was also inconclusive. No obvious accelerants, no."

"Will there be an exhumation to determine who's really in that grave?"

"When we get the okay from the court. And we're rechecking the forensic report from five years ago to see if anything was missed. Forensic tech has advanced a lot in half a decade."

"I chatted with Graham Tibbs's sister, Aria D'Angelo. She didn't seem to care either way about that autopsy. And she's mystified by her brother's vanishing act and still stunned by it all."

"She helped ID the body for us. And we've also been up to Montgomery to interview her. But we didn't get much info." He paused for a moment. "Don't suppose you learned anything else from her that would be helpful?"

"First of all, I should state for the record that she's now officially my client since she hired me to look into this."

"Figured as such."

"She said she and her brother had been estranged for a few years. She also said her brother had a rap sheet. I checked into it. Mostly misdemeanors."

Halabi grunted again. It was a three-grunt interview so far. "From many years ago when he was a teenager. One of those misdemeanors, though, was arson of personal property."

"So I noticed."

"You're thinking what we're thinking, naturally. That with his history, he may have faked his death-by-arson himself." Halabi paused, then added, "Have you talked to his former business partner?"

"Not yet."

"Well, we did." Halabi looked rather pleased with himself that he got there before Drayco. "No joy there, either. The guy allegedly had an alibi for the hit-and-run. He was at a movie theater that night, he says. We haven't tracked down witnesses yet."

"I sense you're leaning toward Tibbs's death being in the 'it was an accident' camp."

"We're trying to track down the driver in that hit-and-run, but it has all the signs of a tragic accident, albeit an odd one. If you can find something that shows me it's not, I'll be all ears."

Drayco spotted a French dictionary on Halabi's desk and pointed it out.

"My wife's idea. Alzheimer's runs in my family. The wife read that learning a new language can help keep it at bay. And since it was that or crossword puzzles . . . "

"What have you got against crossword puzzles?"

"I loathe them, that's what." Halabi jabbed his finger at the book's cover. "Why in the world does any language need two genders? A male desk and a female lamp?"

"Good thing you're not trying German, then. They also have a third grammatical gender, neuter."

Halabi rolled his eyes. "Swell."

"*Vous avez un très joli bureau.*"

Halabi replied, "*C'est un désastre,*" in a very southern accent that made Drayco grin.

He said, "You're of Lebanese descent. Everyone there speaks French and English in addition to Arabic, so you should be a natural."

"I wasn't born there, and I did not get any language genes."

Drayco grinned. "Could have fooled me."

Halabi opened the dictionary, flipped through some pages, and said, "*Merde.*" Then he flipped through some more and added, "*Embrasse-moi le cul.*"

Drayco let out a laugh. "I've never been cussed out by a southern-American-Lebanese cop in French. Sort of French."

Halabi started to flip through the dictionary again, but Drayco said, "Enough already. I'll stop if you will."

The detective stared at him with a poker face that would put the legendary gambler, Johnny Moss, to shame. Detective Lorenzo said that was something that pissed off the other cops. With that poker face, you never knew what Halabi was thinking.

Drayco grinned. "The MPD may not think I'm playing with a full deck, but I'm betting I'll end up with a Royal Flush."

Halabi pointed at the door. "Flush yourself out of here, will you? I don't have a high-priced client, but I've got a bunch of taxpayers I'm accountable to. And no more mystery kidnappings. My plate's full enough as it is."

Drayco took the not-so-subtle hint and escaped out the door. He passed by Sergeant Lorenzo's cubicle again, where the man sat drinking one of the bottles of doogh. He even had a milk . . . make that yogurt . . . mustache as he waved.

Drayco mentally summarized his little "chat" with Halabi. No suspects in Graham Tibbs's hit-and-run, check. The victim's former business partner had an alibi, check. The victim himself had a history of arson, check. The police dropped the ball with Tibbs's alleged death-by-fire years ago, check. Not a checkmate yet, although some might see it that way.

Good thing Drayco wasn't much of a chessmaster, poker player, or a high-roller gambler. Because he never really knew when to quit.

9

Drayco left Halabi's office shaking his head over the man's not quite one-hundred percent belief in Drayco's story, though he'd been more receptive than the MPD. Or maybe Drayco was shaking his head at the detective's bad French accent.

If the police caught up with the hit-and-run driver, then any answers could be forthcoming. Otherwise, Drayco was pretty sure he was one of the few who thought there was a connection between Tibbs-as-kidnapper and Tibbs-as-victim. And that meant Drayco was on his own. With a little help from Sarg.

Drayco slid into his car, the new Generic Silver Camry, or his "GSC," that he'd leased to replace his totaled previous business car. He'd gone back and forth on whether to replace it, but sometimes he needed something more discreet than his classic Starfire.

He popped a CD into the player, a recording he'd special ordered—one of the few-remaining copies of the Bob Bordelon's Bayou Band version of "Twinkle, Twinkle" he thought he heard during his captivity. As he listened to it, he was more convinced than ever it was the same music. He wasn't sure why, but he'd become obsessed with the song.

He played it repeatedly along his route until he pulled up outside a stucco-colored storefront with a corrugated tin awning. The sign above read, "LS Metals," not that the store needed a sign to let you know what was sold there. Metal boxes with rods of all sizes and thicknesses stood next to multicolored metal sheets propped up against the wall. He saw a lot of silver and gray but also items in the reddish family, like copper, brass, and bronze.

As Drayco entered the front door, the displays were even more impressive. He'd never seen so many types of square and round pipes, rods, and flashing. The Tin Man's favorite store?

But if the visual spectacle was interesting, the synesthesia elements from the interior were not. Buzzing from an electric screw gun sent fuzzy maroon tacks into his brain, and the clanging from metal parts was a tsunami of dripping, green-electric triangles. It was an ugly combination, and as usual, he had to fight against allowing the ugliness of his sensory reaction to bias him.

One thing was sure—the shop was filled with various items that would make lethal weapons. That was a downside of being in the crime consulting business, looking at every scene through the lens of its "murder potential." What must it be like to go into a gift shop and just see . . . gifts?

Drayco asked a man loading rods onto a pallet where he could find the owner, Leon Sable, and was directed to a small room in the back of the space. After Drayco had introduced himself and explained why he was there, Sable got up from behind his tanker-style desk to close the door to the office.

The man wore steel-colored pants and a steel-colored shirt to match. By accident or design? When Drayco looked over at the closed door, Sable replied, "My staff doesn't know much about my former business. Or my former partner. I like to keep my past and present separate. Never know how people will react. There were rumors, anyway, and after the police stopped by . . . "

He sat down behind the desk again and promptly began coughing. When he finally stopped, he pointed to a mask lying there. "I have asthma. So I wear that when I'm on the floor."

As he said those words, a machine began buzzing in the background. A small cloud of particulates floated through the main hall, illuminated by the rays of sunlight streaming in from high-up windows.

Drayco looked over at Sable, who sighed, "I know, I know. My doctor told me all the dust and metal shavings in the air might be the death of me. But it's my living, you see."

"I think I do see that, yes. But you said something about rumors?"

Sable frowned. "I don't like to talk about that." Maybe it was from the coughing, but the man's voice was a little raspy.

"The business you and Graham Tibbs owned together. It was a hardware store, wasn't it?"

"Yes, and hard to make a living at it. We were struggling even before the fire. Those big-box things have driven a lot of guys like us out of business, you see. One reason why I switched to metal supply instead. Plus, metal's kind of tricky to order online."

"Customers have to come in and handle what they want in person."

"Precisely."

"Thinking back five years to the time of the fire that burned your business down and allegedly killed Graham, do you recall anything unusual prior?"

"Nothing. And believe me, I've gone over it and over it."

"Did you have any reason to question that Graham wasn't the body found in the fire?"

"None whatsoever. Although . . . "

Drayco waited patiently, but when Sable seemed lost in thought, Drayco prompted, "Although?"

Sable scratched a keloid scar on his cheek. "I wondered what Graham was doing at the store after hours. He was supposed to be packing for a vacation trip the next day, you see."

"A vacation? Where was he headed? And was he traveling alone?"

"Near as I recall, it was a camping trip or something. He liked to fish. Wasn't married and not dating anybody at the time. So I think it was going to be just him, a boat, a lake, and some trout."

"You told the police after the recent hit-and-run that you had no idea he was still alive. Had he not tried to contact you in those five years?"

"Not at all. I'm not sure what I would have done if he had."

Sable grabbed a silver letter opener shaped like a medieval sword and tapped it so hard on the wooden desktop, it made a small dent. "I thought we had a pretty good relationship, could share things. If Graham was in trouble, why couldn't he come and tell me?"

"Since it turns out he wasn't the fire victim, do you think he's the one that burned down the store?"

Sable paused to wipe his brow with his sleeve. "Now, I do. I guess. If it wasn't for that tooth they found, I could have understood the wrong ID being a misunderstanding, you know? But that tooth . . . seems like it was put there as a decoy."

Drayco caught a whiff of something aromatic and traced it to a cup on Sable's desk. A chai latte, if he wasn't mistaken. Drayco asked, "Do you have any idea who might have really died in that fire?"

"None. But I'm dying to find out." His eyes widened for a moment, and he uttered an embarrassed chuckle. "Not the best choice of words."

"The days before Graham allegedly died in the fire, did he appear nervous? Fearful? Talk about someone targeting him?"

"Now that you mention it, maybe. But it's been a long time." Sable's jaw hardened, and a frown returned to his face. "Look, I've been all through this with the police. And I've got a business to run."

"I won't take up too much more of your time. But I'm curious. Do you know the owner of the puzzle store where the hit-and-run took place? His name is Johnny Burdell."

"No, I don't. And I haven't a clue why Graham would have been there, then or now. You'll have to ask that Burdell fellow."

"He's on my list. One other thing—I just left the Arlington PD after a chat with Detective Halabi. You also told the police there'd been a burglary within the two months before the fire. Why no security cameras after, then?"

"One burglary in a couple of years didn't seem like a huge deal. Not much was taken. A lot less money lost in the theft than a good security system would cost. And we were operating on the edge as it was, you see. That's why we only had a bare-bones sprinkler system. And it sure didn't help much."

Sable grew even more defensive. "Those police you mentioned. They grilled me five years ago, and they grilled me again the other day. But my story is the same. I had nothing to do with that fire."

"They probably asked you if it was an insurance scam?"

"I'll tell you what I told them. I could only afford a basic business insurance policy, a pittance. As a matter of fact, I took a big bath on the fire. Came close to bankrupting me. So I had every reason to want my partner alive and for the place not to burn down, you see."

Drayco wasn't yet ready to "see" anything, but he said, "It's fortunate you found the money to rebuild."

"I borrowed from friends and got small business loans, the usual. Did you think I embezzled it or something?"

Drayco didn't answer his question directly. "It must have been a punch in the gut."

"Hell, yes, it was. I didn't know what to do. Part of me wanted to chuck it all and move to Australia to get a clean start. I have an uncle who decided to do that very thing. Did quite well for himself Down Under."

"Plus, there are always the quokkas."

That elicited a brief smile from the other man. "Quokkas kinda look like stuffed animals someone blew some magic pixie dust on and brought to life."

"Probably to balance out all the venomous Aussie spiders and snakes."

Sable grimaced. "Yeah. There's that."

When Sable got a phone call, Drayco waved and returned to his car. After he'd shut the door, he considered what Sable had said. Fact number one, he'd agreed it was incredibly suspicious the police only found a charred corpse and one convenient tooth to ID dental records. Then there was the fact the guy admitted he didn't know what his partner was doing at the business that day, another story that was too convenient and pat. Finally, and something Drayco would check, it didn't sound like an insurance scam.

Perhaps Sable was partners with Tibbs, and they faked the death together. But why? And did Tibbs later double-cross Sable somehow, and that was when Tibbs went on the run? Then, when Tibbs turned up alive again, Sable had to kill him for real this time?

It was mainly supposition and not a lot of substance. Still, Drayco was pretty confident about one thing—none of the hushed voices he'd overheard during his kidnapping ordeal matched the color and texture of Sable's.

So why couldn't Drayco recall the one muffled voice he'd thought was familiar? And because he couldn't, then perhaps his certainty about Sable's voice was off, too. Since the drugs the kidnappers gave him made everything hazy, could he be sure about anything he thought he recalled? Maybe even the face of Graham Tibbs?

No, there was zero chance he'd dreamed up that face only to have his "dream" show up in a newspaper obituary two days later. Tibbs was definitely one of the kidnappers. Now, if Drayco could only figure out how and why.

10

Unlike Leon Sable's industrial building, the Great Games store was more traditional. It had a red-brick façade with white concrete columns and looked like it belonged on a historical film set. Drayco spied the inspiration for the store's name when he was "welcomed" by a plush stuffed Great Dane almost as tall as Drayco inside the front door.

The Great Dane was the least odd part about the shop. A dizzying array of colorful pinball machines lined one wall, while another held shelves stuffed with board games in messy piles. A vintage Victrola perched on top of an antique Singer sewing machine. Next to them, a couple of nickel-operated carousel riding horses looked like they'd galloped over from a county fair.

In contrast to the metal supply shop, it was quieter here, meaning fewer synesthesia headaches for Drayco. But the silence only added to the odd vibe, not helped by the curious man at the counter wearing a shirt printed with cigarette-smoking skeletons.

"Can I help you?" The man ran his hand through his hair with its forest of cowlicks.

"Are you the owner of the store, Johnny Burdell?"

"That's me. Are you here for our big sale?"

"My name is Scott Drayco. I'm actually here to ask about Graham Tibbs."

Burdell's lips formed a hard line, and he splayed his fingers on the countertop. "The cops have been here about that. Are you FBI or something?"

"Former."

"Former? What do you mean by that?"

"I do consulting now. Graham Tibbs's sister hired me to investigate his death."

"Well, now. I'm deeply sorry for his sister. Losing family is hard. But I don't know that I can help her."

"How did you know Tibbs?"

Burdell shrugged. "I didn't. Just some guy wanting to know if I had any idea what this Latin phrase meant. In relation to games or famous codes or whatever. But you can look up the meaning in the dictionary. He didn't need me for that. What the frak?" Burdell leaned even harder on his splayed fingers, making them turn white.

"You were open late the night he was killed."

"Sure. We stay open until midnight most days. Because of all the nerds and geeks who don't get dates." He chuckled and moved one hand to fiddle with his blue square-frame glasses.

"Can you think of any other reason Tibbs might have wanted to see you? If, as you say, he could just look those words up in a dictionary?"

Burdell paused. "You FBI types are pretty proud of your codes and spies and stuff, right? I'm an amateur cryptologist, you might say. Been into games and puzzles ever since I was a small boy. Not just RPG. Anyway, I'd posted in a couple of online forums for cipher geeks. So maybe this Tibbs fellow saw me mentioned there and came to me for help."

"And he only showed you a Latin phrase? There wasn't any other part of a cipher, perhaps?"

"Maybe. Some numbers or something. A yawnfest."

"And yet, you say you're a self-described amateur cryptologist, and you weren't interested in what those numbers might mean?"

Burdell shrugged again. "As I said, yawnfest."

"Did you tell the police about this code Graham Tibbs showed you?" Detective Halabi hadn't mentioned it to Drayco.

Burdell didn't answer right away, turning to straighten a row of creepy Goth Raggedy Ann dolls behind the counter. But when a man entered the shop, Burdell's face brightened, and he waved the customer over. "Phil, here, is a fellow cryptology-loving regular. Phil can tell you I'm known as a puzzle solver and not some kinda noob, can't you, Phil?"

The customer looked from Burdell to Drayco and said, "Sure, Johnny. You're so good, the FBI should hire you, I always say."

Burdell looked smug and told Drayco, "I told you I wasn't making this up. That's why Tibbs came to see me. I've got a reputation as a skill monkey."

The customer looked from Drayco to Burdell and asked, "You still got some of that cactus candy, Johnny? You were out of it last time."

Burdell reached under the counter and handed over a small box.

"Thanks, Johnny. I'm not sure who's more obsessed with this stuff, you or me." Sensing the tension, the customer seemed eager to escape. He made his excuses and headed toward stacks of video games at the rear of the store.

Burdell said, "Look, Mr. Drayco. I'm sorry the guy's dead and all. But it really doesn't have anything to do with me. It was just one of those tragic things. Being in the wrong place at the wrong time."

"Did you see it happen?"

"Like I told the cops. I heard the thump and a car accelerating real fast. Some idiot griefer passing by."

"Griefer?"

"Gamer term. An idiot who goes out of their way to annoy other players."

"Did the car acceleration sound intentional? As if the driver was gunning for the victim?"

"You're the crime guy, not me. I'm just a small business owner trying to make a living. And then this bad thing happens, and all of a sudden the police are here, and you are here, and my business has fallen off. Does that sound like something I'd be part of? Epic fail, man."

"Do you know Leon Sable? Owns a metal supply shop and was the dead man's former partner."

Burdell hesitated. "I don't have any need for metal around here. Unless that fellow sells metal pieces for games or chessmen or such. Does he?"

"Not that I know of."

"Well, there you go."

Drayco was a little irritated by Burdell's half-answers, but he pressed on. "It would be a big help if you could tell me the name of the online forum for cipher geeks where you posted. The one that might have gotten Tibbs's attention?"

"You're not gonna pop in and troll the group, are you? Like a cyberstalker or something?"

"I probably won't post anything. Just conduct research."

"Because they don't take kindly to ganking."

"Ganking?"

Burdell rolled his eyes. "Ganging up on a guy who doesn't have a chance to defend himself."

"I promise not to participate in any ganking."

"Yeah, well, the group's not all that active lately." Burdell hastened to add, "Probably not worth your time."

Another customer who couldn't be much more than sixteen marched up to the counter to pay for a bunch of vintage video games. Seeing the young man buy the "antique" games made Drayco wonder—would the Victrola be in vogue again soon? It would be perfect for playing an original 1930s recording of the "Twinkle, Twinkle" big band arrangement.

Burdell looked over at Drayco with a frown as he rang up the boy's purchases, and Drayco took the hint. He nodded at him, saying, "Thanks for your time."

As Drayco turned to leave, he noted a clothes tree by the door with a colorful puzzle-print jacket and matching cap. He could read an inside label where someone wrote with a sharpie, "Property of Johnny Burdell." Big surprise. That getup made a perfect walking advertisement for his store.

Drayco rubbed the stuffed Great Dane's head on the way out. A little good luck could come in handy.

What to make of Burdell? He'd seemed nervous, but people talking to law enforcement, even private detectives, often felt uncomfortable. Yet, if Drayco's ten years in the FBI's BAU division had taught him anything, it was screaming at him that Burdell wasn't just nervous about Drayco's presence.

More importantly, why would a man like Tibbs, who'd possibly faked his death and been in hiding for five years, suddenly make an appearance at a very public place? And merely to ask about a code? It didn't make sense on any level.

Halabi had asked Drayco if he had proof of his kidnapping, which he hadn't . . . until now. The fact Tibbs showed the puzzle Drayco had solved to Burdell seemed like genuine proof. But why hadn't Burdell told the police about it? Burdell's bragging seemed to peg him as an armchair FBI wannabe, so maybe he'd just let the puzzle bit slip when he'd learned about Drayco's own FBI background.

But if Burdell was hiding info, it was possible he also covered up the fact he'd actually solved what the numbers meant. If so, he was a better puzzle solver than Drayco. The possibility made Drayco cranky, and he slammed the car door harder than he'd planned.

An image of Sarg's comically confused face popped up in his mind as his former partner said, "Sky hug?" in reply to the Latin phrase on the puzzle, *caelesti amplexus*. Leave it to Sarg to cheer up Drayco . . . even when the man wasn't there.

Drayco checked his watch. He was running a little behind schedule, so he had no time for a delayed drive-through brunch. The thermos of black coffee and Snickers bar he grabbed from home would have to do. He wasn't about to be late for his next appointment, one he'd been trying to line up ever since speaking with Aria D'Angelo.

Drayco squinted up at the bluish sky and patchy clouds. Thankfully, the weather was cooperating because his appointment required fair skies and dry ground. He hoped he wouldn't regret the man's choice of a meeting site. *Carpe diem*, they say. Or was it, *carpe automotivus*?

11

Drayco stood at the edge of the dirt track next to the black metal fencing, watching a mud-covered sports car racing around the circuit. A tiered group of bleachers lined up in a row behind him, but they were empty. The only people present seemed to be Drayco and the man driving the car.

Thanks to Aria D'Angelo, Drayco got the phone number for Graham Tibbs's childhood friend, Ezra Layton, and finally arranged a meeting. Even so, it took some diplomacy and a little help from Aria. Drayco was surprised when Layton suggested the track, but sport driving was a passion of his, and he spent a lot of time here.

Layton hadn't told Drayco what car he'd be in, but since only one car currently circled the track, the lone muddy vehicle must belong to him. Drayco studied the car as it zoomed around the large oval, kicking up chunks of dirt and gravel in its wake. Just as he wondered how to get the driver's attention, the car slowed down and pulled to a stop in front of him.

The man inside wore a suit made of flame-resistant aramid fibers like you'd see on professional drivers. The white fabric set off his reddish hair, which wasn't too far off the hair color of Drayco's mother.

Drayco compared him to the photo of a young Graham Tibbs at Aria D'Angelo's house—Graham also had auburn highlights in his younger days. She did say Graham and Layton had been close, but the hair made them look like actual brothers.

The man leaned over, rolled down the window, and called out, "Hop in. Assuming you're Scott Drayco, that is."

Drayco slid onto the right-hand seat as Layton said, "Better buckle in."

It wasn't long before Drayco was glad he did. They immediately picked up speed and within moments, the car's speedometer said sixty miles per hour. With each successive lap, the speedometer crept up a little more until they were pushing 110 in a series of hair-raising turns around the track.

Layton kept giving him side glances as if to gauge Drayco's nerves. He yelled over the engine noise, "You don't look too bothered. Most people who tag along end up turning green right before they puke. Or else they make me pull over so they can escape. It's funny as all get out."

Drayco used his best stage voice to avoid yelling as he asked, "How fast can this thing go?"

Layton laughed. "Let's find out." He shifted gears, and they were soon whizzing around at 160 mph.

"Is this what you do for a living?"

"I wish. No, I manage a shop that sells glass items. What a contrast, huh? From adrenaline to artsy-fartsy."

The buzzing from the engine sent tangerine-colored cactus thorns through Drayco's brain. It was hard to ignore the turbulent sensory input, but he tried to concentrate on the conversation instead.

Layton added, "I love these beasts. They're not toys, no sir. Yet so many people out there treat 'em as such. You have your distracted or careless drivers, sure. But hit-and-run, that's the lowest of the low."

"I agree with you, there."

"Can't see how anyone could leave a person lying in the road like they did with Graham. Not even try to find out how he was. The police usually don't even charge you if it wasn't your fault. Like if someone just walks out in front of you."

They took a few more turns at full speed. With another quick look over at Drayco, Layton aimed for a small ramp off to one side of the track and zoomed over it, making them tilt over on Drayco's side. They were still moving, just sideways.

When Drayco turned to the right, he saw the track as it raced by a foot away from his head. Watching trick driving on two wheels was one thing but experiencing it was something else. It was a bit unnerving.

Layton bellowed out, "Maneuvering on the sidewalls. In car circles, we call that skiing."

Drayco was extra grateful for the seatbelt even after Layton flicked the wheel again, and they were back on all four tires. They continued around the track for another lap, easing up until they were coasting.

"Hope I didn't shock you too much." Layton grinned at Drayco.

"No, but having Graham turn up alive must have been something of a shock."

"Hell, yes, it was. When I heard the news, I didn't know what was worse. That he was alive all this time or that he'd come back from the dead only to be killed for real."

"And you have no idea where Graham's been for the past five years?"

"You kidding me? All I know is, I feel betrayed." Now that Drayco could hear him better, hints of Layton's Alabama origins were more noticeable. He pronounced "betrayed" as if it had three syllables.

"You weren't aware he was in any kind of trouble?"

"If he was in trouble, he knew he could come to me. I just don't understand it. Same with his sister. Family is family. They're there for you when you need 'em."

"And prior to the fire five years ago, you didn't sense anything different about him? Something out of the ordinary that might lead him to fake his own death?"

"Not a thing. We went out drinking two days before. He was joking and laughing as usual."

"So he wasn't the depressive type?"

"Not really. Pretty surprising when you consider his childhood."

"His childhood?"

"A no-account, abusive father. The worst kind, a monster. Every boy wants to idolize his father, right? Needs that father figure to keep him out of trouble and all? His father *was* the trouble."

Layton pulled the car to a stop and joined Drayco in climbing out of the vehicle. Drayco examined the racer close-up. "This looks expensive. Is it a loaner? Or are you the owner?"

"It's my baby, through and through."

"The glass business must pay pretty well." Drayco had researched these cars before he arrived and found similar cars went for close to a hundred grand.

Layton ran his hand along the hood of the car. "I inherited a bundle. Some people spend their money on boats or paintings or furniture. I spend mine on cars."

"Where did you learn how to drive race cars?"

"Graham's the one who taught me everything I know. Got me interested in all of this. I'm not nearly as good a driver as he was. You thinking of getting into it?"

"I prefer flying planes."

"Not me. I'm afraid of flying. Just keep me on the ground."

"It's much more fun being the pilot than the passenger. You should try it."

"Thanks, but no thanks. I get all the adrenaline kick I need with this," he nodded at his car. "If I crash, I might still be able to walk away."

"Unfortunately, Graham couldn't do that. And the driver who hit him hasn't been found."

Layton rubbed his forehead. "So the police said. They also warned me only ten percent of these hit-and-run drivers are ever caught."

"Ten percent of arrests is still better than none."

"I reckon so."

"Graham's sister told me how close you and Graham were. And how supportive you've been of her since Graham's alleged death five years ago."

"Guess we grew closer due to shared grief. And I kind of felt like I had to take care of her since Graham wasn't there to do it anymore."

"She indicated they'd been estranged for a while, though."

"You know how families are. But he'd have been there for her if she really needed him." Layton sighed. "I think her and I are both feeling betrayed. But I know she'll be okay. She's such an incredible woman. Talented, strong, resilient."

"She said similar things about you. She's very grateful for your support."

"Really?" A small smile crept across Layton's face.

"She also said she didn't know Graham's former business partner, Leon Sable. I spoke with him yesterday. Did you have any dealings with him?

"Well, yeah. I approached him about becoming his new partner after Graham died." He corrected himself. "After we *thought* he died."

"So did you, then? Become Sable's partner?" It seemed odd Sable hadn't mentioned anything about it.

"For a time, but it didn't work out. So we parted ways. No hard feelings. Just differences of opinion. Guess I had thought if Graham could work with him, so could I." Layton uttered a morbid laugh. "It just occurred to me. It's not often a guy has two burials."

"Aria D'Angelo suggested a simple ash-scattering private observance."

"That's what I figured. Doubt any one of us wants to go through that funeral thing again. Can you imagine what the pastor would say? 'Dearly beloved, we're gathered here today because the first funeral wasn't real, and this is a do-over.' "

"Graham's sister said you'd been friends with him since childhood. He had some run-ins with the law?"

"We both did. But that's all in the past. People grow up, you know? And neither of us wanted a repeat of jail. Ever. No freedom, lousy food, thugs as roommates, tiny little cells. I didn't have claustrophobia before that, but now … "

"I think I understand." *All too well.* "Going to prison is hardly the best goal to have."

"It's not only that. Graham was beaten up in jail to within an inch of his life. Had to spend time in the hospital. So we made a pact of sorts to stay clean. Not get into any further trouble, kind of looking out for the other."

"I gather it worked?"

"You tell me. I mean, he fakes his own death, comes back, and gets himself killed. Who knows?" Layton smiled briefly again, but it quickly faded. "I've let people lead me astray. It's a weakness I've tried to correct my whole life. Maybe Graham had the same problem."

Drayco noted another car hidden behind the bleachers and looked around but didn't see anyone. Layton followed his gaze and said, "That's my everyday car." He patted the racer and added, "This one I keep in a garage over there." He pointed to a series of buildings on the far side of the property.

If garaging a racecar was anything like hangaring a plane, it was another layer of expense that wasn't cheap. It must have been a decent inheritance. Or possibly, like a lot of hobbyists, Layton spent all of his disposable income on this one thing. Drayco thought of his Steinway, but that was different. His piano was as necessary an expense to him as food. Maybe more so.

Drayco thanked Layton for his time and headed toward his non-Starfire car. He was driving the Starfire less these days since he hadn't got the bullet holes fixed yet.

As he slid inside, he shook his head. What to make of the fact those closest to Graham Tibbs saw few warning signs before the man faked his own death? But someone must have known about the deception. And even more importantly, somebody might have helped him do it.

Drayco cranked up the engine, wishing it were a small plane he could fly somewhere. And not only because it had been months since he last flew beyond the traffic pattern to an actual destination. He'd do almost anything to get out of Thanksgiving dinner tomorrow at Brock's house. It would be one thing if it were just the two of them, but his father had invited several people.

Drayco secretly hated parties or casinos or even opening receptions like Joyelle's art exhibit. It wasn't being anti-social. The problem was the onslaught of colors, shapes, and textures from the voices and music and other sounds echoing off all the surfaces. It was hard to describe to others. He tried to explain it by having them imagine sticking their heads into one of those toy kaleidoscopes as it flung feathery or bristly or bumpy geometric figures at you—all day, every day.

But maybe that wasn't the only reason Drayco dreaded this particular Thanksgiving. Joyelle was going to be there, for one. He still wasn't sure how to deal with that. Plus, he didn't want any more mother hens tsk-tsking about his kidnapping ordeal as if he were twelve.

He'd looked up more details about Aria D'Angelo, and one of her very last performances was around Thanksgiving. It was Mozart's *Magic Flute*, with her signature Queen of the Night role. Coincidentally, Drayco's last performance was also close to Thanksgiving, a few weeks before the thugs carjacked him, injured his arm, and ruined his career.

He toyed with inviting Aria to Brock's shindig but decided against it. It was best to keep your business and personal lives separate. But with her on hand, the other guests might be happy to have her regale them with tales from her performances and wouldn't ask him to play.

He patted the dash of the car. "Sure wish you were a plane, my friend. Sure wish you were a plane."

12

Drayco had gone through every excuse possible to get out of Thanksgiving dinner at Brock's house, but he suspected Brock wouldn't buy the "stomach bug" or "emergency client" routine. Besides, Brock was looking forward to this gathering, and Drayco didn't have the heart to disappoint him.

But just because he'd agreed to go didn't mean he had to be Mr. Social King, so he ducked into the kitchen where he could hang out and handle drink orders. It also allowed him to chat with Seni Saviano, the caterer Brock had hired. Nice fellow. Had an Italian father and a Thai mother, so the grub would undoubtedly be interesting.

Drayco's reprieve was short-lived when Brock hustled into the kitchen and said, "You don't have to play bartender, son." And he pushed Drayco out of his kitchen haven and into the living area where the guests had gathered. Drayco couldn't even use Hoover as a shield since Brock banished the dog to a neighbor's house for the duration of the party.

As he looked around the room, Drayco spied a blonde-haired woman chatting with Brock's new girlfriend in one corner. That's when the real reason he'd stayed in the kitchen with the drinks hit him. And why he wanted to chug most of them himself—Nelia Tyler and Joyelle Babineaux were in the same spot together. Ouch. They seemed to be engaged in an animated conversation, so maybe he could avoid them most of the night.

Fortunately, Drayco caught the eye of Benny Baskin. He motioned Drayco over to where he was standing with his wife, Lailani, dressed in a festive Christmas sweater with exotic red flowers he guessed were from her native Hawaii. And joy of joys, Sarg and his better half, Elaine, were right next to them.

Following the usual innocuous pleasantries, Drayco blurted out that he was surprised to see Nelia there, hastily adding, "Seeing how busy she is."

Benny didn't miss a beat even as he shot a sideways glance at Lailani. "It was Joyelle who encouraged Brock to invite her. Especially since I was coming, too. Be rude not to, right? Not that Nelia herself would have considered it rude. But I figured she could use a break from all the stress of school and work."

Drayco stammered out. "I thought she would be with either her mother or father this year … seeing as how this is the first Thanksgiving since her parents' divorce. And her own pending divorce. That might be—"

"Awkward? Guess they agreed with you, which is another reason Joyelle wanted Nelia here. Nelia's a de facto Thanksgiving orphan this year. Her mother is taking a cruise to the Bahamas, and her father is somewhere overseas with his job."

Sarg butted in to say, "You're still looking tense there, junior. You either need to visit a masseuse or drink one of these." He held up a glass of something blood-red that Drayco recognized from his kitchen drinkmaster wrangling. A cranberry daiquiri.

Elaine rolled her eyes. "Scott works too hard. Like you do, dear. You've had many a tense holiday, yourself."

She shot Drayco a quick look that told him she was rescuing him from Nelia talk, and he was grateful. She added to her husband, "And drink all you want of those daiquiris, Mark. I'm driving." She held up her own cup of steaming hot coffee.

Benny's wife asked, "How's that opera house renovation coming along, Scott? Close to being finished?"

Great. Another topic of conversation he hoped to avoid. "There's been some movement on renovations recently, thanks to Harry Dickerman's money."

"Wonderful! That means we'll all be piling over there soon for its grand reopening concert. Are you going to play on it?"

Drayco opened his mouth to reply, "Not a snowball's chance in hell," or at least a milder version, when Joyelle appeared at his side and said, "That sounds *très fantastique*. In fact, Scott, you should give us a preview of coming attractions with some pre-dinner entertainment and play the piano." She pointed at Brock's Steinway.

That piano was something Drayco had never understood since Brock didn't play any instrument, let alone a piano. Drayco tried to beg off the impromptu concert, but Lailani pressed him on it. "I never get to hear you perform. You must play for us, Scott."

Drayco stifled a groan. But what was there to do? He was all out of excuses today. Trailed by the others, he headed toward the Steinway and slid onto the bench. He had no idea what to choose but fought the urge to crank out a snippet of "Dies Irae." Day of Wrath, indeed.

After rubbing his right arm to help loosen it up and prevent cramping, he launched into an arrangement of "Twinkle, Twinkle Little Star." He played it first in its basic form and then improvised new versions in the styles of Mozart, Chopin, and Debussy.

When he finished, the group applauded, and someone called out, "More," but Brock poked his head in to say, "Dinner will be ready in five minutes."

Drayco breathed a sigh of relief and lagged behind as the others trooped toward the dining area. To his surprise, Joyelle came up to him to apologize. "I saw that look on your face, Scott. I'm so sorry if I put you on the spot. People are constantly asking me to show my work, to be 'on' somehow, so I understand."

She paused, then asked, "Is your arm okay? Do you need to get some cream for it?"

When he shook his head, she added, "I'll take a rain check for a private recital at some point. Without a crowd. One artist to another."

He nodded. "I think we could arrange that."

"Brock told me about the puzzle-guy connection to your strange case. Johnny Burdell, isn't that his name? I love puzzles myself, mainly crosswords. They helped me learn English better." She laughed and linked arms with him as they headed to join the others.

Drayco had to hand it to Brock's choice of caterer. Seni Saviano had outdone himself, and even gourmet chef Sarg approved, getting second helpings. It was unusual fare for Thanksgiving, with oyster kimchi stuffing and butternut squash tabbouleh. But Seni had also added in some unique takes on the traditional dishes, like smoked turkey with apple cider gravy and bacon-crumble apple pie.

They spent a good hour at the table enjoying the food and conversation and staggered up for more drinks on Brock's heated patio. Drayco excused himself to duck toward the back but ran right into Nelia Tyler as she headed out of the bathroom.

He sucked some air through his teeth. Well, he couldn't go the entire night avoiding her, could he? He summoned up an encouraging smile. "Glad you could come today. Benny told me your folks were traveling abroad."

"Dad's on business, Mom's on vacation, and I'm stuck here." She hastened to add, "But this was fun. I'm glad I came."

"That's good. That's . . . really good."

They stood staring at each other, then not looking at each other, and then staring at each other once again. He said, "I suppose this is the first holiday since . . . "

"The big divorce double-whammy," she replied. "Technically, my own divorce from Tim isn't final yet. But it's getting there."

"Holidays are hard on many people. I was usually traveling in my youthful piano days, or Brock was away on business. I spent many a Christmas in a hotel room."

Her tone softened. "I can't imagine. A young teenager, too."

"Could have been worse."

That made her smile for a moment. "There's that one Christmas you told me about—and your rather steamy encounter with that violinist—that didn't sound boring. Borderline legal, considering your age, but definitely not boring."

"Oh, it wasn't."

She appeared lost in thought but then asked, "Are you still composing your own pieces? They are so incredibly beautiful."

The minute she said those words, her face flushed a bright crimson, and he could feel his pulse quickening. The last time he'd played one of those compositions for her, it led to a memorable and steamy night together at his townhome. Which is to say, it was memorable for him. She seemed determined to forget it ever happened.

He said, "I haven't heard much from you lately. I was concerned."

She jutted out her chin. "I'm fine. I've just been swamped."

"Oh, I know, I know. It's just . . . I appreciate how difficult it is for you right now." He ran a hand through his hair. "And my offer to lend an ear when you need it still stands."

She folded her arms across her chest. "Thanks. But I'm not sure that would be a good idea."

"Why not? One friend helping another."

"Friend? Basic friends don't usually have sex, right? Or am I missing a new definition of the word?"

"Look, Nelia, we have to talk about this. We never really did. We just keep dancing around the subject."

She dropped her arms to her side and frowned. "We agreed not to, remember? That whole work-life balance thing? And the divorce? I just . . . can't."

He sighed. "You know I support you in your decision. And with law school and your career."

"I know. And I'm grateful. So let's agree to not talk about this again. To go back to the way things were. Before."

He started to reply, but the haunted look on her face grew deeper, and she gave him a quick wave before heading down the hallway. He waited to give her time to return to the others without him trailing behind. They didn't need any more gossip than there already was about the two of them.

He knew he had to try—for her sake—to go back to the way things were "before." But he also knew how hard that was when you know what a woman smells like, feels like, tastes like—and then have to pretend as if it never happened.

The head start he gave her was even longer than he'd planned, about ten minutes. When he finally headed back, he ignored the mistletoe dangling above one doorway. Who'd hung that up there? It wasn't going to be put to use by him. And he certainly didn't want to think about it being used by Brock and Joyelle.

By the time he returned to the living room, Nelia, Benny, and Lailani had left. Sarg and Elaine stayed long enough to grab some of the leftovers to take with them, which was a big nod to the caterer from picky-gourmet Sarg.

When everyone had departed, including Joyelle, Drayco helped clean up and then said to his father, "Can we not do this again at Christmas?"

Brock grabbed a gin-and-tonic and motioned for Drayco to join him in the study. Drayco eyed the gin, thinking he might need something stronger, but opted for black coffee instead. Since Brock had chosen the leather club chair, Drayco flopped down onto the end of the sofa and swung his legs up to stretch them out to the other end.

Brock said, "If you're referring to that whole piano thing, you did fine."

"This time, maybe. But my arm is too unpredictable. Stress can make it worse."

"Then how do you expect to handle the UMD recital?"

"Honestly? I have no idea."

Brock swirled the gin around in his glass. "Have you figured out that number puzzle yet?"

"No."

"No?" Brock pursed his lips.

Drayco gulped some of the coffee and immediately regretted it since it was volcanic. "I'm having nightmares about it. Giant red numbers that chase me down. I never noticed before how a 'six' makes a good noose, and a 'one' makes an effective shiv."

Brock stared at his son as he continued swirling the gin around, making the ice cubes clink against each other. "You solved the cipher. You'll get the rest of it if it even means anything. Don't sweat it."

Drayco kicked a cushion with his foot. "Maybe it would help if I knew who was behind this."

"You'll figure that out, too. If you didn't have a client, I'd tell you to grab your scuba gear and schedule a vacation to the Bahamas. You haven't taken any time off in, what, a year?"

Had it been a year? Or longer? He couldn't recall when he'd last had a vacation. Maybe his father was right. But if Drayco headed out to the islands, he'd likely just spend the entire time thinking about that damned puzzle.

What was it about him and codes? Was the universal consciousness, or Akashic Records, or whatever you called it, trying to tell him something? He'd had far too many code cases in his career, and cryptography wasn't even his specialty at the Bureau.

As if sensing his son's darkening mood, Brock got up long enough to grab the television remote and turn on a football game. Drayco wasn't a huge fan, but the rigid structure and order appealed to him at that moment.

Was he overthinking the puzzle's interpretation? Or was Brock right that Drayco's "solution" didn't even mean anything, possibly just gibberish? If that was the case, why did someone go to all the trouble to kidnap him to solve it?

Drayco stared at his coffee, set it down, and headed to the kitchen to make himself a cranberry daiquiri. If he was going to spend any quality time with his father, the bitter daiquiri should help that medicine go down. Bitter makes better.

13

Drayco awoke the following day grateful for no new nightmares with terrorizing numbers. Not that his waking thoughts were all sugar plums and puppies. He'd weathered the Thanksgiving gathering better than he'd feared, but seeing Nelia was an unexpected shock. He wasn't sure why, since he could have guessed Benny might invite her to tag along. But the last thing he wanted was for them to part on the heels of an argument.

The best antidote to navel-gazing was work, and Drayco was grateful to learn LS Metals was open the day after the holiday. Apparently, Leon Sable hadn't enjoyed much of a Thanksgiving respite, either.

When Drayco headed into the metal supply store, the man was even more surly and uncommunicative than the last time. Drayco had a feeling his line of questioning wasn't going to cheer the guy up, despite the newly added Christmas tree at the front of the shop.

But then he spied a CD lying face-up on a shelf behind Sable's desk as Drayco entered his office. He walked over to pick it up. "I didn't know anyone else used CDs these days since it's all LPs again. Or streaming on the internet."

Sable pointed to the object in Drayco's hand. "Easier to play than an LP. And the online stuff sounds like shit."

Drayco studied the CD. "Glenn Gould, too. I've got this same Bach album."

Sable crossed his arms over his chest. "We blue-collar types aren't all uncultured yahoos, ya know."

"So you're a Bach fan?"

"Years ago, I dated a girl who played the piano. She kinda got me hooked. Don't know where she is these days, but I've still got those," he nodded at the disc.

Drayco turned it over in his hand. "It's here for you when you need it. And it'll never just up and leave you."

That prompted a small smile from Sable. "Somehow, I doubt you're here to commiserate about music. And old girlfriends."

"I have a few more questions about that hardware store you owned before partnering with Graham Tibbs. The one that also burned down."

Sable's smile vanished. "We discussed that last time, didn't we? Besides, I know where you're going with that one. So I'll head you off. The police suspected arson, but nobody was ever charged. As I told you before, there was no insurance scam. In fact, the arson made it hard for me to get insurance afterward. Rates were through the roof."

"When you say the police suspected arson, that must mean they told you they found accelerants. Or some other forensic evidence."

"I said they *suspected* arson. But they also told me they didn't find conclusive evidence of that."

"Was no cause ever found, then?" Drayco knew what Detective Halabi had told him, but he wanted to see what Sable had to say.

"The cops wondered if it could have been a lightning strike. There was a bad storm that night, but nothing was verified. Or ruled out."

"Were there threats against you or other staff beforehand? Any disgruntled customers?"

Sable had a sudden coughing fit and covered his mouth with his sleeve, with a brief glance over at the mask on his desk. "It's the asthma. Sorry."

Drayco also noted an inhaler lying on the man's desk. But Sable didn't reach for it and replied, "The cops asked me that too, at the time. But no and no. Like I told them, I was going through a rough patch. Hell, life isn't always good to you. And it makes you angry, sure. But it doesn't mean you go burning your own business down. If everyone did that, there'd be a smoking pile of rubble everywhere you look."

"Sorry to press you on this. Difficult questions are what I'm hired to ask."

"And I'm sorry if I stepped out of line. This whole dead-not-dead thing has made me angry. I don't know how to feel. About any of it."

"I'd be surprised if you did."

Sable gripped the armrests on his chair. "My father used to tell me persistence against difficult odds is a form of resistance. Fighting the dark forces of nature. Learning to triumph against them."

"A wise man." Drayco returned the CD to the shelf. "I'm still trying to find out what dark forces had taken hold of Graham. As you said, nothing seemed out of the ordinary on the surface. He was estranged from his sister, but that had been going on for a while."

"It's true Graham and Aria didn't get along. I got the feeling from Graham it was because she was acting all high and mighty. Was too good for him. Maybe a little ashamed of him."

"Did you ever see them together?"

"Just once. And she was fine, then. In fact, she seemed genuinely concerned about Graham. I don't know where he got all those negative feelings of his. Guilt, maybe."

"From his wayward youth?"

Sable nodded. "Maybe a piece of him was afraid he'd hurt her career."

Drayco glanced out the little office window toward the shop's center, with its rows of metal objects. There must have been a recent delivery because the floor was even more crowded than last time.

On a whim, Drayco asked, "Do you ever supply materials to artists?"

"Sure. One's having a gallery show in mid-December. Even invited me to her opening reception."

Drayco's pulse quickened at that. "Is her name Joyelle Babineaux, by any chance?"

"That's the one. Pretty name, isn't it? But how'd you know?"

"Oh, I ran across her the other day. She invited me to the same reception, so maybe I'll see you there."

"It'll be fun to see how she's managed to turn all that," Sable waved a hand toward the shop floor, "into something artistic."

"She must be a regular customer of yours. Did she also come to your former store?"

"I don't recall seeing her there. Unless maybe Graham waited on her. She's a more recent customer. Past year or so."

Drayco chewed on that little tidbit. Perhaps Graham and Joyelle had indeed known each other, which would mean his suspicions of her were on target. How coincidental was it she'd be a customer of the former business partner of the man who kidnapped Drayco . . . and only recently start dating Brock?

He said, "I met with Ezra Layton. He indicated you two were in business together."

"Very briefly."

"You didn't mention this before."

"Didn't feel relevant."

"He was Graham's best friend, so I find it odd he'd be swooping in to be your business partner so soon after Graham's alleged death."

Sable scratched his scar. "You're thinking Ezra was behind both the arson and Graham's faked death so he could be my partner? That's way out there."

"Just looking at all angles."

"Yeah, well, that's one badly bent angle, right there."

"Why did you part ways?"

"Ezra was a little on the lazy side. Expected others to do most of the work. I'm shocked his new business is still around."

"He said he'd come into an inheritance. But it appears he's spent it all on racing cars."

"Figures. The man's not very good with money." Sable wrinkled his nose.

Drayco asked, "Last time I was here, you recalled Graham seeming upset prior to the fire. To follow up on that, were there any shady characters you saw Graham interacting with?"

"There was this one guy, maybe. Saw him and Graham together only briefly, but it was the type of guy you can't easily forget. Had a funny name. Begins with an A."

Sable started coughing again and opened a desk drawer to pull out a bottle of soda he guzzled. "I remember now. Alistair. Alistair Brisbane, as in the city in Australia. I didn't trust the guy, seemed shady. But not like your typical low-life criminal shady. This guy was very self-assured and well-dressed. That's far scarier than some guy on meth dressed in jeans."

The moment Sable said that Graham knew Alistair, it triggered a sudden memory of Drayco's from the kidnapping. The muffled voice he'd heard, the one that sounded familiar but he couldn't identify. He'd been in a haze as he woke up from the drugs when he was delivered to the "prison," but that voice . . . he now realized it was Iago Pryce, Alistair's henchman.

Drayco squeezed his eyes shut and concentrated on that whispered voice. The more he did, the more he had glimpses of the scalene triangles covered in pinkish-orange fuzz, like peaches, that Iago's voice had. If only he'd gotten a glimpse of the rest of his captors—Iago would have been hard to miss, with his six-eight stature, bald pate, and goatee.

The look on his face must have been alarming because Sable hopped up from his chair and put a hand on Drayco's arm. "You okay? I've always heard that 'look like you've seen a ghost' stuff, but this is the first time I've witnessed it in person."

Drayco felt his jaw tightening, but he pasted on a neutral expression as he replied, "It's nothing. I'm fine."

That seemed to satisfy Sable. But Drayco *wasn't* fine at all. The case just took a disorienting one-eighty, and he had no idea where to go from there.

Never in a million years had he imagined his uncle would be behind his kidnapping. What the hell sense did that even make? Sure, the man was as shady as Sable surmised, but to kidnap his nephew? Because there was no way Iago would do something like that without Alistair's knowledge.

Drayco had a pretty good idea of how Brock would feel about it. But he was almost afraid to tell him for fear his father would have a stroke. However, it did explain one mystery—the salted coffee.

Where did Graham Tibbs fit in? Sable said he'd seen Tibbs and Alistair together on one occasion before Tibbs's first "death." And now Tibbs was dead again, this time permanently. Drayco didn't know how to feel about a revelation like this. Angry? Mystified? Betrayed?

It wasn't the type of intel he could share with Detective Halabi or the MPD. For one thing, Drayco didn't have any tangible proof of Iago and Alistair's involvement. Just a whispered voice he'd overheard. No, he was very much on his own on this one.

It appeared he was headed for another round of counterpoint with his Uncle Alistair. Funny thing about counterpoint—the trick was to figure out relationships between voices and how they were manipulated. Drayco felt pretty manipulated right then, but he wasn't about to be played as a fool. Not by his uncle, nor by anyone.

14

With Drayco's emotions pegged to the max, he found it hard to keep them under control. He stopped at an abandoned park in the District as he drove by, wanting to vent some energy. Most people didn't know about the park except for a few of the city's homeless population. One such man was lying on a peeling bench in the far corner, with his head resting on a folded-up jacket.

Drayco tried a number programmed on his cellphone during his mother's murder case, but it was no longer active. Not that he'd expected Alistair Brisbane to keep the same number afterward. However, the scholarship committee at the University of Maryland must have some sort of contact for him, right? Sure enough, after he got in touch with them, they gave him a number to try.

When the familiar self-assured voice answered, Drayco said, "I didn't take you for a common crook. Shady international wheeling and dealing seem more your thing."

He heard only silence on the line for a moment, and then Alistair Brisbane replied, "This sounds like my nephew, Scott. But whatever do you mean?"

"I was kidnapped recently. In my semi-drugged state, I overheard snippets of whispered voices. It hit me that one of those voices belongs to your right-hand man, Iago Pryce. I also got a glimpse of one kidnapper, Graham Tibbs. The man's former business partner told me he'd seen Tibbs with you before his alleged death five years ago."

"I see. Putting two-and-two together, you think I was involved in your kidnapping?"

Drayco almost wanted to throw the phone into the small, brackish pond yards away from him. "Evasion isn't usually your style."

At Brisbane's continued silence, Drayco prompted him, "Wouldn't it have been easier to call me at home if you needed your little puzzle solved?"

A heavy sigh followed a long pause on the other end. "I do apologize for your rough handling. My employees were a bit too intense, I fear. As to why I couldn't ask you for your help, I felt this little tactic was necessary. The risk of your refusal was too great. Plus, the matter was too delicate to handle out in the open."

"All that for a puzzle?"

"A very important puzzle. Although it may not matter now."

"What do you mean?"

"A copy of the decoded message was stolen."

"Let me guess, by Graham Tibbs?"

"By someone I trusted."

"Tibbs went to a games store to find out what the deciphered message meant. Which means he was definitely the puzzle thief. And I find it incredibly hard to believe Tibbs was 'accidentally' killed by a hit-and-run driver coming out of that store at that particular time."

Brisbane cleared his throat. "I see what you are thinking. But I give you my word I didn't have anything to do with the man's death. And Tibbs merely borrowed the puzzle message. But since it wasn't found on his person after he left that games store, someone must have stolen it from him."

"How would you know that?"

"I can't tell you. But my sources are golden."

"What was an allegedly dead man doing working for you?"

"I sometimes help people disappear. Some then show their gratitude by helping me in return. I'm afraid I'm not at liberty to say any more about that, either."

"Not even why this particular man wanted to disappear? I've found a rap sheet for the guy, but it's all long ago, with nothing recent."

"He wasn't involved in crimes recently, no. But he did get mixed up with a bad crowd who did some bad things. He merely feared for his own life. That is all I can say there, too."

Drayco rubbed his forehead with his free hand. This was going nowhere. "You said this puzzle was valuable? Why?"

"It's a treasure map of sorts. A few years ago, something very precious was stolen from an old, dear friend in Uzbekistan. I only want to restore this item to its rightful owner. But if the person who stole the decoded message from Graham Tibbs finds it first, that won't happen."

"Again, I still don't understand why you didn't feel you could ask me point blank to help with this."

"And as I said, this was too important to risk you saying no. Seeing as how it's me, I figured you *would* . . . say no."

"What is this valuable item? How did it end up over here in the States? Or I'm assuming it did."

"I'm afraid I can't tell you that, either, but you were very helpful in decoding the puzzle. I am quite grateful."

"Potentially decoded it. Since I'm not even sure what it means, how could you?"

"We're working on it, but that's all I can say."

Alistair's vague answers irritated Drayco, but there was no way he was giving up. "Who picked the house where I was taken? Why then and there?"

"Graham Tibbs arranged the place. The timing was also his suggestion."

"If you hired Tibbs like you hire other people who 'like to disappear,' then where has Tibbs been for the past five years?"

"Let's just say I have many places where I can keep people hidden away. Think of it as my own private witness protection program." There was a brief chuckle on the other end.

Drayco didn't feel like laughing. "Did you also help with the arson that allegedly killed Tibbs? And plant the tooth so the police would ID the body as his?"

"I did not. That was all arranged by Tibbs."

"Including killing someone else to be discovered in that fire?"

More silence again before Brisbane replied slowly, "He assured me he didn't kill anyone. The individual the police found in the fire had already died of natural causes. A local homeless man, I believe."

"So Graham set that fire intentionally? And used the homeless man as a decoy?"

"That is what he told me. I did not help with the fire, but I do believe his account, then and now."

"Then tell me why a man who went to such lengths to disappear five years ago would risk being seen going to Johnny Burdell's store to ask him about the puzzle? Burdell said he didn't know him, but I have to wonder if he was involved. Or had a closer connection to Tibbs than he let on."

"That was a mistake on my part. I should have kept a tighter grip on Tibbs. I think the man was eager to repay me by helping with my puzzle problem. So he went behind my back to try to solve the code his own way. After all, it was Tibbs who found the puzzle originally."

"And he brought the puzzle right to you, just like that?"

"Even though he could have run off with it himself, knowing its potential value. That demonstrates loyalty."

"Loyalty like you showed my mother?"

This time, the silence stretched out for a long time, and Drayco thought Alistair had hung up. Finally, his uncle said, "That topic is off-limits. Except to say the staff working on the scholarship I set up in her memory—the one that's actually in your name—are looking forward to your recital."

It was Drayco's turn to be silent for a moment until Brisbane just said, "We'll be in touch," and hung up.

A motion off to Drayco's left caught his eye, and he whipped around to see the homeless man from the bench standing nearby and eyeing him. Drayco was six-four, but this man was easily six inches taller and loomed over Drayco as he continued staring.

The fellow said, "I seen you pacing around the park. Looking real angry. Sounding real angry."

Drayco waved the phone in the air. "Sorry. A bad conversation."

The man patted Drayco on the shoulder. "Must be family trouble. Ain't nobody talks to folks like that except family. You gotta resist 'em, man, don't let 'em get you down." And then he turned around and lumbered off, whistling an unidentifiable tune.

The man's whistling made Drayco realize he never asked Alistair about the "Twinkle, Twinkle" song he heard while in his prison. Was that Alistair or Iago or Graham Tibbs or someone else playing it? One of many answers Alistair left to dangle in the wind.

Drayco pulled a photo of a woman with auburn hair and greenish-hazel eyes out of his wallet. It was taken before she first vanished from their lives. She was what, twenty-seven then? To be always and forever young in his mind.

§ § §

Drayco strolled into his townhome, still fuming. But he calmed down long enough to open the back door and make sure Cat had crunchies. She did, but it wasn't food she was after as she strolled in, tail held high, and promptly vanished as she sometimes did for a brief time.

Maybe he could coax her out with some piano playing. Hell, maybe he could coax his sanity out with his piano playing. Following his recent musical obsession, he sat down to play Mozart's "Ah vous dirai-je, Maman," based on the original French children's song that later became "Twinkle, Twinkle." But still no Cat.

He might as well add to the growing pile of failures, so he grabbed the paper with the puzzle solution and settled into his favorite red chair to study it some more. He rubbed his eyes after the numbers blurred together, until he finally pushed the puzzle aside. He glanced over at a deck of playing cards. Maybe he should do some more shuffling therapy for his hand instead?

He didn't feel like doing that, either. But at least he got his wish to toss his cellphone, slinging it onto the coffee table, where it skidded with a loud clanging sound. The "clang" coincided with a ringing at the front door. Should he answer it? Or hope whoever it was went away?

Opting for the former, he opened the door, and Sarg breezed in, sacks in hand filled with containers. He headed straight for the kitchen and ladled out portions of his usual mouth-watering cuisine into dishes he snagged from Drayco's cabinets.

Drayco shook his head. "It's not that I'm ungrateful, but between you and Brock, I feel like I'm surrounded by a bunch of mothering hens."

"It just so happens I have an egg frittata right here."

"This makes two home-cooked meals in the same week. My neighbors will think I hired a chef." But Drayco wasn't about to turn down a gift meal. He grabbed some silverware and a couple of beers and followed Sarg to the dining table he'd actually cleaned off as they feasted on Sarg's gourmet handiwork.

Sarg wisely opted to keep the conversation light and regaled him about his daughter Tara's first semester in her forensic program at Virginia Commonwealth University. "And her professor couldn't believe she had the audacity to question his statement about phenotyping. Only, he was the one with egg on his face."

Drayco rolled his eyes at that. "Okay, knock off the chicken jokes. So what did he say to Tara?"

"That she was right, naturally."

Drayco grinned. "Maybe I should let her have a go at that puzzle of mine. Although I haven't told you the latest."

"What?"

"I know who's behind it. You're going to think I'm making it up."

"Try me."

"Alistair Brisbane."

Sarg's eyes widened. "You're joking."

"Nope. He admitted it."

"What the bloody hell was he thinking?"

"He says it's a puzzle that leads to a stolen treasure."

"I say again, what the hell? Or, more importantly, why the hell? As in, why kidnap his own nephew?"

"He didn't think I'd say yes if he asked for my help."

"Oh, well, he's got me there. I wouldn't have said yes if he'd been my uncle. Not after what he's done." Sarg took a swig of his beer. "All I can say is that mysterious treasure had better be worth it. Like, Ark of the Covenant worth it."

Just then, sounds of tinkling piano keys reached their ears. Sarg stared at Drayco and jumped up in defensive mode as he tip-toed closer to Drayco's piano room. He stopped short at the doorway and started laughing. "Only you would have a cat—well, half a cat—that likes to play the piano."

"I think she's getting better. At first, it was only one key. She has a whole range now. Next thing you know, she'll be playing Bach. Hell, maybe I'll even send her to UMD to play that scholarship recital. She'd raise a lot more money than I would."

"So she's coming inside your townhome more?"

"Whenever she wants to. And she usually wants to when it's raining. I'm just the crunchie-giver most of the time. Although when she had a sneezing fit the other week, I wasn't sure if I should take her to a vet. Or could even catch her to try."

Sarg grinned. "Oh, brother. Isn't that what pet owners do, take an animal to a vet?"

"Am I a pet owner now? Or a pet slave?"

"We had a few cats while Tara was younger, so I'm going with pet slave. And if that feline hasn't sneezed since and doesn't have runny eyes or nose, it's probably fine. Cats have allergies, too, you know."

"Yes, well, I've got an allergy to being kidnapped. By my uncle, of all people."

"So, what's next?" Sarg turned to head back toward the dining table. "It's not like you can go over and barge your way onto Alistair's private island."

"Don't tempt me."

Sarg got a gleam in his eye. "Sure would be fun to try, wouldn't it?"

Drayco groaned. "Not my definition of fun."

"You're just getting soft."

"Not soft. As much as I'd love to traipse over to that island, I don't think it would accomplish anything."

"Maybe, maybe not." Sarg stuffed one last bite of frittata into his mouth then said, "Before I forget, you said something cryptic on the phone yesterday about Joyelle, your dad's new lady friend. What's up there?"

"I found out she has a tie to Graham Tibbs's former business owner."

"Hoo boy. Is that a fact?"

"You were asking what's next, and I suddenly feel the need to know a lot more about her."

Sarg grinned. "I do have the day off."

"Coffee and something in the flour-and-sugar family at the Chantal Cafe afterward, then?" Drayco had noticed Sarg didn't pack any dessert this time.

"If you're buying, yes. And if they still have their famous Lemon Truffle Layer Cake." Sarg was practically drooling.

Sarg's intrusion initially irritated Drayco, but he was now glad his former partner stopped by to rescue him from his gloom. Drayco's blood pressure had spiked while talking to Alistair, and Sarg helped it settle down into only mildly elevated territory.

Between Alistair and Joyelle, Drayco had a cluster of family headaches to deal with. The kidnapping case he'd thought was a matter of a rogue intelligence agency, or some other little spy game, was turning out to be something else entirely. Something far worse for him. So where did he go from there?

15

Drayco held out the key and opened his office, stopping before heading in to give a quick sweep of the space. Sarg peered over his shoulder, "What, no red and green tinsel? Or candy-cane pillows? Better not let my wife and daughter in here. They're OCD about holiday decorating."

Drayco groaned. "I'm already sick of Christmas by September. Stores start selling Christmas merchandise right after the Fourth of July now. It's one long, drawn-out holiday."

Sarg said cheerily, "FourthofHallowThanksMas?"

"Something like that."

Sarg stepped inside and scanned the room. "I haven't been here since those two nice goons dropped by to harass you. You sure you didn't find any bugs afterward?"

Drayco gave him a withering look, and Sarg grinned. "Of course. How could I doubt?"

What Drayco didn't tell his former partner was he'd been extra-cautious ever since, which is one reason he paused before entering. He wanted to give the place a broad sweep first.

Sarg added, "I'm still impressed you took down those two thugs all by yourself."

When Drayco gave him an even more withering look, Sarg just laughed.

After they made it inside and closed the door, Drayco said, "Office, sweet office."

Sarg looked up at the ceiling. "New security cameras, I see."

"Yep. Pointed at the entry. And at my computer." Drayco patted his large desktop. "Not that it would be easy to haul away this baby without anyone seeing you. I think the CPU alone weighs fifty pounds."

"You could just, you know, carry your laptop between your office and house."

"This computer is more secure. And I don't want to install certain database software on the laptop. Plus, laptops are easier to swipe from cars. Or anywhere else."

"Point taken." Sarg pointed to Drayco's filing cabinets. "And you've still got old-school paperwork."

"A habit leftover from Bureau days. It's the same thing when I fly. The new glass cockpits are pretty sweet, but it's good to have an analog backup in case that lovely digital tech fails. Paper maps and compasses tend not to fail."

Sarg raised an eyebrow. "How often do they fail?"

"More than you'd think. Not enough for you to worry about, but I like to be prepared."

"Boy scout motto?"

"I wasn't a boy scout. Traveled too much in my touring days."

"A 'piano scout,' then. Whatever that means."

Drayco nodded at the coffee maker parked on top of a counter. "Make yourself useful."

Sarg pulled out drawer after drawer until he found the coffee grounds and filters and went to work. As Drayco peered at the computer screen, he held out one hand to accept the cup of java that Sarg handed over.

Sarg took a sip of his and nodded his approval. "Kona. Good choice." And then he added, "Find anything?"

"USCIS records show Joyelle Babineaux was born in France. Emigrated a couple of decades ago and is a naturalized citizen, like she said."

"That's a point in favor of her story being genuine, right?"

Drayco switched to another report from a news database. "But then again, there's this. Brock's new girlfriend's former husband died in Europe from a hit-and-run, just like our recently departed kidnapper, Graham Tibbs. Coincidence?"

"When and where did it happen?"

"Before she left, so thirty years. And it was in Tashkent, part of Uzbekistan. Or as it was known at the time, the Uzbek Soviet Socialist Republic. But it also happens to be the same country where Alistair said his friends with the stolen treasure lived."

"Ah, I see where you're going with this. You're wondering if she's a plant via Alistair?"

"Possibly. Or someone else."

"Hmmm." Sarg grabbed the chair in front of the desk and parked it next to Drayco. "Scootch over. I want to log in to some of my Bureau databases."

"What do you think you'll find?"

Sarg tapped on the keyboard, and before long, he let out a whistle. "Something like this, perhaps."

Drayco peered over his shoulder. "Joyelle used to be employed in the CIA along with her husband, Gerard Briller."

"In the days before the fall of the Soviet Union. That explains why they were in that area of Europe. As spies. Says here she left the CIA suddenly."

Sarg accessed another database and scrolled through some files. "Okay. This is interesting. Joyelle allegedly had an affair with a fellow intelligence officer. That's likely why she resigned from the service."

Drayco swallowed some of the coffee, but it wasn't strong enough to hide the sour taste in his mouth. "Now I'm really curious about her intentions regarding my father. Even if she isn't an Alistair plant, is this a pattern with her?"

"I don't know, junior. I agree with you that the timing is odd. But I can't see how her hook-up with Brock could tie in with your kidnapping as a motive. Maybe another case he's working on? He does have high-profile clients. The affair part of the equation, well, we'd have to track down marriage and divorce records. Globally."

"Oh, I will. Maybe today." Drayco looked at the records Sarg had pulled up. "What about her husband? Does it say what type of intelligence activity either of them was involved with?"

Sarg scanned the documents. "Nothing for Joyelle. I see a mention of a resistance group associated with her husband. Something called the Liberty Legion."

"Heard anything about them?"

"No, not a thing. But that's more CIA than FBI."

"Right. Still, if you hear of anything . . . "

"I'll see what I can find." Sarg frowned. "Okay, so let's not fixate on this one suspect. What about other people with possible motives connected to the late Mr. Graham Tibbs?"

Drayco leaned back in his chair. "Other than my uncle or Joyelle, his former business partner, Leon Sable, perhaps. I find it hard to believe he knew nothing about Tibbs's plans to stage his death in that arson. And Tibbs would have had help substituting another body for his own. Unless it was Alistair."

"What's the motive for Sable to be involved?"

"Perhaps Sable was in a shady partnership with Tibbs but later double-crossed him. Sable believed it really was Tibbs in the building, and he was the one who torched it."

"About that body found in the fire. Any ID?"

"No, but I'll leave that up to the Arlington PD to figure out after the exhumation. Alistair said it was a homeless person who died from natural causes."

"Okey doke. Who else might be a suspect?"

"Ezra Layton, Tibbs's childhood friend. Perhaps he was the one who helped Tibbs disappear in the first place, but they had a falling out. Maybe they were partners in crime over Alistair's mysterious 'treasure.' And again, Layton double-crossed Tibbs."

"You said Layton had grown close to Tibbs's sister, the opera singer. Enough to think of her as his older sister. Maybe the hit-and-run was some sort of revenge for her by getting rid of the estranged brother?"

When Drayco rubbed his forehead, Sarg quickly added, "Far-fetched, I know."

Drayco continued, "Then there's Johnny Burdell, the puzzle store owner. Maybe he knew Tibbs wasn't dead all along, and they were in the treasure-hunting scheme together. But he decided he wanted all of the money for himself."

"Didn't you tell me your Uncle Alistair swears Tibbs wasn't associating with anyone?"

"That's what he said."

"And yet he goes to see this puzzle-story guy? Kind of throws Alistair's assertion into doubt if he didn't know about that little visit."

"I'll have to press Alistair further on that. If he'll talk to me again. I'm not buying the whole idea Tibbs was so eager to help Alistair with his quest, he went to Burdell because he didn't trust me to solve the puzzle."

"Feels hinky to me, too."

"While I'm thinking about it," Drayco grabbed a piece of paper and wrote on it. When Sarg looked at it in bewilderment, Drayco added, "Burdell said Tibbs came to see him because Burdell was a 'cipher god' and posted in an online forum devoted to the topic. He swears that's how Tibbs must have tracked him down."

"And that's why this paper says 'The Cipher Circle'?"

"Burdell was vague about this group, as if he didn't want me to visit. But there aren't many such groups, and that's the only active one. I searched through it and couldn't find any Burdell or Tibbs."

"Probably using fake names."

"That's what I figured, too. But I thought I'd just pass this along in case. The Bureau is dealing with a lot of cybercrime these days."

"Will do." Sarg pocketed the paper.

Drayco leaned back and rubbed his hands over his face. "Ah, this whole Joyelle thing. It puts me in a really tight spot. Should I tell Brock what I've found out?"

"Feeling guilty about digging into Joyelle's background, huh?"

"A little. Then again, maybe Brock's done some investigating on his own. Still, the timing feels odd. It's pinging my scam radar."

"It could be nothing. Her former marriage and spook career were a long time ago."

"Unless she's still in the service but not in any branch for which we can access records. In this country or another."

"Yeah, there is that. But give me a little time. I'll contact some associates. See what I can dig up."

"Thanks, Sarg."

"*De nada.*"

"Spanish? Detective Halabi is learning French."

"Okay, then, *je t'en prie.*"

Drayco grinned. "Your accent sounds a lot like his."

"Is he an old southern boy like me?"

"Apparently."

"There you go. Next time I'm in that country, I'll make sure I stay in the south of France."

All joking aside, Sarg was right. Drayco was almost sorry he'd looked into Joyelle's background. His father seemed truly happy with this new woman in his life. But if she had any nefarious designs on Brock, Drayco would be insane if he didn't do something about it.

What if he was wrong? Their father-and-son relationship was rocky even during the best of times. Drayco was actually relieved at the lack of holiday decorations in his office—he wasn't sure he could muster a "be of good cheer" vibe.

Not that Christmas had ever been his favorite time of year. With his mother AWOL, his father gone a lot of the time, and his sister's death, there was never much to celebrate. But the thought of being the one to destroy his father's newfound happiness made Drayco feel like he'd be handing Brock a stocking filled with coal.

But coal or no coal, he knew what he had to do.

16

The bar was poorly lit, dingy, and a little thin on the number of patrons filling out the rear booths, which is the way Drayco liked it. Not so his father, more accustomed to the marble-and-chandelier cocktail party rubbing elbows with the District's rich and powerful. Those places didn't have beer stains on the carpet or the aromatics from bottles of bitters mingling with the smell of burnt cheese.

But when Drayco said they needed to have a chat, Brock had surprised him by suggesting this place, the Burr Bar. They both knew it had places where people can talk privately—and patrons knew to keep out of your business.

He slid into a booth across from his father. "Why not have this talk at your house? Or mine?"

"Because I've got a crew installing the new carpeting today. Damned company couldn't get it down in time for Thanksgiving, so here we are."

Brock held up the glass of Scotch ale he'd started working on. "And because I had a feeling from your tone of voice, I'd need this to wash our conversation down with."

Drayco signaled the server over to order some coffee. He didn't want his brain to be muzzled by alcohol, and he would need the caffeine. But there was no need to reach for the salt because Brock pushed it over to him first.

Drayco said, "I finally figured out who that familiar whispered voice was during my kidnapping."

Brock set his glass down and leaned forward. "Somebody I know?"

"Indirectly. I realized it sounded like Iago Pryce."

Brock's eyes narrowed. "Iago Pryce, as in Alistair Brisbane's hired thug?"

"The very same." Drayco took a sip from the just-delivered coffee before continuing. His mouth was surprisingly dry. "I called my dear uncle. He'd changed phone numbers, but I found one that worked."

"So, what did he have to say?"

"That he was behind it all. He apologized for the 'inconvenience,' but he didn't deny it."

"What idiotic game was he trying to play? To kidnap you over a stupid puzzle? Why not just call you up?"

"I asked him that. He said it was too important, and he was afraid I'd say no."

Brock's face flushed a deep shade of red as he clutched his glass in his hands on the table. "That rat bastard. I'll kill him. I don't care if he is my ex-brother-in-law. Hell, I should march up . . . well boat up . . . to that little island of his and beat him to a pulp. And then ground that pulp into a pulp."

Drayco shook his head. "Wouldn't do any good, I don't think."

Brock pinched his nose, something he did when he was furious and trying to keep from exploding. "Was he the one who killed Graham Tibbs?"

"He said he helped Tibbs 'disappear.' Apparently, Alistair does this for people in trouble. I'm not sure yet what kind of trouble it was in Tibbs's case. But Alistair swore he wasn't behind the death."

"And you believe him?" Brock looked at Drayco with an incredulous expression.

"I'm not believing or disbelieving yet. Reserving judgment."

"Well then, please tell me what was so all-fired important about this puzzle that he couldn't just phone you up in the first place."

"He claims the puzzle I solved—or mostly solved—provides instructions about a stolen treasure of some kind. He refused to say what, where, how, or anything else. Just that it was taken from some friends of his in Europe."

Drayco paused, took a deep breath, and added, "Friends who live in Uzbekistan. Which also happens to be where Joyelle and her husband were stationed when they worked for the CIA."

Brock flopped back against his seat. "You've looked into her past."

"I had to. The timing was too odd."

"What do you mean, timing? We've been dating off and on for months."

"You have to admit the Uzbekistan link is a little too coincidental. And since she was intelligence—"

"You think she's spying on me? Or you? Or is part of Alistair's grand scheme, somehow?"

"She also buys metal supplies from the former business owner of the deceased kidnapper, Graham Tibbs. Name of Leon Sable. More coincidence?"

"There aren't that many metal supply stores around. You know that."

"Her former husband also died in a hit-and-run. And she left the intelligence service after they learned she was having an affair with another agent."

Brock uttered a humorless chuckle. "You really don't like her, do you?"

"Where did you meet her?"

"At the Cipher Club."

"The same club that's patronized by mostly former intelligence agents? And you didn't suspect?"

Brock glared at him. "She told me about her past. The CIA service, her husband's death, all of it."

"Even the hit-and-run part? And the affair?"

"It doesn't matter. That was a long time ago."

"You know how I hate coincidences."

"Look. I can understand you're jealous because of Maura. Not wanting me to replace her."

"I didn't say that. Besides, you've had other lady friends in the three decades since Mom left, and I was okay with those."

Brock corrected him. "You gave off stay-away vibes with each one of them."

Drayco blinked at him. "I did?"

"Every time I began a new relationship, I felt guilty because I knew what was coming with you."

Drayco flipped through his mental file of Brock's former girlfriends. Had he been guilty of those stay-away vibes and not realized it? He shook his head. "I've always wanted you to be happy."

"But only with your mother, is that it?"

"Of course not. She left us and vanished. You don't get over that."

"Damn straight. And I always wanted . . . needed . . . to move on from Maura's betrayal. But you kept dragging me back in, in a way."

"Betrayal? What about you telling me Mom was dead when I was younger."

"We've discussed this before. I believed she was, and all signs pointed in that direction."

They simultaneously picked up their drinks and sipped on them for a few moments without talking. Then Brock sighed and said, "It's just that I feel Joyelle is my first chance at a real relationship in a long time. But you've seemed to resist my chances at finding a partner. Or perhaps in your mind, as I said, a replacement."

Drayco ran a hand through his hair. "I'm more concerned about someone taking advantage of you. And in this case, using you as a pawn of some kind."

"I'm a big boy, son. And for your information, Joyelle told me about her affair. She was quite upfront about it. That should prove she's being honest with me, right?"

"What about the Uzbekistan connection? Wouldn't that indicate a possible link to Alistair and the dead kidnapper?"

Brock frowned. "Sometimes coincidences in life are really just that. I've been around the block a few more times than you have. So I know from first-hand experience."

Drayco gulped down the rest of his coffee, and the vigilant server immediately reappeared at his shoulder to refill the cup for him. Drayco said, "At least she was born in France, as she said."

"Now I'm wondering if you did background searches on all my former 'lady friends,' as you call them."

"No, only this one."

Brock sighed. "You may recall me telling you I met your mother at a dog park. I fell head over heels for her, to use a cliché. Love at first sight. But love doesn't necessarily work out the way you want it to. And love isn't always enough."

Drayco sat up a little straighter at those words. Wasn't that what he'd once told his own former girlfriend, Darcie Squire?

"Look, son, I know this Joyelle thing came out of left field, and I'm sorry I didn't tell you sooner. But I haven't had the best of luck with relationships over the past several years. I wanted to make sure this one was a little more stable before I mentioned anything."

"Still, I wish you'd told me sooner." Deep down, Drayco would like to give Joyelle the benefit of the doubt. But he'd fought hard against allowing any personal feelings to open the door for unintentional biases to barge in. He made that mistake a couple times, and it hadn't ended well.

Brock motioned for the bar server to bring him another ale, and it was apparent they'd be there a while longer. There was no way Drayco would allow his father to drive while his BAC was high.

A chill that wasn't from the inadequate heating in the bar cooled the space between them, and Drayco hated it. He'd spent most of his youth wanting to see more of his father, and now that they could, they often argued when they did.

Brock grabbed one of the menus slotted inside the napkin holder. "Probably need some protein to go with this second ale. The place looks like a dump, but their rib eye is surprisingly good. I'm buying."

Drayco nodded. He could do steak. A little beefy détente would be welcome right about then.

What did Ezra Layton say about Graham Tibbs? That his father was abusive, a "monster." Maybe Drayco and Brock had suffered some rough patches, but Drayco knew he could count on Brock when the chips were down. Sometimes an absentee father, or even a gruff one, was a lot better than the alternative.

17

Drayco had stayed at the bar with Brock longer than he'd planned as they worked through some of the ice between them. Fortified with steak, they'd got their relationship a little more back on track.

When he'd returned to his townhome, he took out his frustrations on his Steinway with Chopin's B-flat minor nocturne. Deciding poor Chopin didn't deserve the rough treatment, Drayco switched to his computer and sat up late using public records hunting for more clues about Tibbs and his friends and family.

It was one of those family members he was meeting this morning since Tibbs's sister, Aria D'Angelo, wanted an update on the case. Ordinarily, he would get her up-to-date via a phone call. But she insisted he brief her in person because she didn't enjoy talking on the phone. She'd added she used to have her manager do that for her and sighed. "I miss having Rowan take care of things."

Before Drayco headed over, he cued up some online video recordings of Aria from her heyday. Even though he wasn't a fan of opera per se, she *was* talented. He also called an opera-expert friend, Dirk Schlezinger, to ask why she hadn't achieved the same level of success as the likes of a Renée Fleming or Joan Sutherland.

He practically heard his friend shrug over the phone. "Who knows why some singers break out, and others don't? Tastes of the day, bad managers or good managers, lucky breaks, maybe someone's harder to work with, the person isn't a good schmoozer. I've known several singers who should have broken through to the big time and never made it, while some lesser talents did."

"Same with the piano, I suppose."

Dirk laughed, "It's who you know sometimes. And maybe still a little bit of who you sleep with."

Drayco winced at that. He'd been lucky to avoid such pressures when he was touring in his younger days. Mostly. He said, "I did some research on her. She has a post-career reputation for philanthropy."

"And how. She's tireless. I think she's hit up just about everyone famous for funds for an opera house and scholarships. But I gather she wants it in her name, not theirs. Has maybe even been a little too demanding about that. An overriding passion kind of thing."

"If you can't get your legacy the way you'd hoped, you try for something else, right?" He felt defensive of Aria. She'd had her career cut short like he had. In fact, he was feeling sorry he might not be able to name his own smallish opera house after her, depending upon what his benefactor agreed to.

After Drayco hung up with Dirk, he warmed up some leftover rib eye from last night's dinner at the bar with Brock. He chased that down with a Manhattan Special soda before heading up to Bethesda, eventually pulling into the familiar gated driveway where he made his way to the front entry.

Aria was in the Christmas-cheer camp, it seemed. The door had a giant wreath with gilded pine and eucalyptus plus some bronze and burgundy berries. Two matching topiaries flanked each side of the porch, each larger than the tiny holiday tree Drayco put on his coffee table—when he bothered putting anything up.

Aria greeted him with a big smile and offered him some espresso, which he accepted. They headed to the cavernous living room and sat on sparkling white chairs that made Drayco wish he *weren't* drinking espresso.

She immediately pressed him on the case. "Have you solved that puzzle thing?"

"Unfortunately, not yet, but I'm getting closer. I know who was behind it."

"Really? Who?"

"A man named Alistair Brisbane. Have you ever heard of him? More importantly, did Graham know him?"

She put her hand to her throat and frowned. "I don't know of him, personally, no. And I'm afraid since I'd lost touch with my brother, I can't really say if Graham knew this man or not."

"Lost touch due to the estrangement?"

"That's right." She sighed. "Not knowing much about my brother—that's as much a tragedy as anything. And it's the main reason I want to make it up to him in death.."

"Family estrangements are a lot more common than you think."

"I suppose so. But I still remember how much fun it was when we were children and how I do miss that. Some of my fondest memories. That was before we grew apart on account of his dangerous behavior."

She picked at her pearl necklace. "That's always how it is, isn't it? You drift away from friends and family due to who knows what? Sometimes you can't even remember why you drifted away. And then they're gone, and you wonder why you let anything get in the way of reconnecting. That will haunt me for the rest of my life. Graham needed somebody, needed me, and I wasn't there for him."

"I think his problems were out of your league, so I wouldn't beat yourself up. If he was involved in something shady—so much so he had to disappear— I doubt you could have helped him."

"Ezra told me that, too."

Drayco noticed the glass piece Graham's friend, Ezra Layton, had given her was missing. He asked about it.

She replied, "Oh, clumsy me, I broke it the same day you were last here. And it was such a lovely piece, too. Of course, I've asked Ezra for a replacement, which I'll pay for."

"I chatted with Ezra at the track where he races his sports car, which is pretty expensive. He said there was an inheritance involved. I've done some checking into his background, but I can't find any rich relatives who might have left him money."

She waved her hand in the air. "I don't want to pry. Who knows? Maybe it was me being too naggy and prying that pushed Graham away. If Ezra ever wants to tell me about it, he will. In his own time."

She peered over at Drayco. "I did a bit of research on you, too. You were a promising young pianist years ago. Whatever happened?"

"A bad accident." That was his stock response whenever he didn't want to go into sordid details about the carjacking. Most people left it at that and didn't press him further.

"Oh, that's just awful. And what a terrible shame. Like something out of *Hamlet*. Or maybe *Rigoletto*. A real tragedy."

"Perhaps. But it helps me know what it's like not to be able to perform after an injury. Similar to your situation."

She smiled at him. "You are a dear young man, Scott."

"I listened to some of your recordings. I can understand how you got your stellar reputation."

She straightened up and broke out into a snippet of "Der Hölle Rache kocht in meinem Herzen" from the Queen of the Night aria.

"That's amazing. And you still sound a lot like those recordings."

"Alas, that's about all I can do these days. Being on stage for hours is too much."

Drayco nodded, knowing all too well. "You're raising money for a scholarship?"

"A scholarship program for opera singers. And also an opera house. I'd be delighted to have it named after me, but I know that seems like hubris. It's all about having to resist the tyranny of age and time. And being forgotten."

"Yet, you have a far greater legacy than most."

"I suppose I do. But the art world is filled with politics, something I'm not very good at. I wasn't invited to sing at a royal wedding. Why? I didn't ingratiate myself, even though I could have if I was that type. And somehow, 'The Three Sopranos' doesn't sound as sexy as 'The Three Tenors,' does it? It's all politics when you get right down to it."

She looked away briefly before turning back to him with a glint of tears in her eyes. "But you didn't come here to talk about me. It's about Graham and this puzzle business. Have you found out how it all ties in with his death?"

"Not yet. But I've spoken with people who might know more about Graham's disappearance and sudden reappearance. Since I have a personal stake in this, I won't quit until I've pieced it all together. You can rest assured on that."

Her face brightened. "You should talk with Christi Allingham, another friend who's known Graham since he was a youth. And maybe more recently, or so I got the impression. She works for the government, I think."

Aria frowned as she thought harder. "I believe it's the Commerce Department. Yes, that sounds right. I suspected there might be a little spark between them. I guess it just never worked out."

Drayco eyed the Bösendorfer piano in the far corner of the room, grateful no one expected him to perform "on command." But it did remind him of one thing. He asked, "Did the song 'Twinkle, Twinkle, Little Star' have any special meaning to your brother?"

She stared at him. "Why, he had a record of it when he was a boy. One of those little sing-song things with those condescending baby voices adults make on such monstrosities. I think our mother gave it to him. They'd sing along together."

"But he didn't have a big band version?"

She looked puzzled. "I didn't know there was such a thing. No, he never mentioned anything like that. Is it important?"

"I have no idea. But it might be."

"After his death ... " She sighed again and then emphasized, "After the *fire* ... they gave me all his personal belongings since Graham didn't have a will. I think they're stored in the attic. To be honest, I haven't gone through them since. But perhaps I shall. And if I find anything, I'll let you know."

"Thanks. I'd appreciate that."

As Drayco made his way down the long front sidewalk, he was intrigued Graham may have had a recent girlfriend no one else mentioned before. Christi Allingham was going on Drayco's list to interview.

He was disappointed Aria wasn't aware if Graham knew Alistair. The man's former business partner certainly knew about that connection. And what about Ezra Layton's sudden windfall to buy all those cars? What if, instead of an inheritance, it was really selling drugs?

Or dealing in stolen goods? He had a rap sheet like his friend, Graham, from years ago. But in the records Drayco dug up, it wasn't anything major. Petty theft, mostly.

He now had a good idea of who played that nursery song during Drayco's captivity. So Graham's mother got a children's "Twinkle, Twinkle" recording for him, and they sang along with it together when he was a boy. Likely not long before her death in a car accident. That could explain its significance to Graham and his interest in other versions like the big band arrangement. Okay. But why choose it to play at the kidnapping house? That must be one serious obsession.

Deep in thought, he tripped over a pair of gardening shears on the sidewalk and did a little twirl on his heel to avoid falling down. The only witnesses to his near-disaster-dance were a couple of crows cawing out something that sounded suspiciously like laughter.

This case was resembling more of a circular hora type of dance. You end up chasing your own tail more than making progress toward your goal. Maybe so, but he wasn't the type to give up on a case with his tail tucked between his legs.

Just then, he looked up and spied a cloud formation that looked exactly like a dog with a curled and tucked tail. He muttered up at the sky, "Thanks a lot."

18

After Drayco parked at his office, he grabbed a cab to take him down to the National Mall. Ordinarily, he'd walk since it wasn't that far, but he didn't want to work up a sweat even in the colder temps.

He'd tracked down Christi Allingham, who did indeed work for the Commerce Department, as Aria D'Angelo had recalled. When he phoned Allingham asking about Graham, she seemed reluctant at first. But she finally agreed when he explained he wanted to find justice for Graham, especially if he was run down intentionally.

Allingham suggested they meet at the National Gallery of Art cafeteria. "I'm a big art fan, so I like going whenever I get the chance. I often have lunch there."

She'd hinted it was also because it was such a public place, and he understood. She didn't know him, and a woman meeting a stranger for the first time *should* be wary. But she'd also added, "Besides, you can sit next to the waterfall through the glass."

Since she'd described what she looked like and what she'd be wearing, he recognized the pony-tailed woman in the blue-and-green plaid suit who'd already snagged a table. When she smiled, it reminded him a little of Nelia Tyler. For a moment, he experienced a wave of depression but chastised himself for wishing it really was Nelia as he sat across from her.

Christi was half-through the lunch she'd bought and apologized for starting without him. "I only have an hour."

"Of course. I'll grab something later."

"Have you tried Mitsitam Cafe over at the American Indian Museum? You really should. It's good, too. Pacific salmon with this wild berry sauce. And some delicious bison chili."

He asked her about her job. "Miss Allingham, you mentioned on the phone you work in GIS. As in geospatial analysis?"

She wrinkled her nose. "Most people's eyes glaze over when I tell them what I do. Yes, geospatial analysis, visualization of large data sets, and advisory assignments related to the effectiveness of government programs. We develop and maintain mapping tools, including the National Broadband Availability Map."

She warmed up as she talked more about it, and her eyes sparkled. "I research new management practices for application to programs or operations. Then we craft office analytical capabilities and internal dashboards to report on effectiveness and productivity of government programs."

She stopped herself with a little laugh. "Sorry. I warned you. Boring, yes?"

"Doesn't sound all that boring. And I would imagine it involves quite a lot of training."

Christi sat up straighter with a smile. "A PhD from the University of Denver. I'm quite proud of that. Most people in that program are men."

"How did you and Graham meet?"

"We knew each other in high school. I was a physics geek, and he was interested in science for a while. But he started slacking off. Got lazy, involved with some bad stuff."

"I'm aware of that. Various misdemeanors."

"After school, I heard he did some jail time. Not long, but long enough." She stared at the waterfall for a few moments. "And then you say he faked his own death five years ago? I just can't believe it. What in the world for?"

"He'd apparently gotten into trouble again and wanted an escape route."

"I knew he had a rough past. But he truly wanted to make a fresh start in life with his business." She frowned. "I understand that business was failing, I believe. So I can see how that would make it easier to disappear. But by trouble, I don't think you mean financial trouble, yes?"

"I'm not sure at this point."

With a nod, she added, "Honestly, though? I couldn't see him wanting to ever go back to prison, even for some minor infraction. So maybe it wasn't something he *did* that was bad. Maybe he'd *witnessed* something that was bad. Like the witness protection program, yes?"

He was a little bemused at her ending so many sentences with "yes." He replied, "That's a possibility. I've spoken with Graham's sister. She hinted you and Graham might have had a romantic relationship at one time?"

Christi slowed her dipping of a tea bag in hot water as she again studied the waterfall behind the glass. "We dated for about a year. When we were seniors. But I got accepted into UWM—the University of Wisconsin where I did my undergrad work—and Graham didn't want to go to college. He seemed to be at loose ends. No real ambition, just drifting. Later, when I heard he'd gone into the hardware business with his partner Leon Sable, I was pleased for him. I thought he'd finally found what would make him happy."

"But it didn't?"

She pulled her gaze away from the waterfall to stare at the liquid in her cup. "He invested twenty years in that business. I guess he found some measure of happiness."

"You don't sound convinced."

"It's hard to run a small hardware store these days. Not with so much competition from the giant chains, yes?"

"You heard this second-hand?"

She sighed. "We ran into each other six years ago. There was still a little of that spark left over, and I'd just come off a divorce. So we kind of hooked up again."

"You must have been devastated when the fire happened, and everyone thought he'd perished."

"Well, of course! I was horrified when I heard the news. But by then, we'd broken up for the second time. He was getting darker, angrier, more moody. I just couldn't take it. Not so soon after my divorce."

"And you have no idea why his moods changed?"

"No, but when he allegedly died in that fire . . . I wondered if it was suicide. Then I learned he was alive all this time. And now he's dead again? It's emotional whiplash. I don't really know how to react anymore."

Her eyes watered, so he reached over to a napkin holder and grabbed a couple he handed to her. She thanked him and added, "Why did he disappear? People don't usually do that unless they're running from something, yes?"

Then her watery eyes took on a more haunted look. "You don't think . . . that is . . . we broke up not long beforehand . . . "

"Things weren't going well for him by that point, but I doubt it was on account of you." Or so Drayco's Uncle Alistair had led him to believe.

"Then it must have been something pretty bad. Poor Graham. He could be a lot of fun to be around when he wanted to be."

"When he started to get 'darker, angrier, more moody,' as you said—did he talk about feeling threatened?"

She shook her head. "When I hinted around, he'd clam up. But he did say this one odd thing."

"And that was?"

"I'm paraphrasing. But it was something like, 'Do you think there's any room in heaven for people involved with someone else's death, even if they're innocent?' "

"By someone else's death, did he mean murder or an accident?"

"He didn't elaborate. That was it. And then he changed the subject."

A sudden commotion caught their attention as a loud crash reverberated throughout the marble-and-glass space. Two patrons had bumped into each other and sent their respective trays, plates, silverware, and glasses flying everywhere. The ensuing argument between the patrons led to a security guard running in and separating them as they stomped off, leaving the poor cafeteria workers to clean up the mess.

Drayco waited for the little drama to die down before asking his companion, "Did Graham ever mention Johnny Burdell? Or Alistair Brisbane?"

She thought about it for a moment. "Burdell sort of sounds familiar, but I can't place it. Except . . . maybe something about the environment? Sorry. But the other name is quite distinctive, hard to forget. He never mentioned that man to me. But I overheard a phone conversation once where the name came up."

She repeated the name aloud, "Brisbane. I've always wanted to go to Australia. But who doesn't, yes?"

Drayco held back a laugh. He had no doubt his global-oriented uncle had been there, but he doubted it was for the surfing, kangaroos, or their world-famous opera house. Plus, he was still amused at her habit of ending so many sentences with "yes."

He asked, "But you couldn't tell what it was about?"

"Graham was agitated, ranting at first. And then he lowered his voice, so I couldn't hear anything."

"One more thing. You said you dated Graham in high school. So you must have known Ezra Layton, Graham's best friend?"

She scrunched up her forehead. "Ezra was on the football team. I had a thing about avoiding those types. Overheard too many stories from other girls about unwanted sexual advances. And worse."

"Anything specific to Ezra?"

"No, nothing like that. As far as I knew, he was pretty clean. Except for some of the same misdemeanors as Graham. They were pretty close back then, those two."

They chatted for a while longer about her job and her own half-feral cat, a ginger tabby, before she had to return to her office. Since he was in a cafe, he grabbed some food and sat back down to do some people-watching as he liked to do.

Maybe he was too fixated on his case because when he spied a man with a slight resemblance to Graham Tibbs, Drayco felt his pulse quicken. Surely Tibbs wasn't going to turn up, again and again, like in a cheesy horror film something along the lines of *The Man Who Wouldn't Die?* At this point, Drayco wasn't counting anything out.

19

Drayco stopped by his townhome to check on the mail and to do some web surfing. He looked up all the local environmental groups, searching for membership rolls, photos, or social media postings. Finally, he found something that made him stop and stare.

Christi Allingham was right about Johnny Burdell being associated with environmental causes. Or at least one particular conservation group, the Potomac Conservancy Pact. But there, in a photo from one of the group's meetings several years ago, Drayco saw someone else familiar. It was the late Graham Tibbs. And he was seated right next to Burdell.

After checking the organization's website for contacts, Drayco got the phone number of a staffer named Mary Acherly. After introducing himself, she said, "Is this a legal issue? I can put you in touch with our attorneys . . . "

"Not an issue for an attorney, no." He referred to the online photo he'd found. "Was Graham Tibbs one of your members?"

"Graham Tibbs? Well, since our meetings are a matter of public record, I guess I can look that up for you." Drayco could hear the woman tapping on a keyboard on the other end of the line. "Here we are. He was active a few years ago. But then he let his membership lapse."

"Unfortunately, he died recently in a car accident." Best not to add it was a little more complicated.

Acherly replied, "Oh, lord, I'm so very sorry to hear that. Well, in checking the records here, it seems Graham came to several of our meetings. Volunteered for a committee studying recycling. He worked at a hardware store and reported seeing a lot of waste that bothered him."

"I see. And I also believe you have another member by the name of Johnny Burdell? I saw him in an online group photo."

"Oh yes, he's a much more recent member. I've met him. Please don't tell me something's happened to him, too?"

"No, he's still alive and well. Did Tibbs and Burdell know each other?"

"I'm searching through the minutes. Ah, yes. They both spoke at one particular meeting on a topic they shared strong feelings about. Looks like they might have coordinated their attack on the board's proposal. So they must have known each other."

"What type of proposal were they attacking?"

"Let's see here." More sounds of tapping on the keyboard. "It was when the board wanted to get a new carbon tax for businesses passed by the county. Johnny and Graham both owned businesses, and they disagreed with that particular proposal. Funny how folks are all for the environment until it affects their bottom line."

Drayco thanked Acherly and hung up. Well, then. Burdell denied knowing Graham Tibbs, the same Graham Tibbs mowed down in front of Burdell's store. And yet, it seems they knew each other pretty well. If so, then Burdell's song-and-dance about Tibbs only learning of Burdell's "expertise" in an online cipher-geek forum was also a lie.

Maybe it was time to have another crack at Mr. Burdell.

§ § §

On his way over to the Great Games store, Drayco spied a black car that might be tailing him. It had tinted windows and a temporary license tag. Just as he was trying to decide whether to follow it, it seemed to evaporate into thin air. A "ghost car?"

No, he was sure he saw it. Probably turned off onto a side street. He was still jumpy from the kidnapping, that was all, and it was likely just some diplomat.

Drayco parked the Starfire and headed into the puzzle store, but he didn't see signs of Johnny Burdell anywhere. Just Drayco's luck to get him on his day off. Drayco strolled up to the counter, where an unfamiliar man stood watching him expectantly. "Can I help you?"

"I'm looking for Johnny Burdell, the owner."

"You mean the soon-to-be-former owner."

Drayco frowned. "Former owner?"

"He up and quit. Well, quit running the place, which is why I'm here. He plans on selling the store soon, I take it."

"So you're the new—"

"Manager. Frederick Oak."

"O-a-k, like the tree?"

"Yes, but you're not going to make an acorn joke, are you? Because I am so sick of acorn jokes." Oak spoke in a long drawl that would put Ezra Layton to shame, but not a southern drawl, just a drawl-drawl.

Drayco took a whiff of the air. "Is that *pine* air freshener?"

"It's not like oaks give off any scent, do they?" The man grinned as he tugged on his brown-and-gray beard. He added, "I don't suppose you're in the market for a puzzle and games store? I can let Johnny know."

"Not right now, thanks. But where did Burdell go? And why all of a sudden?"

"Didn't say. Only that he had to get out of town. I assumed it was a family thing, but Johnny didn't want to talk about it. And I'm not the type to pry. Gossip's for old biddies." Oak simultaneously crinkled his nose and twiddled his thumbs.

"Had he been having family problems, perhaps?"

"When had he not? Johnny's always having woman trouble. I've known him for a while now. I used to manage another game store up in Baltimore."

"What kind of woman trouble?"

Oak frowned. "You're asking a lot of personal questions there. I'm not sure how much I should say about all that. Gossip again, you know. Small minds with little to do."

"This wouldn't be gossip since we're talking about a possible murder investigation."

"Murder? Surely Johnny isn't involved—"

"A man was killed in front of this store."

"You mean that hit-and-run? Thought it was just an accident."

"It might be much more."

"Geez, I don't wanna get mixed up with any murder thing." Oak frowned again. "I don't have an attorney, but I could get one."

"I think it highly unlikely you'd be a suspect. In fact, the more helpful you are to me, the more I'll be able to help find the real culprit."

"Are you police?"

"Private investigator. The hit-and-run victim's sister hired me."

Oak thought about that for a moment. "Not sure I can help, but the woman trouble I mentioned? Maybe one of those women ran over that fellow because she wanted Johnny blamed for it."

"Any woman in particular?"

"His ex-wife, maybe. I think Johnny still carries the torch for her. But I predicted that one wouldn't last from the get-go."

"Why is that?"

"The ex and Johnny's sister were at each other's throats all the damned time. Johnny was caught in the middle. Shame, really. Deep down, Johnny's a good guy. The kind who wants to be better."

"Did Johnny leave any address where he could be reached?"

Oak eyed Drayco skeptically. "Again, no offense, but I'm not really sure who you are. Why don't you give me your number? I'll call him up and tell him you want to talk."

Drayco pulled out a business card from his wallet and handed it over. "Burdell belonged to the Potomac Conservancy Pact environmental group, didn't he?"

"A big passion of his. I joked about him being a tree hugger due to my name, which he didn't find funny. I thought it was pretty hilarious. But he was always going on about global warming, the plastic in the oceans, polluted water, things like that. He and his ex shared that passion if not the other kind."

"How long ago were they married?"

"Let's see. Five years, maybe? It's so easy to lose track of time. One day you're holding your new baby, and the next, he's six inches taller than you and playing basketball for the high school team."

Oak added, "Johnny was crazy about Vi, but they were oil and water, you know?"

Drayco frowned. "Vi?"

"Her nickname. I think she goes by her maiden name now. Keating."

Drayco noted that a set of display shelves from his last visit were missing, replaced by a rack of the latest video games. He pointed them out, "Rearranging already?"

"Oh, you mean those books? A bunch of how-to stuff and history and such. Books like that don't sell all that well, you know? People who come in here want video games or board games or yard games. Not books. That was Johnny's thing. He loves vintage stuff."

"I don't suppose he's also into big band music, is he?"

"Big band? Like Duke Ellington, Benny Goodman, and all that?"

"That's right."

"Don't know. Since he liked old stuff, why not? If he gets in touch with you, you can ask him."

Drayco thanked Oak for his time and headed out into the cool early evening air. It was warmer than a typical late November, but still not the tropics. As he leaned against his car, he processed this newest wrinkle.

It seemed highly unlikely Burdell would suddenly decide to sell the store he loved and then "disappear." Not so soon after Graham Tibbs's death. Was he complicit in the death somehow?

If Detective Halabi didn't know about this little turn of events, Drayco should pass it along. At least he'd get some more bad French cursing out of the man, so there was that.

He slid into the driver's seat with a sigh and cranked up the heat, a fitting metaphor. With his disappearance, Johnny Burdell had cranked up the heat on the Tibbs case. Maybe Drayco should have another go at Alistair and see if he'd helped "disappear" anyone else lately?

20

Sunday, November 28

"This is quite possibly the worst idea you've ever had." Drayco looked over at his father, who was dressed uncharacteristically—black shoes, black slacks, black shirt, black jacket, black hat, black gloves. Not that it would have mattered much since the overcast sky obscured the moon. They looked like typical burglars dressed in their matching black garb. And, in fact, they kind of were.

Brock replied, "You didn't have to come along."

"I almost didn't."

"What changed your mind?"

Drayco shook his head. "As if I was going to let you do something idiotic like this by yourself. On account of me, I might add." He wasn't about to tell his father Sarg had wanted to do this very thing—and Drayco almost took him up on it.

"Pinning your shady uncle down on dry land is near impossible—as you have found out. But I'm determined to get answers about why he kidnapped you. And what the hell this game is all about. I refuse to believe it's only about a measly puzzle."

Drayco also wasn't accustomed to seeing his father turn red with anger, and this made twice in recent days—and both were over Alistair. He said, "I doubt we'll get past his security, but it's a pleasant night for a boat ride on the river."

Brock smiled a fraction. "I wouldn't count your old man out just yet. Thanks to your intel, I have a pretty good idea of the island's security detail."

That was to say, Drayco's *aerial* intel. He flew over the island in a rented Cessna a few months ago out of curiosity. He'd put the plane on autopilot long enough to take some zoomed-in photos of the place.

It took up sixteen acres with a private beach and two marinas with docks. At the time, the leafed-out trees made it harder to spy the house in the middle of it all from the air, but he could just catch a glimpse of the Federal-style home and its nearby helipad.

Drayco held out his hand to his father, who was still up on the pier, to take some of the cases he was carrying and help load them into the cuddy boat. Once the gear was on board and his father hopped in, Drayco opened one case and whistled. "You brought along quite a kit of high-tech spy gear. I'm surprised."

Brock shot him an amused look. "You think I'm a doddering old man who's forgotten all the Bureau tricks?"

"Not at all. But you're always by the book."

"Nothing about this entire situation is by the book. And there's certainly nothing about your shady uncle that's by the book."

"Assuming we make it to the island and slip in without being detected, what do you hope to find?"

"Answers."

"What if he isn't prepared to give them?"

Brock rubbed the back of his head, and Drayco asked, "What aren't you telling me?"

"I pulled a few strings, and I won't say with whom. But I learned Brisbane is out of town."

"So what answers do you expect to learn if he's not even there?"

"A paper trail. Despite the fact he's a master at hiding his dealings. But again, that's nothing you don't already know."

Drayco cranked up the motor, and they headed out from the dock in Alexandria into the Potomac River, navigating by the boat's GPS. They traveled about an hour following the river to where it dumped into the Chesapeake Bay. From there, it was only a few miles farther to the north.

As they got closer to their target, Brock made a slashing motion across his throat, and Drayco cut the engine. Pulling out paddles, they guided the cuddy to the island's southerly dock and tied the boat to the cleat as quietly as they could.

Taking a lay of the land from the surface level as opposed to his previous aerial scan, Drayco noted a turret-style structure five feet taller than the trees. It resembled an old lighthouse. It was separate from the main building, a sprawling home with several wings he could see from his vantage point. It likely had even more wings and rooms in the rear.

Drayco looked around the area for motion sensors and spied a couple closer to the house. He almost wished there was a sliver of moonlight to help him see the type of sensor being used. Since most of them had the same basic setup, he and Brock would try the infrared laser trick. Or maybe a little silicone spray or an air duster, depending upon the sensor's range. But if Alistair had any underground detectors, they'd be out of luck and quickly detected.

Once up on shore, Drayco and Brock slipped on the backpacks filled with tools. They crept up the wooden stairs from the dock to the grounds, taking cover behind some trees along the shoreline while they assessed the situation.

Most of the rooms in the buildings were dark, with just a couple of lights inside one room at the farthest end away from their location. That was a bit of luck in their favor. They could try the door nearest their current location that led into an unoccupied room.

Drayco pulled out a pair of infrared binoculars he trained on the door area. He noted two security cameras mounted to cover that area and held up two fingers to Brock. His father strapped on a pair of night vision goggles to see for himself.

Drayco studied the door entry. He was relieved it didn't use biometrics and was a wireless system. They had a direct line of sight to the sensors, which was another big help. When Drayco whispered those details to his father, Brock nodded and pulled out a mini spectrum analyzer. With luck, they'd find which frequency the wireless cameras used and then send interference back to the system.

Drayco glanced at Brock. They'd had a discussion in the boat, with Drayco saying, "You know using these jammers is illegal, right?"

And Brock had growled in reply, "What he did was illegal, so we're fighting fire with fire. And I doubt he'll be turning us in if he finds out."

With the plan of attack in hand, they locked in on the frequency, initiated the jamming, and hurried to the door. Drayco pulled a magnet out of his pocket in case there were also magnetic door trips, and he needed to override those signals. He handed it to Brock so he could grab his lock-pick kit and made quick work of the door lock.

They entered the building in hyper-stealth mode. Drayco used the night vision goggles to spy any interior motion sensor devices. When he thought he saw one above an archway ahead, he pointed the infrared light beam at it to blind the sensor. That would allow Brock to examine the rest of the room.

Since they didn't hear any alarms, Drayco hoped that was a good sign. But alarms could still be silent when tripped.

There didn't seem to be any temperature sensors and no fog machines, something he'd worried about. Since Uncle Alistair lived on an island, he probably had some expectation of infrequent attacks. This had led Drayco to hope Alistair didn't feel the need for Fort Knox-style security. So far, he was right.

They scurried through the first room, which wasn't all that interesting. Looked like a sunroom, with the pungent aroma of new cedar paneling. It was unfurnished save for a few wicker chairs.

This led them into a hall, and they checked each door, one by one, until they found what appeared to be an office. As offices went, it didn't look like it would be as forthcoming with Alistair's secrets as Brock had hoped. But nothing ventured, nothing gained.

After they closed the door behind them, he and Brock each took a separate filing cabinet and flipped through folders using hand-held red flashlights. Drayco still wasn't sure what type of paper trail Brock wanted to find. But he was game to give it a try, and they'd already come this far.

Drayco's cabinet held old contracts, expense logs, and business correspondence. Fairly routine. He took photos with his cellphone of the documents and memorized certain details in case something happened to the phone.

Drayco did find one thing interesting, a recent flight log taken via a private jet to and from the UK and Ireland. It was a series of flights dating from around the time his mother reappeared and then disappeared again. Drayco memorized the tail number of the plane listed on the logs.

When the blower to the heating system's air handler switched on, Drayco's heart jumped. He'd been on covert ops before, but he'd never been this jittery. Maybe it was having his father there? Or maybe he was just getting lax, so he willed himself back into laser-brain mode. He couldn't afford to twitch at every creaking board or window rattle.

He resumed flipping through files, even as he was itching to explore other areas of the property. When they'd arrived, both docks were empty of other moored boats, and the lights they'd spied in the house could be on timers. It was quite possible there was no one else on the island with Alistair away.

A split-second after he had that thought, the sound of a door opening followed by footsteps approaching from down the hall reached their ears. Drayco and Brock froze in position, exchanging glances and not daring to move a muscle. The footsteps slowed as they approached the office, and Drayco held his breath.

After a couple of agonizingly long seconds, the steps continued down the hall and then turned around and headed back in the original direction, past their room. Drayco breathed a quiet sigh of relief. But there went the chance to investigate other areas of the compound.

They continued to search through files for a while longer. But after finding little of interest, Drayco whispered to his father, "You do know he likely has offices in several locations. And gigabytes of info stored in encrypted digital files."

Brock sighed and whispered back, "And I'm thinking we should probably try some of those other avenues instead."

"You're giving up here?"

"Not giving up, per se. Just coming to the realization you were right. This was probably a horrible idea."

They listened again for the footsteps. Not hearing any, they cracked open the door, peered down the hall, and retraced their way back into the sunroom.

They headed toward the dock after exiting through the same rear door and jamming the cameras again to avoid being detected. Drayco made sure to use the infrared on the motion sensor now they knew someone was on the island.

Just as they were inches away from the landing, a floodlight flipped on from the rear of the house. A man's voice called out, followed by a warning shot from a gun.

Not wanting to waste any time, he and Brock scrambled into the boat and paddled out as quickly as they could before starting up the motor and peeling away. As Drayco looked back, he saw a figure silhouetted on the dock, hands on his hips, staring out after them.

21

Maybe it was the surreal trip to Alistair Brisbane's island that had given Drayco very surrealistic dreams, but they made him sleep later than he'd planned. He'd been doing that far too many times lately.

So much for some time at the piano to get ready for his upcoming audition. After a few phone calls, he barely had time to shower and put some black salted coffee in a travel mug before he dashed off for his meeting with Benny Baskin, Esquire.

Baskin had scheduled the little chat to discuss a previous case they'd worked on. But Drayco also wanted to ask Benny about a different case, an arson, that Benny was involved with not too long ago. With luck, the attorney could dig into some legal files to find something on Leon Sable's two former businesses that burned—potential insurance fraud with either.

Sable said he was underinsured for the first fire and completely uninsured for the second, which would be "proof" he had nothing to gain from setting it—unless it was to cover up a murder. Sable had also said the police didn't find accelerants. But there were many creative ways to hide arsons. Drayco had heard of many such ways during his FBI days, from using potato chip bags set on fire to intentionally short-circuiting an appliance.

He'd just pulled up to Baskin's office building in his Starfire when he got a call on his cell. Looking at the number, he gritted his teeth and then answered.

The familiar amethyst-colored filament tones of Alistair Brisbane greeted him. "Iago tells me we had some uninvited visitors last night to the island."

"Is that a fact? How very strange."

"Iago didn't get a good look at them, but he managed to spot part of the boat's registration number. He traced it to a marina in Alexandria. The boat was a rental, but Iago teased out the name of the person who rented it."

"Teased out? You mean strong-armed, don't you?"

"Iago can be very persuasive when he wants to be. The renter's name, by the way, was Brock Drayco."

"Brock's gone night-fishing before. That wouldn't be too unusual."

"Perhaps he was fishing this time, too, but for a different species of prey. Iago thought he saw two men in that boat. And I believe I can guess who the other man was."

"Were you at home at the time?"

Brisbane chuckled. "I think you already know I wasn't. But I have to compliment you and your father. First, that you made it to the island without being seen. And then to make it past the security I have in place to deter visitors. Tell me—what did you hope to find?"

Drayco thought briefly about his mother. But he also realized lying to his uncle wouldn't accomplish anything, so he spoke the truth. "Brock hoped to uncover what the kidnapping and treasure were really about. You're not his favorite person right now."

"And I doubt I'm yours, either."

"Having a relative arrange for my kidnapping is a first for me, I'll grant you."

Drayco wanted to deflect the conversation and attention away from Brock, so he added, "But I'm more interested in the puzzle I half-decoded. It's driving me nuts. I don't know what it means, and I can't break it down further. You said you might have an idea. Since you owe me on this, care to share?"

"You do make a good case. But alas, my initial impressions on the matter were incorrect. My interpretation of the decoded message led to a dead end. I'm afraid I can't be of any help."

"So your mysterious treasure is still out there?"

"I haven't seen it come up on the black market."

Drayco had a good idea his uncle would know a lot about the black market, so he took his word. For now. "By the way, Alistair, does the tail number N234QR mean anything to you?"

Alistair chuckled. "You *are* pretty good. I registered it under an anonymous LLC."

That confirmed Drayco's suspicion his uncle had his own private jet, lucky stiff. But the information could come in handy at some point.

Drayco said, "I'm glad you called. There's something else I wanted to talk to you about. Someone claiming to be my 'agent' went behind my back with the UMD concert committee to change the pieces I was going to play. I only learned this morning when they phoned me. And my audition is tomorrow. You can bet I wasn't the one who called them about this."

"And you think that someone is me?"

"You arranged this whole scholarship concert. Why wouldn't it be you?"

"I've been guilty of many things, but I assure you, this isn't one of them. I will look into it, that I can promise. And I wish you the best of luck."

Brisbane paused before adding, "However, I wouldn't recommend trying that little island stunt again. We've made some new security additions."

Drayco hung up with Brisbane, shaking his head. He could pretty well imagine what those additions were. Biometrics, noxious fog blasters, fiber optic sensors. Maybe even trained Dobermans or Bullmastiffs.

After a glance at the time, he hopped out of the car and took the stairs to Benny's floor two steps at a time. He flung open the door to the hallway and crashed into a woman heading past him at that moment.

He stammered out, "Oh, excuse me, ma'am. I . . . " Then he saw who it was.

Nelia Tyler stared at him. "You're in a hurry this morning."

He gave her a weak smile. "Sorry about that. I'm a little late. You know how Benny hates tardiness." Drayco tried to tell himself his heart was racing from the stairs instead of seeing her again.

Nelia kept staring at him, but said, "I'm heading that way. Maybe I can plead your case."

But she didn't move right away and stood there biting her lip. "Benny told me what you'd relayed to him. About your uncle's involvement in your kidnapping. Why hasn't he been arrested?"

"For one thing, proof. For another, well, it's complicated. In fact, I just got off the phone with him."

Her jaw dropped. "You're still talking to your uncle? After all of this?"

"I need to keep him on my radar. Might be a lot harder to get to the bottom of this strange business otherwise—the kidnapping, the coded puzzle, the likely murder of one of the kidnappers."

"Brisbane could be behind that, too. Why do you trust him?"

Drayco couldn't really answer that. Was it only because the man was the brother of Drayco's mother? He wasn't even sure he knew how to explain it to her. Or himself.

He replied, "My uncle's a savvy operative. I doubt he leaves trails leading back to him for most of his shady dealings."

"You realize that makes it more likely he killed Graham Tibbs to remove one of those trails, right?"

"But it's not his style. And he sounded genuinely surprised by the death."

"I hope you know what you're doing here, Drayco."

He nodded. "Me, too."

She studied his face. "Did you ask Brisbane about your mother's whereabouts? Or if she's even still alive?"

This time, he just shook his head, marveling. She always seemed to be a mind reader. Of *his* mind, anyway.

She pressed him, "Are you afraid to find out?"

"Afraid isn't the right word." Her question made him unexpectedly angry, and he lashed out without thinking. "Just like fear isn't the reason you stayed with your abusive husband all those years."

Her eyes narrowed. "We're not going to do this, are we? Be at each other's throats from now on out? Just because we can't be—"

"Together?"

"No one gets everything they want in life." Her shoulders sagged and her frown faded, making her look deflated.

He glanced up at the ceiling for a few moments and then gave her a slight smile. "Right now, all I want is for Benny Baskin not to kill me. He packs a lot of wrestler-muscle in that four-feet-nine of his." Drayco looked at his watch. "I'm now fifteen minutes late."

She returned his half-smile. "I said I'd plead your case. I'll tell him you got stuck in the elevator."

He did a double-take, not sure if her offer to lie for him was genuine or if she was pulling his leg. But they headed into Baskin's office together, where the attorney was pacing past his massive barge-sized desk as he carried on a loud conversation on his cellphone.

After a few more grunts and eye rolls, he rang off and tossed the phone on his desk. "See what you made me do? I had to take a call from that idiot, Borman."

Berry Borman was one of the most legendary—and not in a good way—prosecutors in the District. Drayco had also butted heads with him on a few occasions. He shot Benny a sympathetic "mea culpa" glance, prompting the attorney to reply, "Don't go using those puppy dog eyes at me, either. Although since they're blue, guess that makes you a Siberian Husky."

Drayco barely got out, "Sorry I'm late—" before Nelia jumped in, "He was stuck in the elevator."

Benny looked from one to the other and rubbed his non-patched eye. "Since you're late, I had a little extra time to look up this Leon Sable fellow you were asking about. As you know, public records don't disclose investigations against businesses. Unless they resulted in charges. But an attorney friend of a friend told me Sable was on the Virginia Attorney General's radar. Two business fires relatively close together . . . that's quite unusual."

"But they didn't find anything?"

"Nothing they could take to court. They were mostly interested in the second one due to the body found inside. But you know more about that than I do."

"Some, but still waiting for more reports from the Arlington PD."

Benny frowned at Drayco. "I wish you'd let me go after Brisbane. I know I could find something, even if it's a violation of a minor legal code."

"Thanks, but he can afford a whole host of Bennys. Nothing would ever stick."

Benny studied Drayco. "You doing okay, boy-o? Kidnapping's kind of a big deal."

Drayco rolled his eyes. "Oh, for god's sake. I'm completely surrounded by mother hens. Or is that mothers hen? I'm not sure what you call a bunch of hens."

"A peep. Or a brood. Groups of chicks are a clutch."

Drayco and Benny both stared at Nelia, but it was Benny who asked, "How did you know that?"

"My uncle has a farm."

"Is his name McDonald?"

She laughed. "You're close. It's McNair."

Benny fiddled with his string bow tie. "Overalls, sheep shit, and pig slop. Sounds like fun."

"Hate to disappoint you, but it's a modern farm. UAVs, LED lights, automated control systems."

Her UAV reference gave Drayco an idea he filed away for future reference. Maybe a drone would suffice instead of storming Alistair's island next time.

Nelia was also right that Drayco shouldn't really trust his uncle. But what had Alistair meant with that comment about his interpretation of the decoded message leading to a dead end? Alistair hadn't exactly cautioned Drayco not to pursue the puzzle any further. Did that mean he was still waiting to see if Drayco could solve the whole puzzle business for him?

He might be waiting a long time because Drayco still hadn't figured out what the damned thing really meant. And part of him was beginning to think he never would.

22

Drayco decided it was time to talk to Graham Tibbs's childhood friend, Ezra Layton, again, not at the track this time, but at the man's glass shop. Between Leon Sable's metal supply store and Layton's glass shop, the former seemed a more appropriate business choice for an adrenaline junkie like Layton.

Stained-glass windows fronted the place, which was a cliché, albeit an attractive one. Maybe it was the time of day, but when Drayco walked inside, he was the only other person there besides Layton.

Drayco strolled over to the counter, where Layton said, "If it isn't the private-eye pilot. Surely I answered all your questions last time."

"Mostly. But here's one for you. How in the world did you decide on a glass business?"

Layton laughed and said, "It's something I fell into. I bought the business from an elderly woman eager to sell it at rock-bottom prices. I needed a job, this seemed pretty easy, so I just went with it." He added with a grin, "You'd be amazed at how many sexy women are into glass."

Drayco looked around the shop, noting the glass theme was everywhere, from the stained-glass front windows to the rainbow-colored ceiling light fixtures. A locked display case held an assortment of figures grouped by color—turquoise, red, amber. An even more impressive variety of glass vases, plates, and some contemporary-looking blobby things perched on wall shelves and square display stands throughout the space.

Drayco said, "I'm afraid to walk around in here."

That made Layton chuckle even harder. "I'm insured. Feel free to move about the cabin."

"Aria D'Angelo told me about the glass piece you'd given her. Unfortunately, she also said she'd broken it recently."

"That's too bad. I'll have to get her something to replace it. She really liked that piece, too."

"Are you also an opera fan, Ezra?"

"Reminds me of cats in heat. I hate opera music."

Drayco grinned. "That makes two of us." Okay, so maybe hate was a little too strong. Plus, as long as composers and arrangers made opera transcriptions for the piano, Drayco was okay with it.

At Layton's raised eyebrow, Drayco added, "Well, I appreciate the skill, the musicianship, and the drama."

"Kinda wish she were into something else, even '60s rock, that would be fine. Or folk or country." Layton thought for a moment. "Wouldn't it be something if she was one of those Madonna or Lady Gaga types?"

"Perhaps she would have had more success in those genres late in her career. They're not as picky about voices as opera. If that were the case, she could probably even get away with singing after her vocal injury."

"She deserved better than having it all end that way." He beamed as he said, "And she's still in her prime. Could have gone on a long time. Or as they used to say when I was growing up, she's 'fine as frog hair split four ways.'"

Drayco smiled briefly at that. He'd have to write that one down. "Did you know Johnny Burdell?"

"Not personally. But him and Graham were into those tree-hugging causes. Wasn't really my thing. Plus, I'm not a fan of games and all that. Way too dull. I like my hobby a lot better."

"Have you heard from Burdell lately?"

Layton grabbed some stock and rearranged it on the counter, explaining, "Too close to the edge. A hazard around here." After he seemed satisfied, he replied, "I've never talked with him directly. Maybe I should, since Graham was killed outside Burdell's shop. Maybe he'd have some answers for me."

"You're going to have to find him first since he quit the shop suddenly. I haven't been able to track him down yet."

"He quit? Now, why would he do that? Graham said Burdell loved that place."

"I was hoping you could tell me."

"Nope, sorry. But if for any reason he should contact me . . . "

"Do let me know."

Drayco mustered the courage to pick up one of the glass blobby things. Looked a little like a rainbow-colored Klein bottle, folded in on itself. "Did Graham ever mention the name Alistair Brisbane? Or Joyelle Babineaux?"

Layton scratched his head and sounded out the names slowly. "Briz-bane? Bab-in-know? Nope, sorry again. Never heard of either one."

Drayco took a step back and bumped into a square display stand. In desperation, he reached over just in time to catch a glass sculpture as it slid off toward the floor.

Layton didn't seem phased, like a man who'd seen it all. "Nice catch. But you can understand why I don't want kids in here." He pointed to a sign near the door that read, "No children under twelve without a parent or guardian."

He walked around to inspect the glass figure, and for the first time, Drayco saw he had a limp. Layton followed Drayco's gaze and said, "Horse-riding accident. My first attempt at horse jumping. You know, rails, hedges, and the like. I told you I was an adrenaline junkie."

Drayco was relieved when Layton inspected the glass piece and was satisfied. Drayco said, "I spoke with Christi Allingham."

"Ah, yes, Christi. I suppose she told you they were an item in high school. Hooked up again not too long before Graham's first 'death.' "

"She mentioned it, yes. I'm surprised you didn't."

"What? Oh, if you're thinking she's the one who mowed Graham down, you're wrong. She was out of his league."

"Why do you say that?" The way Layton's expression turned both wistful and angry made Drayco think Layton had a thing for Christi, too.

"Heaps smarter than he was. Graham and me were buds, but doesn't mean I'd call him a genius."

"If she's that smart, couldn't she have arranged an untraceable hit-and-run?"

"No way. They broke it off before the fire at his business. She'd moved on with her life. We all did."

Wary of making another wrong move, Drayco stepped closer to the counter. "Speaking of that fire, a possible arson, Leon Sable had a previous store burn down from arson. Did you know about that?"

"Sable didn't discuss it, but Graham mentioned something. I thought nothing of it."

"And it didn't occur to you after Graham's fake death that maybe Sable was involved?"

"Okay, okay, so maybe it did occur to me. What, you think since Sable tried to kill Graham once but failed, he made sure he got it right this time?"

"I didn't say that. But I have to keep all options open."

"Yeah, I get that."

"Last time I spoke with you, you said you partnered with Sable for a time, but it didn't work out. Differences of opinion."

"It wasn't like I suspected he was a lunatic murderer or anything. Still, he does have a bit of a temper. And he wasn't quite as broken up about Graham's death as I was."

"Then you think he was glad or, at least, relieved Graham had allegedly died?"

"Maybe. But if Graham was alive this whole time, then maybe Leon and Graham were in on it together, you know?"

Layton picked up a glass stein on the counter and held it in his hands. The letters "G" and "T" were etched on the side. "In high school, Graham and I used to sneak out of class. Had an older friend of a friend who owned a bar and let us have beer. So I had this made for Graham. It was to be a birthday present the same year he 'died' in that fire. God, I miss him."

Drayco thanked Layton for his time and threaded his way around the various displays to avoid knocking another one over. Once outside, he mused over Layton's possible interest in Christi Allingham. Maybe they'd been partners in more ways than one.

He also thought again of Layton's assertion that Graham Tibbs and Johnny Burdell "were into those tree-hugging causes." The Potomac Conservancy Pact staffer had helpfully verified it, and that fact seemed to put a lock and chain on the whole Burdell-didn't-know-Tibbs line. But why had Burdell tried to hide their connection?

Everyone also denied knowing Alistair, but plenty of lies were swirling around this case already. Maybe one player in this drama actually did know him, but wasn't about to admit it.

Drayco's uncle hadn't been as apoplectic as Drayco feared over his and Brock's little recon mission. What in the world had possessed his father to even come up with that crazy idea? It's not the kind of thing Brock went in for anymore, so why did he want to do it? In retrospect, it was an insane thing to do.

Brock said he was motivated to find answers to Drayco's kidnapping. And what had Drayco hoped to gain from their little island "excursion?" It wasn't like he'd find his mother ensconced there in a kitchen baking cookies. Yet, they hadn't had the chance to explore the rest of the compound, had they?

Maybe it *was* an insane move on their part, but Drayco took a little bit of comfort in it. A sort of proof his father loved him in his own weird way. Not that he'd really doubted it. But the tensions from years of distance between them wouldn't be easily massaged away. Not then or now.

§ § §

Drayco stood in front of the chain link fence and studied the property beyond. After checking the real estate records, he was shocked to find the ruins of the burned-out hardware store, formerly owned by Leon Sable and Graham Tibbs, were still standing. The place *was* a recent target of a Fairfax County public hearing on blight abatement and scheduled to be demolished soon. But not yet.

Part of the problem was trying to get back taxes from the woman who owned the land, currently living in Greece. When Drayco tracked her down, though, she was perfectly fine with him looking at the property. But without a key to the padlock on the fence, he wasn't sure how to proceed. That is until he found an enormous gaping hole in the fence around the back.

Judging from graffiti on the former parking lot and some walls, he had a pretty good idea local teens frequented the place and were possibly the source of the hole in the fence. That would also explain a rusting barrel filled with empty beer cans and a few bongs.

Even with twilight half an hour away, Drayco could easily see his way inside the husk and examine what was left. The charred main walls were still standing—barely—thanks to being constructed from reinforced masonry and a bit of extra help from the "minimal sprinkler system" Leon Sable had mentioned. But they also looked like they could give up the fight and collapse at any minute.

Several of the twisted steel joists and girders still hovered above the building, forming the "bones" of a steel skeleton. They almost gave the impression of arms holding the carcass together to keep it from falling apart.

Most of what was once been shelves, tools, and paint, all of which helped fan the flames, were long gone. Scavengers likely stole anything of value left—unmelted copper wire, silver, titanium, nickel, wrought iron. The place was now just a sooty concrete slab piled high with the detritus from a thermodynamics scientist's nightmare.

Drayco wasn't sure why he'd wanted to come here. Maybe because he had an increasingly empathetic link to the late Graham Tibbs. Or he was just feeling sorry for the poor homeless man who'd allegedly served as Graham's "stand-in," left behind, lost, and largely forgotten.

From the police report, Drayco had a pretty good idea where the body was found on the fateful day. He inched around a blackened pyramid of unidentifiable rubbish to what used to be the center of the store. That should have been another clue in the original fire investigation—the victim was in the middle of the store, not near a window or door trying to escape the blaze.

What type of trouble could Tibbs possibly have become involved with for him to take such a drastic step? Even if the homeless man was already deceased, the planning involved in dragging him into the store, planting Tibbs's tooth on the man, then torching the building was complicated and risky.

But then again, it *had* worked, hadn't it? Everyone believed Tibbs had perished in that fire, and with Alistair's help, he was able to "disappear."

Drayco did a three-sixty to size up the ruins. Even five years later, there were hints of the acrid smell of burned wood mixed in with black mold and urine-soaked cardboard, thanks to those "beer-soaked" teens. Not that it really mattered since the place would just be a memory soon like Graham Tibbs himself.

One thing did seem out of place, though, and Drayco headed for it. The wall behind the scorched former counter sported several uniform-sized holes with a pink powder around them. Upon closer inspection, the substance wasn't ash but brick residue.

Each of the holes was roughly the same, and when he stepped back, he noted they lay in a regular pattern. That wouldn't happen naturally, fire or no fire. It was far more likely from someone drilling holes looking for something, plus the pink powder—free from mold, dirt, rain, or soot—indicated a recent search.

It might just be thieves searching for any remaining copper wire, but he doubted it. All of that would have been stripped out long ago. This looked like it was done within the past week, give or take—and Graham Tibbs's death was just a little longer than that. If someone believed Tibbs found Alistair's mysterious treasure, would they think he hid it in a wall safe here?

It seemed pretty far-fetched. But eager treasure hunters had been known to dig up graves, dive into sunken ruins, and climb down treacherous mountain cliffs. Well, if Tibbs did hide something here, it was long gone, too. A dead end in more ways than one.

As Drayco headed toward the back of the ruin and the rear wall, his feet crunched on some paper, and he reached down to rescue a sheet that looked new. It was the newspaper page with Graham Tibbs's obituary. Well, now. Drayco's hypothesis about the brick-treasure connection was looking a lot less far-fetched.

Just then, he heard more crunching. But this time, he hadn't moved, and the sound seemed to come from the back of the property. More of those teens coming returning for another party? Or another scavenger, maybe.

A brief movement caught his eye. He looked over in time to see part of a sneaker-clad foot withdrawing through the same opening Drayco entered earlier. He started to run after his mystery visitor, but an instinctive forewarning made him stop in his tracks.

With a loud rumbling, bricks in the remaining rear wall cascaded down like dominoes as that section of the wall caved in. Drayco jumped back to avoid being buried but ended up slipping on some of the burned boards and almost fell forward head-first into the tumbling debris. He regained his balance just in time to take another step back and just missed the clay-and-mortar avalanche by inches.

As dust and mortar from the bricks swirled around him, he held his breath and staggered out the opening into the old parking lot. But he couldn't stop the coughing fit the dust brought on, and by the time he straightened up again, there were no signs of the intruder. Was it just another teen and a stupid prank gone wrong? Or had the person who'd excavated the holes in the wall returned for another try?

Drayco entered the building again long enough to take a few photos with his cellphone camera of the wall behind the counter, as well as the new rubble pile and the remaining ruins of the building. He looked in vain for the newspaper obituary in hopes he could get some fingerprints off of it. But it flew out of his hand during the wall collapse and now lay entombed somewhere beneath the rubble.

By coming here in the first place, he'd risked danger and failure and ended up with plenty of both. But it somehow reminded him of Graham Tibbs's favorite saying, that necessity is the mother of taking chances. Drayco had looked up that quotation when Aria D'Angelo mentioned it, and it was attributed to Mark Twain. But wasn't it Twain who also said a person with a new idea is a crank until the idea succeeds?

With one last look at the wreckage of the ill-fated hardware store, Drayco headed toward his car, still keeping an eye out for anything, or anyone, suspicious. He couldn't count out a teenage prank or just bad timing. But if Drayco was the real target of the wall collapse, then maybe he'd hit a nerve with someone.

23

This was an even worse idea than Brock's crazy trip to Alistair's island. Drayco should never have said "yes" to this whole scholarship recital. When he got up earlier in the day, he'd picked up the phone and put it down several times to call it all off, last minute or not.

He had the perfect excuse, too, after his little drama yesterday evening at the remains of the burned hardware store. He was lucky he hadn't injured his gimpy arm any further when the wall almost fell on him, but he still sported a few new aches in his good arm.

Besides, he had a client and a case, his top priority and his real job. The piano bit . . . that was in his past. Not to mention the fact this recital business wasn't just a bad idea, it was the definition of insanity. But, setting aside any loyalty—or lack thereof—to his Uncle Alistair for setting up the thing, Drayco couldn't back out of it now.

After spending the morning psyching himself up for the first public musical performance pressure in years, he made his way up Rhode Island Avenue and US-1 to College Park. Once there, the scholarship committee liaison who greeted him was gracious, which somehow made it even harder to take. He'd almost prefer she be distrustful or condescending.

She showed him to the green room behind the stage, where Drayco filled the sink half-full with hot water. He leaned over it to plunge his right arm inside, turning on the tap to add a little more water until it covered his entire lower arm.

Usually, he timed his soaking sessions by the minute for good measure. But instead of looking at a timer, his mind kept drifting back to the case. Alistair, kidnappings, puzzles, treasures . . . and if Brock's new girlfriend was involved, espionage might also be in play. So why was he wasting time here?

The liaison popped her head into the green room to tell him the committee was ready for him. How long had he been soaking? About fifteen minutes, he guessed. But would it be enough? That was the "million-dollar" question—the amount Alistair had given to endow the scholarship.

The committee he was to play for was very understanding about the repertoire mix-up when they realized whoever provided the revised list hadn't done so with Drayco's knowledge. Since that list came via someone claiming to be his agent on the phone, they were even more mystified.

Unfortunately, an after-hours answering service took the call and didn't get a name or return number, so the committee—and he—were still in the dark about the identity or motives of the culprit. Had the attempted intervention been well-intentioned? Or an attempt at sabotage?

Not that it would matter if he didn't do well regardless of what pieces he played. The setup was like a traditional contest "jury," with the committee seated in the row below the stage. And like most juries, they were essentially there to pass judgment. Alistair had questioned why this committee step was even necessary.

But Drayco knew the music school staffers were well aware of the injury years ago that cut his concert career short. They wanted to save themselves the embarrassment of a gimpy pianist having to quit mid-recital, leaving ticket-holders disappointed. It wouldn't reflect well on the music school or the university.

It was years since he was up on a concert hall stage alone with a piano while an audience waited expectantly. What would it feel like? Time to find out.

He strolled out on stage, but he wanted to turn right back around and escape to the green room when he saw the piano. They'd told him it would be an older-model Steinway, but this was a shiny new Kawai.

The action would likely be stiffer and tighter than he was used to—requiring more muscle and finger strength.

He forced himself *not* to turn around and gave a quick bow. He slid onto the piano bench and sat still for a moment to focus his thoughts. Then he launched into Bach's Prelude and Fugue No. 9 from the Well-Tempered Clavier, getting lost in the notes as he'd hoped he would. When the last sounds of the Bach faded away, he leaned back a little with a smile. That had gone better than he'd feared.

He placed his hands on the keyboard to play the next piece when the air handler for the heating system cranked on with a loud whooshing sound he could hear on stage. Shades of what happened on Alistair's island all over again. The noise was annoying, but the fluttering gray-brown veil with silver dagger crosses it sent into his brain wasn't helping. Great. Why now?

He plowed ahead and made it through a couple of Chopin études from Opus 10, the third and the twelfth, the so-called "Revolutionary," which buoyed his confidence. His right arm was throbbing, but that was normal these days after playing for twenty minutes. Next, it was time for Debussy's Suite Bergamasque. He took a deep, calming breath and eased into the opening Prélude. So far, so good.

He reached the Menuet section, feeling the adrenaline rush of what came next, the iconic "Claire de Lune." But right as he started the movement, he felt the familiar cold tingling sensation tunneling up his wrist and arm. The cramping exploded with full force, making his fingers curl up into his palm.

It took every ounce of control he had not to pound his fists onto the poor hapless piano. Instead, he stopped, took a deep breath, and swung his feet around on the bench to face the committee. They glanced at each other with knowing looks.

One member cleared her throat and said, "We could give you a few minutes and try again?"

Drayco rubbed his arm to stop the contractions. "I don't think that's going to help, but I can go soak the arm in warm water again."

The committee members looked at each other again, nodded, and appeared relieved not to discuss it with him further. He gave them a little wave and headed back to the green room. Should he give it one more try? In the great cosmic scheme of things, would it matter now if he did? Or didn't?

He made his way to the sink and ran more hot water from the tap. Sarg was right—Drayco rarely ran away from a challenge. Well, he wasn't about to start now, injury be damned. One way or another, he was going to make this work.

After only five minutes of soaking, he dried off and headed back toward the stage. It was now or never. But when his second attempt ended in even worse arm cramping only two minutes after he started playing, he stopped again and slid off the bench with a grim smile. "Obviously, this is a problem. However, I think I may have an idea . . ."

24

Drayco woke up the next morning wondering if the concert audition had all been a dream. But when the full reality hit him, he let out a groan. He should have listened to his instincts and canceled the audition months ago.

Humiliation, rejection—he'd experienced those feelings many times, just not with the piano. But that wasn't quite right, was it? At home, it was a daily occurrence thanks to his injured arm—he just didn't have an audience to witness it. Hopefully, the compromise he'd worked out with the committee would suffice.

Time for the best therapy he knew, to get back to work. He wasn't hungry but grabbed some Manhattan Special espresso sodas from the fridge. As fortification went, they were as good as anything else. Caffeine, sugar, carbonation—what more did you need?

After a short drive, Drayco parked beside LS Metals. Once inside, he waved at the clerk near the door and pointed at a man in the rear of the shop. As Drayco headed toward Leon Sable, his target looked up with an exasperated frown. Drayco handed over a chai latte he'd snagged from a drive-through coffee shop.

Sable stared at it for a moment before accepting it with a nod of his head. "Thanks. I could really use this right now."

"Leon, I've recently learned that despite the denials of Johnny Burdell, he did know Graham from their involvement in an environmental group."

Sable slurped some of the latte, then said, "And you want to know if I'm lying, too?"

"Just wondering if the three of you hung out together."

"As I told you before, I don't know the guy. But when I read the obit in the paper again, a day or so ago, well . . . "

He paused and took another sip of his drink. "It finally sank in about where Graham was hit. And then I recalled Graham talking about Burdell once. It wasn't about puzzles. Had something to do with recycling or some such thing. I guess that's the treehugger group you mentioned."

"Burdell never visited your store before the fire?"

"Not that I recall. Well, while I was there, anyway. I did have some days off. And no, we never 'hung out' together."

"You weren't part of that environmental group?"

"Nope. Doubt they'd want me. Metals create a lot of pollution. Leaching of metals in the water and soil and such. I'm not proud of that, but there's worse out there. Plastics that never decompose, toxic chemicals, radioactive crap."

"So you don't know how long or how well Graham and Johnny Burdell knew each other?"

"You should ask Burdell about that."

"I did, but now Burdell has disappeared. Or left his store behind, anyway."

"Maybe it's built on some sacred Indian burial ground. Who knows? Bad luck? Cursed? Maybe he's just ready to retire. Hell, I'm almost there, myself."

"What about Ezra Layton? Did he ever mention Burdell? Or the same environmental group?"

Sable coughed, then cleared his throat. "I don't recall. Ezra and I had little personal interaction outside work. I liked Ezra enough, despite his laziness. Even though our business partnership didn't pan out, we parted on good terms. I think he bought a glass business or something after that. It's kind of froufrou for him, but whatever it takes to make a living."

"I've been there. It's very . . . glassy. Dangerously glassy."

That made Sable grin. "I'll bet."

"Leon, I'm curious if Graham ever mentioned a girlfriend named Christi Allingham?"

"Sure, they were off and on. I met her once. Seemed nice but above his league." Sable uttered an embarrassed laugh. "Sounds kinda bad, Graham being dead and all, but there it is."

"I don't suppose Ezra Layton ever expressed an interest in dating Christi?"

"What?" Sable rubbed a hand behind his neck. "He never said. Near as I recall. Guys don't always talk about that stuff."

"Did Graham have any other girlfriends in his past? Ones that might have a vendetta?"

"Graham didn't date much. I can't remember him being with any woman for more than a few weeks. Maybe a month or two. Even Christi was hot-and-cold."

"Why is that?"

"When you're running a business, you work long hours. One reason I'm not married yet. Almost came close once, though. Sure wish I hadn't broken things off with Vi. Ezra didn't like her. Should have ignored his advice to break it off."

As the sound of a female voice reached his eyes, Drayco looked up to see a staffer chatting with a familiar platinum-blonde woman. She was bent over as she studied some metal rods in various colors, brass, copper, silver, and bronze. He thanked Sable for his time and made a beeline for the woman.

He waited until she straightened up to say, "I imagine you come here often for your work."

Joyelle Babineaux looked up, startled, as her eyes darted around the space. "Why, fancy meeting you here, Scott." She reached over to give him a quick French-style kiss on either cheek. "This is my go-to place for supplies. Can't beat the variety or the prices. I'm particularly fond of their copper sheets since they work so well for *repoussé*."

"*Repoussé* as in pushed?"

"In a way. *Repoussé* techniques use hand tools or hammers to create three-dimensional reliefs in sheet metal."

Drayco pointed at the rods she'd been scrutinizing. "What will you make out of those?"

"I have a new commission. A woman in McLean is building this huge garden complex at her house. Tennis court, pool, fountains, the works. She wants two sculptures to go with her designer's plantings."

Joyelle picked up one of the rods and rolled it around in her hands. "The client also has a beach house. I'm thinking maybe something in the marine animal family. Maybe a dolphin."

He looked at the rod she was holding. "Guess that's why you're the artist, and I'm not. I can't quite envision a dolphin coming out of that."

She laughed. "By the time I get through with it, it will beg for mercy. Lots of pounding, twisting, and soldering."

"I'm surprised Brock hasn't asked you for a sculpture yet."

"I'm working on him. He has the perfect spot in his foyer. Maybe I'll even make a sculpture of him since he's such a handsome man. A perfect model, with his athletic build and the way his tanned skin shows off his short grayish hair."

Drayco tried not to squirm at her descriptions of his father's physique. "How did you and Brock meet?" He'd asked Brock the same question but wanted to see if their stories matched up.

"At the Cipher Club."

"I looked up their recent schedule. They're known for their parties for former alphabet soup people like my father . . . and you."

She tilted her head to study him. "Did Brock tell you that? Or have you been checking up on me?"

"I know about your intelligence background. And your late husband, Gerard Briller, and his hit-and-run death."

Joyelle sucked air through her teeth. "As you can imagine, that's a painful topic for me. I'd really rather not talk about it here. But maybe later we can sit down and get drunk over it."

She grabbed a couple of rods from the shelves and scurried off to the front counter to pay for her purchases. Drayco watched her until she exited the store.

A voice at his shoulder boomed, "Scaring off my best customers, are you, Mr. Drayco?"

"We were just getting caught up."

Sable narrowed his eyes. "Hmm. Well, I guess we'll see each other at Joyelle's upcoming exhibit, right?"

Drayco half-smiled. "And maybe they'll have chai lattes."

Sable thanked him again for the drink, and Drayco headed outside. Joyelle must have made a pretty quick getaway since he didn't see her anywhere in the parking lot. He stopped in front of the store and picked up some wrought iron finials. Surprisingly sharp. Yep, lots of impressive potential weapons in this place.

His Uncle Alistair said he kept tabs on his "disappeared" people. And that Graham Tibbs hadn't been in contact with anyone—even Graham's former business partner, Leon Sable, something Sable himself confirmed. Yet, Graham *did* contact Johnny Burdell. Whom else might he have talked to without Alistair knowing?

It wasn't out of the realm of possibility Graham Tibbs contacted Joyelle. Drayco had the feeling she'd deny knowing Tibbs if he asked. For that matter, she'd probably also deny knowing Alistair.

Was Graham's visit to Burdell the first time since the arson "death?" If not, and if Graham Tibbs made a habit of contacting old friends, then Johnny Burdell or Leon Sable could still be in play as a co-conspirator in whatever scheme they were involved with. Burdell or Sable could also be behind Tibbs's ultimate demise.

Suspects, speculations, suppositions. But no smoking guns.

Drayco replaced the finials on the display table and picked up a coil of steel wire. It reminded him a lot of piano wire, which reminded him again of the audition yesterday. He tossed the coil on the table and headed back to his office for some additional database research and to call up more of his contacts.

Ah, the exciting adrenaline rush of the detective life—computers, paperwork, phone calls. Of course, there was always the occasional kidnapping to spice things up a bit.

25

It was only five-thirty in the afternoon, but twilight had come and gone. That was one of the many downsides to the autumn time change as if the colder temps and stark brown trees weren't enough. But it was good for stargazing and getting out the telescope because of the clearer seeing at night . . . unless the gray skies settled in, as they often did along the mid-Atlantic coast.

Drayco looked up toward a thankfully cloud-free sky to see a small meteor blazing a trail, flaring for a second or two before it was gone. Didn't certain ancient civilizations think that was a bad omen?

Another side effect of autumn was that more shops closed up early, around six, but not the Great Games store. Drayco had considered calling up the new manager, Frederick Oak, to see if Johnny Burdell had returned but thought better of it. Sometimes, the element of surprise worked best.

Drayco also checked into Oak's past and drawn a blank as far as any scandals were concerned. But the chance Oak and Burdell were partners in something shady together wasn't nil.

The other reason to check out the puzzle store again was that Drayco had no luck in tracking Burdell down via other means. So much so, he was beginning to suspect this was another of Alistair's "helping a man disappear" schemes. But maybe if he asked nearby store owners if they had recent dealings with Burdell, they could offer some insight.

Drayco started with a couple of businesses across the street from Burdell's former store, but no joy there. The various staff all knew the guy, but everyone Drayco talked to said the same thing—Burdell was eccentric and hard to get to know. Whether it was him being standoffish or shy or anti-social, they weren't sure. Maybe that was why they were shocked to hear he'd left the store and was going to sell since he was so passionate about it. And as far as they knew, Burdell's store was doing well financially.

As he exited an antiques shop and looked over at Great Games, Drayco couldn't help but think about Alistair's puzzle. He still hadn't figured out what the damn thing meant . . . that is to say, the "solved" version with the words for numbers and the Latin phrase.

Yet, hadn't Alistair also said whatever doors he'd believed Drayco's "solution" might open remained firmly shut? That seemed to imply the treasure Alistair sought was still out there somewhere. Whatever it was, someone felt it was worth killing for.

Drayco stopped on the sidewalk to look up at the sky, hoping for more meteors and not just another man-made satellite cluttering up the view. But movement closer to the ground caught his attention, and he turned to spy a man headed toward the puzzle store.

He couldn't see the man's face, but his build and walk seemed familiar even in the darkness. If Drayco wasn't mistaken, the man was also wearing a puzzle-print jacket and matching cap. They looked identical to clothing hanging by the door with Burdell's name on them that Drayco saw on his first visit to Great Games.

Relieved to have tracked Burdell down, Drayco darted across the road as fast as he dared without spooking the guy. But at that exact moment, he heard an unmistakable high-pitched whine—something he recognized from his FBI training when they'd practiced different driving techniques. It had the same purple-helix sound of a car engine in low gear picking up speed.

Burdell didn't seem to notice, deep in thought. Throwing caution to the wind, Drayco ran toward him, shouting out a warning. He got close enough to almost grab Burdell's coat. But the car just accelerated faster and struck Burdell so hard, his body flipped over the vehicle onto the street.

As the car whizzed past, it swerved toward Drayco and grazed him, knocking him over on his back. Lying there, trying to catch his breath, he realized he was seeing more stars—the kind you get from hitting your head.

The antiques store owner apparently saw what happened and rushed over to help Drayco stand up. Then they both scrambled toward Burdell. But it was immediately obvious from the unnatural angle of his neck and his unblinking stare it was too late for anyone to help the unfortunate man.

The store owner grabbed his stomach and soon threw up on the sidewalk. Drayco reached into a pocket to pull out a handkerchief. Handing it over to the retching store owner to wipe his mouth, he patted the fellow on the shoulder and made sure he was turned away from the street.

Drayco went over to Burdell and knelt down beside him to try to find a pulse, even though he knew it was useless. By then, a larger crowd had formed on the scene. Drayco made sure no one touched the body, even as he wanted nothing more than to go to the dead man and close those staring eyes.

Drayco's own eyes were still blurry from the fall, but he rubbed them until he could see well enough to call 911 on his cellphone. As he waited for the authorities to arrive, he concentrated and tried to visualize the seconds before the hit-and-run and, playing it over again in his mind. Was there anything he could have done to prevent the tragedy?

Maybe his reflexes were a little too slow. Or perhaps he was too lost in thought over that damned puzzle to have been on high alert. He'd come close to having a grip on Burdell's jacket, just a couple of inches beyond his grasp. Two inches that stood between Burdell and death.

The emotional pain was bad enough, but he was also aware of aches and throbbing in his left shoulder and left leg and probably some new bruises. He rubbed the back of his head, but no blood. And no signs of a concussion—no headache, confusion, dizziness.

Was this going to be another hit-and-run that would end up labeled as an accident by the police? Because Drayco was pretty damn sure it was intentional. Two hit-and-run cases in the same spot, two weeks apart. Statistically possible, but highly improbable.

Whoever that driver was had targeted Johnny Burdell and maybe Drayco himself. But why? A coded puzzle lay at the center of Drayco's kidnapping, and a puzzle store was at the center of two mysterious deaths. If Alistair's "treasure" was at the heart of all of it, then it was looking to be as cursed as King Tut's gold.

In the distance, Drayco heard the sirens of approaching emergency vehicles. The night air felt suddenly colder, and he turned up the collar of his coat against the chill.

If the case hadn't already been personal because of his kidnapping, it was definitely personal now. Come hell or high water, Drayco would get to the bottom of the tragedies. And maybe in so doing, he could somehow find closure for the late Johnny Burdell—lover of puzzles, cactus candy, and environmental causes.

What had Frederick Oak said? "Deep down, Johnny's a good guy. The kind who wants to be better."

Drayco glanced over at the paramedics who'd swarmed out of an ambulance and were bending over the body. An unexpected moment of intense grief hit him full force. Whether he could have saved this man or not, he'd have to leave that to kismet or the Akashic Records or whatever deity was running things in the universe.

Right then, he had a lot more police reports to fill out. And another long night ahead.

26

Since Sergeant Gus Lorenzo was nowhere to be found, Drayco deposited a fresh case of Persian doogh yogurt drinks on his desk. Then he continued his trek down the long hallway toward Detective Halabi's office. Although Drayco's leg was still sore from the hit-and-run, it wasn't so bad that he had to limp.

But his painful shoulder was another matter. When he'd told Brock about the incident, Brock had practically forced him back to see Dr. McDonnell again for an X-ray, and Drayco had given in on that one.

Thankfully nothing was broken, but Drayco hadn't been able to find a position in bed that wasn't painful. Still, the shoulder wasn't what made him almost take a rare sleeping pill. He was afraid he'd have a parade of nightmares as he reached out to Johnny Burdell, the man's coat slipping through his fingers time and time again.

He yawned as he headed toward Halabi's office, hoping the dark circles under his eyes weren't too noticeable. At least, he hadn't needed to make an appointment with Halabi this time since the man had contacted Drayco first.

As he strolled into the police detective's office, Drayco said, "*As-tu mangé des beignets aujourd'hui?*"

Halabi replied, "*Trou du cul,*" a bit haltingly.

"Bravo. You know how to curse in French."

"I want to learn the most interesting bits first. That way, I can give my colleagues a hard time without them knowing."

Halabi studied Drayco as he eased himself into a chair and added, "That was quite an adventure you had last night. You've become quite the hit-and-run magnet."

"That's pretty much what Sergeant Lorenzo and Sergeant Persinger said to me last night." Drayco had stayed on the scene for a few hours helping fill in any details he could to help the police investigating the incident. They'd been thorough and professional, despite the gibes at his expense.

Halabi picked up a paper and waved it in the air. "I printed this out before you came. The only other witness, an antiques store owner, verified your account. Accelerating car, swerving toward Burdell, striking both of you."

"I got the impression they were definitely targeting Burdell."

"Are you sure Burdell was the intended victim and not you?"

"Not one hundred percent, no. Or maybe it was a two-for-one deal."

"The report says you didn't get a good glimpse of either the car or driver." Halabi peered at him. "Seems unlike you."

"It was dark, and I was too busy taking a fall to the ground." Drayco tried not to let Halabi's tone of voice get to him. Not when something else kept nagging at him, some little detail his subconscious was trying to tell him that he couldn't quite tease out of that murky pool.

Halabi sighed. "The antiques store owner didn't get any details, either. Except it was a dark car."

"That was also my impression, such as it was."

"Well, don't be too hard on yourself. Might come to you later. If so, let us know."

Drayco pointed at the stack of papers. "I didn't have the chance to talk to Frederick Oak, the new puzzle store manager. Did he know why Burdell was returning to the store when he was hit?"

Halabi shook his head. "Burdell hadn't called ahead. Oak was quite shaken up by it all."

Drayco leaned back in his seat and was immediately sorry when he hit his shoulder on the chair. He must have winced because Halabi said, "That witness said you hit the ground pretty hard."

"Hard enough. Nothing broken, so I call that a good day."

"Uh huh." Halabi frowned. "Interestingly, the report also said you were going to talk to Oak to see if Burdell had reappeared. I didn't know he'd disappeared."

Drayco started to shrug but caught himself in time. "Disappeared might be too strong a term. But he suddenly decided to sell his store. And I was unable to contact him."

"That might have been a detail we should know about it, don't you think?"

"It was on my 'to do' list, I swear."

Halabi snorted. "This year's or next?"

Drayco ignored him. "Who benefits from Burdell's will? Maybe that's the simple answer to all of this."

"Oddly enough, his ex-wife. The man also had an older sister. I can imagine how that went over when she found out. Actually, I won't have to imagine. We're going to have a chat with both the ex-wife and sister today." His tone turned a little darker. "And we would prefer to be the first to talk to them."

"I'm too busy nursing my boo-boo."

Halabi didn't crack a smile. "I understand you're a victim in all of this, too. But what I don't need are tainted witnesses."

"That's good because I don't taint. I merely question and observe."

Drayco changed the subject to avoid more dagger-stares from the other man. "Have you exhumed the grave that allegedly held Graham Tibbs's body?"

Halabi nodded. "Got some DNA from the bones. But no match in any police databases."

"No reports of someone missing at that time who might fit the victim's build?"

"No, but turns out it doesn't matter. We tried one of those online ancestry things and got lucky. Found a match to a relative, and it looks like the deceased was a man known to be homeless. Mentally ill. He'd been seen in the same area as Tibbs's business."

"No dental records for an exact ID?"

"Other homeless people in that area who knew the victim said he didn't have any teeth. Fell out from meth or some other nasty shit."

"That makes the planting of Graham's distinctive tooth premeditated."

"Agreed. I also had our forensic guys use the latest tech on the exhumed body and do a thorough job this time. Didn't seem to be foul play. No bullet fragments or ligature marks on the bones, no skull or neck fractures."

"Was there enough lung tissue left to tell if there were any asphyxia lesions or tract mucosal damage? Or soot?"

"Yeah. But no such airway inhalation damage according to the CT scans. There were signs of a heart problem. Anyway, he was dead before the fire. It's likely the poor guy died of natural causes—"

"And Tibbs just took that opportunity to help make his own 'death' look real."

"Exactly."

"You do know this makes two hit-and-runs in the same case?"

"As I recall, you don't like coincidences. Neither do I. I'm wondering now if Burdell was the intended victim all along. And poor Graham Tibbs was hit by mistake."

It was odd to hear Halabi say that since Drayco awoke with the same idea. The two men were about the same height and build. Maybe Burdell killed Tibbs, wanted the treasure for himself, and then a third partner mowed him down.

Drayco said, "I didn't see any traffic cameras outside Great Games along that stretch of road."

"We haven't had a lot of reasons to put one there. You can bet it's been bumped up the priority list." Halabi grimaced. "We'll find that driver. Or drivers. Hell, since Burdell has two women involved with his story, I wouldn't be surprised if the driver was a woman. That whole Bonnie and Clyde thing. Isn't there always a woman involved?"

"You've been watching too many movies." Drayco was pretty sure Nelia would have Halabi in a headlock right about then, a thought that made him smile. He added in French, "*Vous avez une araignée au plafond.*"

Halabi groaned. "French slang again, yay. But if there's anyone with a few loose screws around here, it's you, Drayco."

27

Drayco got a call from Aria D'Angelo, who'd read about Burdell's death in the news. She sounded anxious over the phone, so he made the trek to her house to fill her in and see how she was holding up.

When he arrived, soft music played in the background. Something from the baroque, but a piece he couldn't quite pin down. At first, it was instrumental, but he thought he recognized the composer when a voice started singing. Rameau, perhaps?

She looked at him, noticing his puzzled expression, and said, "'Tristes apprêts.' Sad preparations. From *Castor et Pollux*."

She'd made drinks for both of them and handed over a cup of spiced apple cider. From the sour, woody aroma wafting his way from her direction, she'd added something a little more potent to hers.

She sat down and took a sip. "Two hit-and-runs at the same place. This man, Johnny Burdell . . . do you think he was behind my brother Graham's death?"

"Perhaps, but it doesn't explain who killed Burdell."

"Someone shady, no doubt." She shook her head. "I can't say I'm surprised. My late brother ran in some bad circles in his younger days. We were both raised Catholic, but I guess it didn't take with Graham. I do pray for his soul every day."

Drayco noted a lighted candle on a table in the corner, next to an icon of the Virgin Mary. He asked, "And you think Graham was still involved with these people?"

"Who else? Some nasty connections, I fear."

"What kind of nasty connections?"

"Maybe mob, maybe not. I can't be sure. I didn't know this Burdell gentleman, and I still have no idea why Graham was coming out of his store the day he was hit. It's hard to imagine how someone who loves games might have something to do with criminal enterprises. It's absurd, don't you think?"

She sat her drink on an end table and added, "Or maybe I'm being naïve, and that saying is true. The quiet ones are the most dangerous."

"It's also possible Graham was an innocent victim in all of this, and Burdell was the target."

"You think so? It would do my heart so much good to know my brother wasn't some monster."

She grabbed her cup again to take a few more sips of her "extra-spiced" cider. "The news report said someone else was hit. Were they involved too?"

"Uh, that would be me."

Her eyes widened. "You were hit? I had no idea. But you look fine."

"Just a few bruises here and there." He didn't want to mention his shoulder was killing him. "If we're talking about out-there possibilities, there's also a chance the car was aiming for me and not Burdell."

"I don't understand. Whatever for?"

"Hard to say unless I've asked someone the wrong questions, and they don't want me to find the answers."

She put a hand to her throat. "I didn't plan on you getting hurt when I hired you. Perhaps I should call it off and write you a check for the work you've already done."

"If it's really what you want to do, that's fine. But this has become too personal for me to just let it drop."

"It sounds like you're going to keep digging no matter what."

He nodded. "Being kidnapped and almost run down by a car does that to you."

She stood up and said, "Maybe I can help. I'll be right back."

When she left the room for a couple of minutes, it gave Drayco more time to inspect her opera memorabilia. It was truly like being in a museum of Aria D'Angelo's career, and he felt like he should pay her for admission and not the other way around.

He'd been thinking more seriously about naming his Opera House on the Eastern Shore after her. He'd even asked his financial benefactor if he approved. It seemed fitting somehow—her career, like his, cut short by circumstances beyond her control. They shared a passion for music. And they both had scholarships being set up in "their" honor.

When she returned, she handed over a piece of paper. "I found a folder the other day that had letters from Graham. Going back years, of course. When people still wrote letters."

Drayco studied the paper. "It mentions Johnny Burdell here."

"The name meant nothing to me at the time, and I'd forgotten all about it. But it shows Graham knew him."

Drayco read a little more of the note. "It talks about a project they were going to work on together. But no details."

"Graham always had his schemes. Wanting to find the next get-rich-quick thing." She pointed at the paper, "It also mentions Burdell's wife. So maybe she's the one you should ask? Maybe she got Graham and this Burdell fellow involved, then wanted any spoils for herself."

"You're suggesting she'd kill Graham and her ex-husband to get what she wanted?"

"It's the femme fatale, isn't it? I sang many such roles in my day."

He smiled and started to reply when she added, "And don't say it can't happen in real life. I watch all those true-crime shows on TV."

"Burdell's ex-wife is on my list to interview next."

"Excellent. Now, if you'll excuse me again for just a moment." She left briefly and this time reappeared with another round of drinks.

After she sat back down, she said, "There was another reason I wanted to speak with you. I need your advice."

"Oh? What about?"

"Well, I hesitate to mention it. I might have just been imagining things."

"What sort of things?"

"It may be nothing. But yesterday, I took a taxi to my favorite clothing store at Mazza Gallerie. When I returned, things weren't quite right."

"In what way?"

"Some pots in my back garden were rearranged. It even looked like someone removed the pool cover and put it back, but not the way I left it. Plus, the bushes in front of a rear window were disturbed. As if someone was trying to find a good place to break in."

"Did you see any signs they were successful? Anything missing?"

"No, at least I don't think so. But maybe they were just careful. I'm not sure how they got in the yard to begin with. Perhaps they used a ladder to climb over the fence?"

"Did you report this to the police?"

"That's where I need your advice. I was wondering . . . perhaps you could look around first? I'd hate to bother them if I really am just imagining the whole thing. That 'crazy opera singer,' you know."

"I hope the police would take it more seriously than that. But yes, I'll be happy to look around for you."

"Oh, thank you, Scott. It would put my mind at ease."

She showed him to the back entry, where he headed out to first check the fence around the perimeter. But there didn't appear to be ladder indentations in the ground. Any potential thief might have used a rope ladder, but that would be tricky during daylight hours.

He also checked the pots, the pool area, and all the first-floor windows but again, no signs of forced entry. When he made his way back inside and reported his findings, she smiled. "Well, I guess that's good news. Maybe I'll hold off calling the police, after all."

"I don't think they'd mind if you did. And perhaps adding security cameras would be a good idea, too."

"I've been meaning to do that. It seemed so unnecessary with the gate and fence."

"As you say, peace of mind would be worth it."

She nodded. "At any rate, I'll look forward to hearing how your conversation with Johnny Burdell's ex-wife turns out. Why, you'll probably have this case solved the day after."

"Cases don't often wrap up quite that quickly."

"I have faith in you." She tilted her head. "Any luck with that puzzle?"

He was hoping she wouldn't ask about that. "Not yet. But I'm not giving up on that, either."

"You must call me the minute you solve it. I just know it's at the heart of my brother's death."

But was it? Perhaps it was all a wild goose chase, and the real reason for the deaths of Graham Tibbs and Johnny Burdell—since Drayco was sure now they were linked—was something far different.

He was still obsessed with the fact Burdell denied knowing Graham Tibbs when Drayco first talked to him. Why would he not want to acknowledge that fact unless he had something to hide? Something that tied him to Tibbs and not in a good way.

Maybe Aria and Detective Halabi were both right about the femme fatale angle. He was very much interested in talking with the ex-Mrs. Johnny Burdell, although at this late hour, it might have to be tomorrow. What he needed right then was a unique perspective on things, and he had a pretty good idea of where to get it.

28

The server ushered Drayco to a table close to the edge of the rooftop terrace in Rosslyn. Due to the building height restrictions in the District, if he ever wanted a bird's-eye view he always had to go across the river into Virginia.

His seat was next to one of the pyramidal space heaters that dotted the open-aired space like Egyptian obelisks in an urban oasis. Maybe future civilizations would one day dig up these heaters and wonder about their significance. A religious icon for worship? Geographical marker? A child's toy? Well, this modern-day human was very grateful to benefit from their very mundane but welcoming warmth.

He absorbed the views, some of the nicest around even at night. Or maybe especially at night. You couldn't see the National Mall in the dark from here. But there's no way you'd miss the spotlights from the Capitol, the Lincoln Memorial, and the Washington Monument.

It was even easy to see where the Potomac River snaked through the darkened landscape because of the water's lack of illumination. Hovering above the river was a moving stream of white landing lights and strobes from the planes on approach to National.

The views weren't the only reason he chose this spot. It would be a lot harder for someone to jab a syringe into him up here, especially with witnesses. He still wasn't sure if his situational awareness was back on track, so why tempt fate?

A pot of purple-ish things on the terrace floor also caught his attention. They looked like purple cabbages. He grabbed his cellphone to look them up. Ah. They were called *Brassica oleracea*, or ornamental kale. As he flipped through the details on his phone, someone plopped into the chair across from him.

Drayco's jaw dropped as he noted his new companion. The man nonchalantly signaled to the server.

Brock asked Drayco, "You ordered yet?"

He shook his head.

"Great. My timing is perfect." When the server arrived, Brock ordered some coffee "extra hot," a pastrami on rye with Dijon mustard, and caramelized onions on the side.

Brock and the server looked expectantly at Drayco, who blurted out, "Make that two." At least they'd both have onion breath. When he looked around and didn't see a salt shaker, he added, "And some salt?"

After the server hustled off, Drayco rubbed his chin. "Are you following me?"

"I like this place a whole lot better than the last one." Brock looked around at the view.

"You didn't answer my question."

"You were almost run over. And coming so soon after your kidnapping, I might add. By the way, I had to learn from Detective Halabi you might have been targeted, not Burdell."

"Halabi? What, does he think he has to call the daddy on the wayward little boy who keeps getting into trouble?"

"For your information, the case of my own I'm working on has an Arlington connection. I'd rung up Halabi earlier about it. He was just returning my call."

"Ah. I see."

"What I want to know is, *why* did I have to hear about this from Halabi? Are you still upset with me after our little argument the other night?"

Drayco hit his shoulder on the seatback and tried not to wince. "Didn't want to worry you. You've been a little smothering after the kidnapping. I don't know who's worse, you or Sarg."

"Sarg. I'm a blood relative. Caring is supposed to be in my DNA. So how's the case going? And by that, I mean I want to hear everything except any talk about Joyelle. Unless it's to apologize for suspecting her motives."

Drayco sighed. "Okay, I'll tell you everything. If you let me know where Joyelle was last night."

The server arrived with the coffee, and Brock stirred in some sugar and cream before answering. "We did have plans. But she had to cancel when something came up. A deadline project she's working on for a client, so don't read anything into it."

The cap on the salt shaker was loose, so Drayco ended up dumping more salt into his coffee than he'd planned. He took a sip and grimaced. "How can you be so sure about her?"

"You did profiling-type work in the Bureau. So did I. But I've been at this a lot longer than you have. I wish you'd give me some credit."

Not wanting to start another argument, Drayco changed topics. "I might have neglected to tell you something else. Uncle Alistair called me. The day after our little outing to his island."

Brock growled. "What did he say?"

"Not much. He admitted he was impressed with our snooping skills after getting past his security. But he hinted it wouldn't be possible again."

"He should thank us for showing up the weaknesses in his system."

"In a back-handed sort of way, I think he was."

After the sandwiches arrived, Drayco filled his father in on his case between bites, summarizing, "The motives are hazy, and the suspect list is short. First up, I'll arrange to have a chat with Burdell's ex-wife and his sister."

Brock scooted his chair a little closer to the nearest heater. When he noticed Drayco's half-eaten sandwich, he said, "Are you going to . . ."

Drayco pushed over the plate, and Brock grabbed the sandwich and wolfed it down. He wiped his mouth and said, "This Burdell character. The odds of another hit-and-run at the same location are longer than me turning into a purple unicorn."

"I'm convinced the two are linked. I just don't know how yet."

"You'll figure it out." Brock patted his stomach and then pointed at Drayco's. "You getting enough to eat? You only ate half your meal. And you look thinner. Something wrong?"

"I had a late lunch."

"Then why did you come here?"

"I don't know. Maybe I hoped it might help my perspective on things."

"Don't you usually play Bach for that?"

Drayco said, "Variety. Spice. Life." He gestured toward the sky. "And stars. Sort of."

"Hmm." Brock pointed at one of them. "What's that one?"

"Vega. Part of the constellation Lyra."

"You could get a job in astronomy if you ever tire of the sleuthing racket."

"Searching for black holes instead of blackguards?"

Brock chuckled. "You and Joyelle share the same sense of humor. I hope you can get to know her better. See her like I do."

Drayco just nodded and took another sip of his salty coffee.

Brock stared up at the sky. "Your sister Casey loved to go stargazing."

Drayco nodded. "One of our many shared interests. I suppose that happens even with fraternal twins."

"I miss her terribly. I know you do, too. But you don't have the regrets I do."

"Regrets?"

"I wasn't there for you or her as much as I should have been after Maura left us." A hint of anger crept into his tone. "The little twelve-year-old girl needed her mother while she was battling cancer. But Maura never came back."

"You know why, now."

"Her reasons don't matter. But I have little room to talk, right? I wasn't the best substitute. I don't know, Scott. Maybe it was Casey's death that was the final straw. The thing that pushed me away from caring so much."

"Yet you do care. You're very passionate about your work. And you've done a lot of good through it."

"But I know I've been a disappointment to you. That's what matters the most."

The server popped in again and took their dessert orders. When their tiramisu arrived, Drayco and his father ate it mostly in silence, gazing up at the stars, the few they could see through all the light pollution.

It surprised Drayco that his father remembered his Bach habit, but Brock was surprising him a lot lately. The little nagging feeling of guilt about Joyelle bubbled to the surface again. Maybe Joyelle was a second chance for Brock in more ways than one, something his father really needed in his life. So why couldn't Drayco just let his suspicions go?

29

Friday, December 3

Since Drayco's "different perspective" opportunity at the rooftop grill hadn't gone as planned last night, he'd returned home, taken Brock's reminder to heart, and played some Bach instead. Rather than calming him down as it usually did, it only made him more irritated. Bach never irritated him. So why now?

Bach was a puzzle solver, with the way he created complex contrapuntal lines he would mesh together, sometimes backwards and upside down. Johann Sebastian would probably have figured out Alistair's little number puzzle in nothing flat. Maybe that was it.

After hauling his aching bones out of bed, Drayco hopped in the shower, hoping the warm water would soothe the pain. And it did help, some. But he definitely didn't have an appetite for microwave macaroni and cheese with ketchup.

He grabbed some breakfast-on-a-bun from a drive-through and ate it a little angrily as he pointed his Generic Silver Camry toward Chantilly, where he'd made an appointment to talk to Johnny Burdell's sister. Maybe it was the angry eating, but he didn't notice the same dark car from a few days ago seemed to be following him until it screeched off onto Route 28, and he missed a chance to follow. Route 28 south . . . toward the National Reconnaissance Office, part of the spook network. Coincidence?

The vehicle was definitely real and *not* a "ghost car." This time, he had the presence of mind to glance at the plate in his rearview mirror. There was no front plate, but he did catch a temp tag in the back. So, was it a new car, or was the driver using a fake tag to avoid ID? Well, if this was another kidnapping attempt, it had failed.

He headed onward to his destination, which turned out to be a rather unremarkable house, a colonial with slate-gray siding, a bay window that took up one-third of the façade, and a plain brown fence. The only feature of interest was a hunter's-green door that looked out of place with the gray.

Connie Burdell Spanton might be ten years older than her brother, but her smooth skin, artful makeup, and dyed lilac hair made her look younger. The siblings shared the same Grecian nose and pale brown eyes, but their clothing choices hinted at sharp personality differences.

Whereas Johnny's attire had tended toward the nerdish eccentric, Connie could have stepped out of the latest fashion magazine spread. Her jewelry didn't look expensive, but there was plenty of it. She wore a matching blue-stone necklace and earrings, heart-shaped nose and eyebrow studs, and various knuckle rings.

She ushered him in with a tight smile and herded him toward the front room next to the bay window as she said, "I don't have oodles of time to spare. And I'm not sure how I can help. I told the police yesterday everything I know."

He stopped beside a large aquarium filled with purple, orange, and bright blue fish. "This is impressive. From the colorful fish species, I'm guessing saltwater?"

She nodded. "Saltwater fish are so chichi, aren't they? But I'm proud of this. I'm helping to save a few species. By breeding some endangered ones, like this fellow here." She pointed to one fluorescent specimen. "Nicknamed blue-eyes. Kind of like yours."

"Did your brother have a hand setting up your aquarium?"

"He was a big enviro buff. So I guess you could say he inspired it. But this tank was my idea from the start."

She leaned over to peer through the glass. "They're so beautiful and wild. Not a care in the world. Just swim and eat. In fact, I've decided to have Johnny's cremains scattered over the Atlantic. The perfect milieu for it." She pronounced it "meal your."

Before Drayco could even ask about funeral arrangements in Burdell's will, Connie gritted her teeth and added, "That is, if his ex-wife will let me."

Drayco eased onto a curved aqua-colored armchair that reminded him of ocean waves, taking pains to avoid banging his shoulder. "Did you know he was leaving his estate to his ex?"

"Not a clue. How many men have you ever known to do that? Johnny and Vivianna hadn't even seen each other in a couple of years."

"Are there other family members who might also have benefited?"

"Some cousins in south Florida. But I'm the only family he kept in touch with." She tilted her head at Drayco. "You don't look like a private detective. Way too cute."

He didn't miss a beat, replying, "It's a disguise."

That made her smile, and she held up her ring-less left hand. "I'm a relatively nouveau ex, too, so if you ever get bored . . . "

He smiled briefly and tried to change the subject by studying a scrap-metal rabbit sitting on the bay window ledge. He picked it up. "This is unusual. I know a shop that sells materials like this, LS Metals. Also an artist who creates objects from metals, Joyelle Babineaux. Do you know her or the metal store owner, Leon Sable?"

"Don't think so. My interior decorator picked that thing out. I was tired of ennui-decor, so I asked her to do avant-garday. You like it?"

"It has a certain bunny-ish charm." He returned the rabbit to the ledge and spied a few other "avant-garde" touches—a spaghetti chandelier made of green industrial electrical cord, a red lip-shaped chair, a triangular bookcase. He said, "I hope the police interrogation wasn't too unpleasant."

"What? Oh, not really. They contacted me, sure, to tell me about Johnny's death. But they didn't ask a lot of questions. As I told them, I have no idea why he'd be targeted. I'm confident it was all an accident."

"You said you were the only family Johnny stayed in touch with. You got along well?"

She chewed on her lip. "We didn't always get along great. Know any brothers and sisters who do? But the back-and-forth was kinda fun. Can't believe I'll never get the chance to argue with him again."

"Sounds like you spoke with him often."

"Maybe not often enough."

"Did Johnny ever say anything about a treasure code or map?"

Her eyes widened, and she shook her head vigorously. "But you'd better ask his ex-wife, the Psycho Bitch, since he left everything to her."

"I can understand why you'd be bitter. As you say, few exes leave their estate to a former spouse."

"I never trusted her. They weren't suited, and I wondered if she hooked up with him for money. Business owner and all that. But I'm the one who supported him through thick and thin. And here he leaves his money to a woman who divorced him."

Drayco must have signaled his next question because she beat him to the answer. "Yeah, she divorced *him*. You'd think that would make him even angrier with her, right?"

Drayco fingered the little rabbit sculpture. "Did Johnny ever talk about a man named Graham Tibbs? He knew your brother through an environmental organization."

"Graham Tibbs? That's an unusual name." She grabbed a little net from a panel under the tank that she raked through the water on top. "You'd think I'd recall it if I'd heard it. Do the police think he's the hit-and-run driver?"

"Not exactly. He was killed in an identical accident. At the exact same spot a couple of weeks ago."

She frowned. "Then you must think this wasn't an accident."

"I was hired by Graham Tibbs's sister to look into his death. And if this is related, I need to know."

"Can't imagine such a thing. Johnny murdered? That's what you mean, isn't it?"

He nodded. "Did Johnny ever mention being spooked about something? Or any threats?"

"He was as dull as they come. That puzzle store was the big excitement in his life, his *raison d'être*. It was the only thing that kept him going."

She put the fish net down and waved her arm toward the door. "Look, I hate to rush you, but I have another appointment. I don't want to be late."

He returned to his car a little bemused over the encounter. Connie's attempts to inject French terms into sentences, even mispronouncing them, as in "raisin deet," smacked more of pretension than genuine interest. At least Detective Halabi was making an effort to really learn the language. But what was with all the French in Drayco's life?

Connie Burdell said she didn't know what was in her brother's will. That would put her firmly in the suspect camp if she hoped she'd be the beneficiary. She'd also seemed ill-at-ease about the ex-wife, not that Drayco could blame her. It was quite an odd move to make on Burdell's part.

He was beginning to see what Frederick Oak had meant about Burdell's "woman trouble." After talking to Connie, he couldn't wait to check in with the "Psycho Bitch" to hear her side of the story. He just hoped she didn't know any French.

30

When Drayco finally reached Johnny Burdell's ex-wife after several futile calls, she told him to meet her at an address in Vienna. The property was her ex-husband's house—now hers, thanks to the inheritance. He was sure he'd written the address down correctly, but when he arrived, the place couldn't be farther from the man Drayco had met. Or his eccentric store.

Burdell's home was the middle structure of three plain gingerbread houses in a row, flanked by one on the left with pink siding and blue trim and another on the right with blue siding and yellow trim. Burdell's was the mildest of the trio, with a beige and orange paint combo.

The woman who met Drayco at the door also didn't match the image Drayco formed from his encounters with Burdell. Johnny Burdell had looked very much the geek, but his former wife, Vivianna Keating, was vanilla to Johnny's pistachio. Her black leggings and gray tunic sweater were more "normal," with none of Connie Burdell's pretensions.

But when Vivianna ushered him inside, the interior of the gingerbread house morphed into the kind of place where Drayco imagined the deceased puzzle store owner would live. He felt as if he'd stepped into the land of *Willy Wonka*, a vibe enhanced by the Candy Land painting that took up the main wall.

There wasn't much room to sit down in the crowded space, which was just as well since Drayco didn't see any chairs. Okay, there was one, but it was covered with boxes of vintage board games.

An old wooden bicycle wheel hung from the ceiling, suspended above a vintage carved wooden horse wearing a Santa costume. The floor sported shoe lasts, a wooden train set, and plastic balls of various sizes. But the creepiest items were the life-size doll heads perched on a makeshift plywood table. What was up with Burdell and weird dolls?

Vivianna looked at Drayco with a bemused expression and said, "Can you see why I left him?"

"I take it you didn't share his love of all things . . . puzzled."

"I most certainly did not. I think he also had a bit of the hoarder in him, as you can see."

"Begs the question as to why he left everything to you in his will."

"I have no earthly idea. Unless he had the will drawn up while we were married and never got around to changing it."

She picked up a plush octopus toy with a thin, worn coat. "Or maybe it was because he hated his sister so much. He was always ragging on Connie since she made a big show out of supporting him. But she was very judgmental and condescending to him in person."

"She didn't give me that impression. Made it sound like they had the usual types of disagreements."

"I'll bet she blamed me for everything too, didn't she?"

When Drayco didn't immediately reply, Vivianna added, "That woman is crazy, mark my words. The type who snoops through all your drawers and closets when she thinks you're not watching. After Johnny and I got engaged, I received a real 'poisoned pen' letter. It had a white powder inside, so I took it to a chemist. Harmless talcum, but how was I to know that? It was unsigned, but I knew it had to be her."

"She didn't seem thrilled about the estate situation."

"Oh, I'll bet. But the joke's on her. When Johnny's attorney contacted me, I asked how much we were talking about. It's not a huge amount."

"Even after you sell the games store?"

"He had gobs of debts. The attorney *thinks* proceeds from selling the puzzle store might just cover them. Honestly, I don't know where he spent his money."

"Gambling, maybe?"

"I wouldn't be surprised. He was lousy with finances and always in debt up to his eyeballs. Gave a lot to environmental causes, though. One shared interest we had in common."

She sighed. "But I can use every dollar that comes my way. I run an animal shelter, which isn't cheap. I rely mostly on donations and grants since the money I'd saved up from my former law practice is long gone."

"Law practice?"

"Animal law. Big surprise, eh?"

"Animal law, as in veterinary malpractice?"

"And custody disputes, housing disputes, consumer protection, animal cruelty, etc. Not lucrative, but highly rewarding."

"I would imagine." Drayco stepped on a squeaky bunny toy and hastily moved aside. "Thanks for agreeing to talk to me. I'm assuming the police contacted you, too?"

"To tell me about his death, yes. They didn't have many questions for me once I told them I had no idea why he might be targeted. They asked me about an alibi, if you're wondering." She eyed him with suspicion. "Unless you've talked to them already?"

"What did you tell them?"

She smiled briefly. "That I had had dozens of witnesses, mostly of the four-footed variety. I don't have a lot of staff, so I rarely leave the rescue facility. My apartment is on the second floor above the office there."

"You divorced Johnny about five years ago?"

"That's right. Believe it or not, I really loved the guy. But to risk a cliché, love is blind. We weren't that compatible from the start. Then it got worse right before the divorce. But I don't think it was on account of the divorce. Or that's what I tell myself."

"What do you mean?"

"He'd gotten angrier, kept more to himself. Didn't want to talk much. He seemed to change overnight."

"Do you have any idea what caused the change?"

"He was odd and eccentric, so who really knows? Maybe the business was struggling then. We didn't talk shop much."

"Did he ever mention the names Graham Tibbs, Alistair Brisbane, or Joyelle Babineaux?" Drayco hated to add that last one. But he'd be a lousy detective if he didn't pursue that angle.

"I don't think so. The police asked me about Tibbs. And I'll tell you what I told them. It does sound familiar."

"How so?"

"Just familiar. But no, I didn't know any such person."

"Your ex-husband was killed in the same way and at the same location as Tibbs."

"That's what the police said."

"And you had no inkling Johnny might be involved in any criminal schemes with or without Tibbs?"

"Johnny was too much of a nerdy type to get involved in a big crime scheme. Maybe it was revenge from a disgruntled customer? Someone who thought they were cheated out of some money over a rare whatever they gave him to sell? Because I can't imagine anything else."

"Yet soon after Tibbs's death, Johnny up and quits his store, looking for a buyer."

"What?" She looked genuinely surprised. "The police didn't tell me that."

"I'm not sure they knew about it."

"Now that's odd. He loved that store. It was his whole life. It would have taken something truly awful to make him want to give it up."

"Did Johnny have any lady friends after your divorce?"

"I never heard about it if he did." She sighed. "Not that I've had much luck in that department. But breaking up with my recent beau was a mistake. Leon was a pretty good catch."

Drayco's ears perked up. "Leon? As in Leon Sable, who owns LS Metals?"

"Why yes, that's him."

"Did you know Graham Tibbs was Leon's former business partner?"

She shook her head. "He just mentioned his former partner had died tragically. He didn't want to discuss it, and I didn't press him."

She got a pensive look on her face. "Then Tibbs's death must have been hard on Leon. Maybe I should look him up again to see how he's doing."

On one of Drayco's trips to Leon's store, something he'd said rang a bell in Drayco's brain. "Did he call you 'Vi'?"

"Yes, why?"

"When I spoke with Leon recently, he mentioned an ex-girlfriend named 'Vi'. Sounded rather wistful."

"Really? Maybe you just misread him. But still . . . I should check up on him."

Drayco looked around the room again at the piles and piles of memorabilia. "What in the world are you going to do with all of this?"

"I'll put ads in magazines that feature games and antiques in hopes there might be takers. If not, I guess an estate sale."

"It might help my investigation if I could look through some of these things."

She frowned. "I need to get back to the shelter." But after taking another look at the mess, she added, "But, if you think it'll help with your investigation, then maybe you should. To find justice for Johnny."

"You'd trust me alone with this?"

She nodded. "When I got your call, I looked you up. Impressive. Somehow, I think all of this," she waved her hand around the room, "would be safer in your hands than a sticky-fingered estate sale crew."

"I promise I'll leave everything in the same condition I find it."

"Too bad." She grinned. "The place could use a good clean. You'll be sure to lock the door on your way out?"

After she'd left, Drayco surveyed the piles that formed the rubble of Johnny Burdell's life and had a few second thoughts about offering to look through it all. But it was better than dumpster-diving. *Mostly* better.

Vivianna Keating didn't behave like a woman trying to hide something. But then again, she'd dated Graham Tibbs's former business partner, Leon Sable. If she knew she was the beneficiary, but not the small amount of money involved, perhaps she and Leon were in cahoots and killed Burdell in a scheme to get his inheritance?

It made a pretty convoluted motive, for sure. But greed can make bizarre bedfellows, and Leon and Vivianna both needed funding. It was also possible they were putting on a show for Drayco—that they weren't exes.

One thing was sure, Burdell's sister and ex-wife weren't besties. Not even close. Which of their stories was closer to the truth? Vivianna said Connie made a big show out of supporting her brother, but was very judgmental and condescending to him in person. On the other hand, Connie had claimed Vivianna hooked up with Burdell for his money.

With a sigh, Drayco started his search in the front room, methodically looking at each item and trying to put everything back just as he'd found it. If the front area was daunting, the rest of the house wasn't much better. Five hours later, Drayco was ready to call it quits when he found a ledger poking out from under the microwave.

"Where else would you put it?" he said aloud.

It was mainly household purchases, and it appeared Burdell had tried to balance his budget, if badly. But the very last page—the most recent entry one day before Burdell's death—caught Drayco's attention. Scrawled in the margins were the words, "I've had it. This is insane. I should never have said anything. Why did I make that call? I'm next, I know it."

Drayco re-read the note several times, but its meaning didn't get much clearer. What should he not have said? What call should he not have made?

Drayco tucked the ledger under one arm, took one last look around the byzantine, eccentric mess, and made sure to lock the door on his way out. Maybe the note made little sense yet, but one thing was certain—Burdell had a pretty good idea he was in the crosshairs. And now, that odd little note would serve as his epitaph.

31

Drayco's breath formed mini-clouds that hung around him like rising pillars of regret. He hoped this wasn't another horrible idea he'd live to regret later. But this is where she'd said to meet him.

As he laced up his rental skates, his companion said, "Isn't this an amazing place for a skating rink? Out here on the Mall, with the gallery in the background. It's such a little gem. Especially at night, when it's hardly ever crowded."

Drayco couldn't disagree with Christi Allingham, seeing as how they were among only a handful of partakers on this particular evening. And she was also right about the backdrop, nestled amid the National Gallery of Art Sculpture Garden, with hefty sculptures standing guard—like Alexander Calder's red *Cheval Rouge* and Tony Smith's *Moondog* and its octahedral shapes.

He asked, "You've been here before?"

"All the time. Well, when it's open during the cold months." He noted that she'd had the foresight to wear a warm knitted beanie, unlike himself.

As he finished up lacing his skates and got ready to put on his gloves, she stared at his left hand. "Not married, I see?"

"Not that I know."

She laughed at his rather lame joke and smiled a little too brightly. The Pavilion Cafe next to the rink was still open, so maybe she'd imbibed some of their mulled wine before he arrived? Otherwise, why the sudden flirting? This was a far different reaction from her than when they met at the National Gallery's cafe.

She pointed toward the rink. "You've lived in the District for how long, and you've never skated here?"

"It's been eighteen years—I think—since I last skated anywhere. And I wasn't a pro then." The music playing from the speakers changed tunes, making Drayco add, "At least they're not using bland elevator music."

Christi shook her head. "No, it's 'O Mio Babbino Caro' from *Gianni Schicchi*. I love that opera."

As he stepped tentatively onto the ice, he said, "Then you must have got along great with Graham's sister, the opera singer." It wouldn't be easy to ask her questions while concentrating on skating, but he was game to try.

"Never met her. She was gone a lot when Graham and I dated in high school. And by the time we hooked up again a few years ago, he wouldn't even talk about her."

Christi's first steps into the rink weren't tentative at all. She moved like a pro. She said, "I gather there was an estrangement. Too bad. I would have loved to meet her. It was because of her that I got interested in opera. When I found out what she did for a living and all."

"You didn't have any interest in studying music?"

"I've been a map freak all my life. Begged my parents to get the *World Almanac* every year for Christmas. I think I had a map from every major city on the planet hung on my wall."

"Then it's easy to see how you got involved with GIS. Different types of mapping."

"Quite true, mostly digital. But you should see my home office. It's still covered in paper maps." She skated a little circle around him and laughed.

"Cheaper than wallpaper."

"I'm not so sure. I'm on a first-name basis with all the staff at the National Geographic Museum down on 17th. Especially the gift shop crew."

"Was Graham as fond of maps as you are?"

"Like everyone else, he thought it was weird."

"Was he fond of games and puzzles, then? That's more mainstream."

"He was bad at math and not a nerd at all. Not sure what we saw in each other. Even now, I'm a bit of a geek with my job. But geeks are sexy now, yes?" She skated another circle around him, this time a little closer.

"You told me last time you recalled the name Johnny Burdell from environmental causes he and Graham were involved with. How deep was Graham into those causes?"

"You mean, was it like those Seaway Sentinels people? The ones who ram whalers and sabotage commercial fishing vessels?"

"Something like that."

"Graham could be a little intense. Once he got into something, he really got into it. So, I don't know. Maybe."

As they skated around the oval, he made the mistake of looking at the fairy lights framing the National Archives across Constitution Avenue. He felt his feet begin to slide out from under him, and just as he was bracing for a hard fall, Christi grabbed his belt and yanked him upright.

After first thanking his lucky stars he'd avoided a broken ankle, he thanked Christi for her assist. "You're a lot stronger than you look."

"Pilates." She grinned. She slipped her arm through his and expertly matched her skating rhythm to his to keep them both stable.

"I know you said you avoided Graham's best friend, Ezra Layton, in high school, but he and Graham stayed friends. So Graham must have talked about him when you hooked up again recently."

"Graham wasn't much of a talker and kind of secretive. Maybe it was his rough childhood, those misdemeanor arrests and all."

"I'm curious. Did Ezra ever ask you out?"

For the first time, she lost her rhythm, and he braced for a fall for both of them. Fortunately, the skating gods took pity on them, and they resumed their former pace.

She replied, a little breathlessly, "No, why?"

"I got the impression he might have. I know what you said about football players, including Ezra. But people do change."

She broke away from him to do a toe-loop jump and then circled around to link up arms once again. Drayco wasn't a skating expert, but her form looked pretty good. It was kind of nice to be outside, having a bit of fun for a change. So he decided to just enjoy the experience for a few minutes and put the detective persona on ice. The twinkling fairy lights cast artistic pillar-and-ribbon patterns on the rink, and it was a little magical. But then, he'd always loved Washington's monuments at night, and this was no exception.

Sadly, though, he wasn't here for his own entertainment. He asked, "Did you hear about Johnny Burdell's death?"

"You mean Graham's environmental buddy?"

"That's the one."

"Did he have something to do with Graham's death? Was he arrested for the hit-and-run?"

"He was killed in a hit-and-run himself."

"Oh, my god." Her skating slowed to a crawl and then to a stop as she turned to face him. "You think their deaths are related?"

"I'm not sure. It could be a coincidence."

"Maybe it's my geeky nature, but those odds don't measure up."

"I'm inclined to agree with you. And you're sure you don't recall Graham ever mentioning Burdell outside their environmental interests?"

She looked away toward the National Archives building as she thought about it. Finally, she shook her head. "Sorry. Wish I could help, but I'm drawing a blank."

She sighed and slowly started skating again, once again linking arms. "I'm realizing there's so little I knew about Graham."

They skated in silence for one entire revolution around the rink before she said, "Let's talk about something more interesting. You, for instance."

"Me? Not sure I'm all that interesting."

"Are you kidding? A private detective? And I did a little research. The geek in me, you know. You played the piano? For a living? I mean, how did you get from one to the other?"

"That's a long story. And perhaps one saved for another time."

"I'll look forward to hearing it someday."

Drayco hastily steered the subject back to the case. "I don't suppose you've ever heard the name Joyelle Babineaux?"

She looked sideways at him. "One of your girlfriends?"

"Ah, that would be a hard no."

"Then I can happily say I've never heard of her."

They paused to lean against the railing and watch a young girl who couldn't be more than seven or eight as she executed some pretty complicated leaps. Christi pointed to her and said, "A triple salchow. She's very good."

"Maybe we'll see her performing at the Olympics someday."

Christi got a dreamy look on her face. "When I was her age, I spent two hours a day skating. Took lessons and did pretty well. But not that good. Like most skating girls that age, I dreamed about the Olympics."

"Don't skaters usually retire around age twenty-five or so? I think your career will last a lot longer than that."

She laughed. "I guess so. And I like to think I'm making a small difference. All those spatial relationships and linear networks help us understand planet Earth better. Like how its physical processes shape human activity."

"After I met you last time, I did a little research of my own on the whole GIS concept. The data is used in just about everything—education, health, real estate, public safety, insurance, manufacturing. Even retail."

She smiled up at him. "Now you're making me feel like a geeky goddess."

He made a slight bow before her. "Your highness."

She bit her lip and asked, "I don't suppose your phone number is easy to find? In case I think of something else to add to Graham's case. Or for any other reason."

He took off a glove, fumbled through his pocket, and pulled out his wallet. He handed over a business card that she stuffed down her shirt. So, he wasn't dreaming it. She was definitely flirting. Well, if Nelia was a lost cause, why not? Christi was pleasant enough company.

But if he were honest with himself, his heart wasn't in it. One-night stands weren't his thing. And what about Nelia? He had no idea whether Nelia was seeing anyone else while waiting for her divorce. She'd said she wasn't ready for another relationship, but maybe it was just with him? He hadn't entertained that notion before, and he didn't like the way it made his blood freeze.

Thankfully oblivious to the maelstrom of confused thoughts swirling around in his head, Christi linked up arms again and pulled him toward the rink's center. He forced himself to focus on the case and what, if anything, his questions to Christi had revealed. Maybe he was just tired, but he wasn't connecting the dots very well at that moment.

But as he peered over the barrier, trying to get a glimpse of the shadowy sculptures, he thought about their materials. Tony Smith's *Moondog* was aluminum, and Alexander Calder's *Cheval Rouge* was steel. Wonder what Joyelle Babineaux thought of them? Good art or bad art? Was there any chance the metals came from Leon Sable's shop? Probably not, but metal was turning out to be something he found lurking around every corner in this case.

For now, he and Christi had another forty-five minutes of skating they'd paid for. The crisp, cool air and the re-learning of an old skill might do him some good. That, and a cup or two of the mulled wine afterward.

32

Saturday, December 4

Sarg grabbed the thermos and refilled Drayco's travel mug before placing it back in the Generic Silver Camry's cup holder. Drayco took a few sips, grateful to Sarg for even thinking of bringing along coffee. But their trek was going to take them forty-five minutes to an hour, depending upon traffic, from the District into Fauquier County, Virginia. Caffeine fortification was welcome.

Sarg said, "Did you get up early enough to see that psychedelic sunrise this morning?"

"You make it sound like I always sleep 'til noon."

"The life of the bachelor detective. Out all night, sleep all day. Like a tomcat."

"For your information, I was up at five. Did a run along the Tidal Basin and even got in an hour of Chopin. Well, an hour total, including the breaks I have to take."

"Don't you have that recital audition coming up soon?"

Drayco shook his head. He wanted to forget it for now, not get into psychoanalysis about what happened. "Thanks for coming along. I could have done it on my own."

"Sure, sure. But if this was the place your kidnappers took you, who knows what else might be lurking around? Backup, my friend. Always backup."

"Our first stop isn't my little prison. It's a carillon. It's not open to the public, but the family who owns it makes sure it's played regularly. Often on Fridays, the same day when I heard it during my captivity. And some Saturdays."

"The latter of which also happens to be today. Natch. But will you be able to tell if it's the same one you heard? You said you'd listened to every carillon within hundreds of miles."

"I couldn't find any recordings or videos online of this one. Can't be sure until I hear it in person."

They pulled into a circular driveway leading to a tiny parking lot, only big enough for a couple of cars. But they were alone. Their target was dead ahead, down a short brick pathway.

As they climbed out and approached, Drayco studied the building. It looked like a layer cake. It had a hexagonal pinkish concrete base unit with small windows that must house the carillon keyboard and a timer mechanism. The hexagonal concrete tower perched on top probably housed the chimes. And that was further topped by a copper dome sporting a weathered green patina.

Drayco looked at his watch. They had a few minutes to wait until the top of the hour, but they still peered up at the tower as if it might somehow go off early. Maybe their concentration on it was why they didn't hear the growling . . . at first.

They both whipped around to see an enormous black dog with its teeth bared. Sarg whispered to Drayco, "You didn't happen to bring any sausages, did you?"

The dog continued to growl, not giving any ground. When it crouched down with its muscles pulled into attack mode, Drayco said in a calm but firm voice, "Hey!" and dropped his arms to his sides.

The animal paused for a moment, and then Drayco added in a softer voice, "You look like a nice pup. I'll bet you live around here, don't you? It's a lovely morning to be out and about, isn't it?"

The dog's ears perked up, and its muscles began to relax. Drayco knelt down and held out his hand, palm up. "I'll bet you'd like some head-scratching, wouldn't you?"

The animal hesitated and then crept along the grass until it got within a hand's width from Drayco, who allowed the dog to smell his hand. Then the tail started to wag, and Drayco scratched the dog's head and ears, making the tail wag even more. "See, I knew you were a nice pup."

Drayco heard a faint voice calling out in the distance, and the dog turned toward it. He looked at Drayco and then back toward the sound. Drayco said, "Someone is calling you, pup. You run along now. It was nice to meet you."

The dog gave one last glance in their direction and then bounded away, making Sarg shake his head. "Does having a feral cat show you how to do that?"

"Brock's German Shepherd is a rescue and can be prickly. But we get along pretty well."

"You should hang out your shingle as an animal whisperer."

"If detecting doesn't work out . . . " Drayco shrugged. Or would he turn instead to astronomy, as Brock had suggested?

"Well, you'd be a natural. What kind of dog was that, anyway? Largest one I've ever seen. Mastiff? Great Dane?"

"Looked like a wolf-dog hybrid to me."

"Oh, that's just great. Why couldn't it have been a Chihuahua?"

Dealing with the dog caused Drayco to forget about the carillon, so it made both him and Sarg jump when it went off. The song it began to play had the same first opening notes as "Twinkle, Twinkle, Little Star," C-C-G-G-A-A-G, but it soon morphed into a tune Drayco didn't recognize. Great, Drayco was starting to hear that damned nursery song everywhere.

Sarg studied him. "Can you tell if it's the same carillon?"

"It has the same grainy, rusty orange-and-blue squished ovals with spikes the other one did. I'd bet good money on that."

As they listened, Drayco noticed the bronze doors leading inside looked slightly ajar. He pointed it out to Sarg and headed straight for it. Sliding his hand between the two door panels, he opened it wide enough for them to enter.

Inside, a keyboard stood in the central rear part of the open room. It was not a digital carillon, as Drayco had guessed, because a woman sat perched on the bench. Drayco put his finger to his lips to alert Sarg not to say anything. They should let her finish the piece to avoid startling her—and let everyone in the vicinity know something was awry.

The extra time allowed Drayco to study the instrument, similar to others he'd seen before. Two keyboards, one for feet and the other for hands. The keys were spaced much farther apart than a piano keyboard so they could be struck with closed fists. Plus, all the steel wires and cables were a clue this wasn't an ordinary piano or organ keyboard.

He waited until the piece ended and cleared his throat. But even that unexpected sound was enough to make the woman jump off her seat. She stood staring at the two men with wide eyes. "We're not giving tours right now. You'll have to come back some other time."

Drayco gave her his best disarming smile. "Sorry to startle you, Miss—"

"Cardena. Vina Cardena." She wasn't what he'd expect from a carillonneur. She had short auburn hair with bangs that looked like they were cut along the edge of a ruler, bright-pink lipstick, and tattoos of dragonflies on her neck.

"We didn't know there was anyone here since I thought this was a digital carillon. And there weren't any cars out front."

"My brother dropped me off." She added with a jutted jaw, "And he'll be back soon."

Sarg had apparently gauged her reaction enough to know it was a good time to pull out his FBI badge. "I'm Agent Sargosian. And this is my associate, Scott Drayco."

She looked from Sarg to Drayco. "I'm not sure I should be talking to you. Do I need a lawyer? Or maybe I should have you talk to the Gunnison's lawyers. The Gunnison family owns this carillon and the property."

Drayco asked, "And they hired you to be their carillonneur."

She blinked at him for a moment at the use of the correct term. "Yes, they did. But what's this all about? I don't know too many criminal carillonneurs."

Drayco grinned. "Neither do I, but there's always a first. By the way, we just encountered a rather unfriendly black dog outside. Does he belong to you?"

"Oh, you must mean Oscar. He lives a half a mile away, but his owners don't keep good tabs on him." Vina eyed the two men. "And you escaped unscathed?"

Sarg piped up, "Thanks to Drayco, here. Has a way with doggos."

That made her frown a little. "Then you must have some sort of magic since Oscar can get pretty fierce. He's been known to bite people, so I call him the Demon Hound. What, are you some kind of warlock?"

She actually seemed serious, and from Sarg's twitching face, Drayco suspected he was holding back laughter. But the expert FBI agent had a pretty good deadpan expression when he needed it.

Vina glanced at Sarg, and her gaze fell to his left hand, where she noticed the wedding ring. "You're married."

"So my wife tells me," Sarg replied cheerfully.

"Oh, okay." And she moved a little closer to him as if he would somehow protect her from Drayco. Those muscles on Sarg's face were twitching hard now. Poor Sarg. He and Drayco were getting a lot of wedding ring—or lack thereof—attention lately.

Drayco pressed on, "Were you here playing here a couple of weeks ago? It would have been on a Friday, November 19."

She didn't even have to think about that, nodding right away. "I'm here Fridays and Saturdays most weekends."

"Did you notice unusual visitors to the area? An unfamiliar car, perhaps?" Drayco described Iago Pryce, Alistair's right-hand man, and Graham Tibbs. "One of the men would be tall, about six-eight, and bald with a graying goatee and mustache. The other man is more heavy-set, with thinning blond hair and a small V-shaped scar on his chin."

Sarg added, "And the car would be an older-model sedan. Biggish."

She stepped a little closer to Sarg again as she replied, "I think I saw that car. This place is out in the boonies. We've got a lot of farms and businesses that supply the farms. Think pickup trucks and Jeeps. Not too many boat-sized sedans."

Drayco asked, "And the two men?"

Vina replied to Drayco even as she was batting her eyelashes at Sarg. "Sounds about right. It was dark, but there's a security light out front by the road. They drove past it, so I could see inside the car for a moment. They were big guys. A little scary-looking."

"Had you noticed them before? Or since?"

"That was the only time. But as I said, I'm only here on weekends." She smiled at Sarg. "FBI? That sounds exciting. And really romantic."

The muscles on Sarg's face almost turned into spasms, and even his right eye was twitching now. Drayco pulled out a business card and handed it over. She took it but barely looked at him as she continued her Sarg-worship.

Sarg cleared his throat. "That's all we have now. Do give Mr. Drayco here a call if you think of anything else," and he grabbed Drayco's arm, pulling him toward the exit.

Once outside, Drayco grinned. "I think you have a new fan."

"It's the wedding ring. Some chicks are attracted to married men. Just as a lot of married women seem to be attracted to you, your mighty Warlockness."

That made Drayco want to both laugh and wince. So he opted for wince. "Anyway, looks like we're on the right track with the location."

"Now, all we have to do is find the place they held you prisoner." Sarg studied the open field around the carillon, with a forest of obscuring trees at the edge of the property. "Easy peasy."

Drayco headed to the car where Sarg stopped him. "How about I drive so you can look around better? You said you got a brief glimpse of the front of the place."

"Good idea. But let's be methodical about it." Drayco called up the GPS map, and they picked the nearest roads to try first. Drayco nixed a dirt road, adding, "The ride wasn't that bumpy."

After the seventh road, several dead-ends, and rows of more endless trees, Sarg said in exasperation, "Everything looks the same around here. Maybe we shoulda brought a drone."

They'd driven a quarter mile down the eighth road when something caught Drayco's eye, and he said, "Stop."

Sarg pulled over and followed Drayco's gaze toward a house half-hidden down a gravel driveway. He asked, "That the one?"

"Maybe. One way to find out."

They continued down the driveway, parked, and got out to study the house's peeling red doorway. Drayco said, "The brief glimpse I got of my prison included a door a lot like that."

Sarg surveilled the area. "Nice and spooky. Good Gothic setting. Seen any good ghosts lately?"

"Maybe we'll run into a ghost butler." Drayco pulled out his pick kit, which made Sarg say, "I guess it's okay if you do it instead of me."

"What, forgotten how?"

Sarg glared at him. "Funny. Nah, Director Onweller would be furious if he found out I'd broken into a house. And one not related to a case. Even then, we'd need a subpoena."

"If you want to wait in the car—"

"You kidding? This is the most fun I've had in months."

Drayco made quick work of the old lock, and they headed in, with Sarg keeping one hand by his side near his hip holster. The place comprised five bedrooms, a living room, a den, and a farmer-sized kitchen. All the rooms were empty except for a few old wooden chairs—until they entered a small, windowless room with mildew on the walls, one twin bed in the corner, and a bathroom with no door.

"Bingo," Drayco said.

"You sure?"

"Absolutely. This is the place."

Sarg tried one of the light switches. Nothing happened. "So they had the utility company turn on the electricity long enough for your little stay and then turn it off again?"

"I heard a buzzing sound before they hauled me inside the house. Could have been a generator."

"What about the plumbing? Unless someone's still paying the water bill."

Drayco looked out a window and spied the tops of a couple of green tanks nearby. "Gravity-fed septic system. And maybe a well or cistern. Since we're way out in the middle of nowhere, makes sense."

"Huh. Wonder why your kidnappers picked this place? Doesn't look like it's been lived in since the fifties. Did you see those painted metal cabinets in the kitchen?" Sarg shuddered.

"Guess they needed somewhere isolated, away from prying eyes. But we'll look up the property owner later, just in case."

"Alistair?"

"I doubt he'd hold on to a property this godforsaken. But who knows?"

As Drayco continued to look around the room, he felt a tingling sensation at the back of his neck and reached up to rub it. Sarg must be keeping a close eye on him because he asked, "Something wrong?"

"Just those ghosts, I guess." He wasn't the type to get PTSD, not over something like this. But his palms were sweating all of a sudden. And that made him furious. "Guess I'm having some not-very-nice thoughts about a certain family member."

"You and me both. Your Uncle Alistair had better hope he and I never meet in person."

They conducted a more thorough search of the building, including a brief trip up into the attic, home to dozens of mice and hundreds of spiders. Finally, they decided they'd seen everything they could—especially when Sarg slipped on the attic floor and got covered in dust and cobwebs, prompting a sneezing fit. Good thing they didn't have Leon Sable's asthma.

Once safely in the front of the house again, Sarg eyed Drayco. "I think I'll also drive back." He hurried to add, "Give you a chance to look around some more. In case you see something else."

Drayco knew Sarg was being over-protective again. But he had a point. Drayco needed to continue looking around, but he was also wrestling with emotions that might affect his driving—anger at his captors and Alistair, frustration with the damned puzzle, and worry about Brock and Joyelle.

Plus, there was something else he couldn't quite put his finger on. Maybe a hint of his claustrophobia returning? Continuing angst about his mother? The excruciatingly embarrassing piano audition? With a shake of his head he pushed all those thoughts aside.

He flipped on his satellite radio until he found a polka station, making Sarg smile. With his former partner's favorite music blaring out of the speakers, they headed down the road and toward the District. At least one of them would feel relaxed.

33

Master-chef Sarg knew the locations of the best diners and restaurants off the beaten track. So it was no surprise when he turned the car off the interstate and into a small town unfamiliar to Drayco. But the restaurant Sarg chose was apparently a "hog" heaven, with a horde of Harleys parked outside.

The interior was clean, small, and packed. They made a lunch out of some of the best chicken and dumplings Drayco had ever tasted. If he were ever back this way, he'd have to try their Shenandoah Stack with mac 'n' cheese pancakes. No ketchup required.

Drayco picked up the check since Sarg was doing him a favor, and Sarg protested. But when Sarg learned Drayco was going to pay a visit to Graham Tibbs's childhood friend again, he said, "I'll let you pay if you let me come along. If you can stand me a while longer."

Drayco poked him in the arm. "Does Elaine approve of your playing detective sidekick on your day off? I'm guessing the honey-do list is longer than *War and Peace*."

"Why do you think I want to tag along with you? Not that re-sealing the driveway doesn't sound like a super fun project."

"Ah, that lovely creosote aroma."

"Everyone at the Bureau stays upwind from me for weeks. Can't get that smell out of my hair. I think it even gets into my pores."

After Sarg grabbed some food to go, they headed off to see Ezra Layton, who hadn't wanted to meet at the racing track again, much to Sarg's disappointment. He was even more bummed when he learned they were meeting Layton at his glass shop. Sarg sighed, "Maybe they'll have something I can get Elaine by way of apology for not getting my hands dirty today."

"Not hands, no, just everything else." Before they went inside the store, Drayco handed Sarg a roll of duct tape so he could pat himself down and get rid of the remaining dust and cobwebs.

When Drayco introduced Sarg to Layton as his former partner, Layton asked, "Cop partner?"

"FBI."

Layton's eyes widened. "Is the Bureau involved now? I thought it was just a hit-and-run."

Drayco explained, "He's consulting." Sarg gave him some side-eye, making Drayco hastily add, "The Bureau isn't officially involved."

"That's a relief." Layton nodded, but the tension lines on his face deepened, anyway.

Drayco turned to Sarg, "Mr. Layton has a pretty sweet racecar."

Sarg whistled. "Like a NASCAR racer? I'd love to see one up close since I'll never be able to afford it. Those are way too pricey for my blood."

Drayco asked Layton, "You said it was thanks to an inheritance?"

Layton pursed his lips. "Not that it's any of your business, but yeah. I do okay with my shop. Save a little here and spend it over there. It's a matter of priorities. Plus, I don't have kids. So you could say the car's my baby."

"Leon Sable said running your own business can be an uphill battle. Must be tough."

"As I said, I do okay."

"Last time we spoke, you said Sable has a bit of a temper. Did Graham ever mention Sable getting violent toward him?"

"Not really." He glanced over at Sarg who was inspecting a vase of colorful glass flowers. Making sure Sarg wouldn't pull a Drayco and tip over a display?

Layton turned his attention back to Drayco. "Look, I know I suggested maybe Leon and Graham were in on that arson thing together. But back when I thought Graham was killed in the fire, I wondered if Leon murdered him."

"Any particular reason why?"

He shrugged. "Money. Bad blood. Jealousy. You name it. But since Leon didn't get any insurance money, I pushed it out of my head. Hell, there must be easier ways to kill somebody without wrecking your own business."

"The police looked into that angle and didn't find anything."

"Maybe they didn't dig hard enough."

"Have the police been around to talk to you again in the past few days?"

"No, should they?"

"Whether they should or not is up to them." So, Halabi's team hadn't interviewed Layton yet. That was a surprise. "However, three days ago, Johnny Burdell was killed outside his puzzle store in a hit-and-run. The same place and the same method of death as Graham."

Layton raked his hand through his red hair. "That doesn't sound good."

"Last time I saw you, you were going to pay a visit to Burdell, hoping he might have some answers for you."

"You asking if I contacted him?"

"Did you?"

"Thought about it, sure. But I've been too busy with my shop. And taking care of my car." Layton sucked air through his teeth. "Look, maybe you should ask Leon. He dated Burdell's ex-wife, Vi Keating, for a time."

Drayco had filled Sarg in on his visit to see Vivianna Keating, and Sarg shot him a meaningful glance. Drayco asked, "Ezra, have you thought any more about trouble Graham might have got himself into? Something that would prompt him to disappear and be targeted once he showed up again?"

Layton stared down at the counter as he drew his index finger along the surface in a rectangular pattern. "Since his and Leon's business wasn't doing well, maybe burglary or robbery. Or some other money thing."

"Why would you say that?"

"All those troubles with the law Graham and me had early on."

"You think Graham lapsed? Was sucked into a criminal scheme?"

"Who knows? But it's too late to find out, isn't it?" Layton kept tracing rectangles on the countertop, back and forth. "Wish I could have Graham here again. Maybe I could have put a stop to it."

"You really think you could have prevented his death?" Immediately as he said it, Drayco had the thought, *Just as you could have prevented Johnny Burdell's?*

"I don't know. Graham and me shared a little too much in common. Like trusting the wrong people." Layton lifted an arm to wipe his red, watery eyes with his sleeve.

"The wrong people?"

"It's too bad I'm not gay. You know why? I'll tell you why. It's women who've ruined my life. Older women, mostly. A word of advice . . . " He uttered a humorless chuckle. "Stick with the younger ones."

Drayco pulled out a business card. "If you think of anything else about Johnny Burdell, give me a call."

"Sure." Layton held onto the card by the edges and stared at it as if expecting it to burst into flames.

Before they left, Sarg took the opportunity to look around the store and picked up one item with a triumphant "Aha!"

When he brought it over to the counter to pay for it, Drayco looked at the glass bowl with a raised eyebrow. "Um, nice?"

Sarg crowed, "It's a Brixo soda-lime glass bowl. In rainbow colors. Elaine's been wanting one. It's your dad's fault since she coveted the one he had at Thanksgiving."

"I think it belonged to the caterers."

"Well, she wanted it. And here it is."

They headed to the car with Sarg's purchase swathed in bubble wrap and a Styrofoam-padded box that Drayco secured in the back seat. As they buckled in, Sarg asked, "So if Burdell's ex-wife was dating Tibbs's ex-partner, that seems interesting, don't you think? A conspiracy to get the mysterious treasure of Alistair's?"

"It occurred to me, too. Great minds and all." Drayco looked over at the box to make sure it was secure. "You up for one more quick stop? Since you mentioned Tibbs's ex-partner, that is."

"You bet." Sarg reached over with his hand hovering over the GPS. "Gimme the address, and off we go."

Drayco complied, and as Sarg was punching in the coordinates, Drayco popped a CD into the player. Sarg stared at it. "What's that?"

"Ernst von Dohnányi's 'Variations on a Nursery Tune.' "

Sarg listened as the first dramatic, stentorian measures began. "I don't hear a nursery tune."

Drayco pressed the forward button through the introduction section until he reached the theme. Sarg rolled his eyes. "'Twinkle, Twinkle,' again? Man, you're seriously obsessed."

§ § §

As they drove up to LS Metals, Sarg groaned. "Do not let Elaine see this place. My honey-do list will be longer than an encyclopedia."

They found Leon Sable in the fenced-in outdoor space in the back. Surprisingly, he had a smile on his face when he looked up and saw who it was. "Mr. Drayco, I hope you've brought good news about Graham's case."

"We're still investigating. My friend, Marc Sargosian, was very interested in your shop when I told him about it. He's working on some projects for his wife." Drayco looked over at Sarg, who gave him an exasperated look.

But Sarg dutifully stepped into his new role as hen-pecked-husband and said, "You know how home repairs are. There's always something."

"Are you looking for anything in particular?"

"Got a suggestion for metal trim around windows? Oh, and some rustic planters."

"Aluminum's good for the trim. You have a capping machine?"

"I have access to one."

"That's good. And for the planters, maybe some 14 gauge milled steel. Might need grinder and welder gear."

"No problems, there."

Sable said, "Follow me," leading them to some tall shelving.

As Sarg pawed through the aluminum stock, Drayco asked Sable, "Your posted hours indicate you're open late, until nine."

"Most days. Gotta keep up with the big-box stores. That's partly what killed me with my former businesses. Couldn't match their hours. And inventory."

"Are you here at closing every day?"

"Not every day. My assistant manager and I take turns."

"What about three evenings ago?"

Sable frowned. "That kind of smacks of alibi fishing to me."

"Johnny Burdell was killed in a hit-and-run."

"Burdell . . . that's the guy who owns the puzzle store, right?"

"I asked you about him last time. You said you didn't know Burdell but had overheard Graham mention him."

Sable scratched the scar on his cheek. "If the police are interested in me, they should ask me themselves."

Great. Two potential suspects Drayco had now tackled before Detective Halabi. "They aren't. Not right now."

"I'll tell you what I would . . . will . . . tell them because it would be easy enough to check. Yeah, I closed that night."

"Were you alone?"

"No other staff at the time. I'd have to check my records for any customers, credit card receipts, and such. It's not the type of info I'm comfortable giving out."

"We'd need a subpoena for that, anyway."

"Did you bring one?"

"No, I just ask questions and try to find answers. Although I have a feeling the police might drop by when they discover you once dated Burdell's ex-wife, Vivianna Keating. That's the 'Vi' you mentioned to me in passing last time we met, wasn't it?"

Sable stood still for a moment. "Vi's last name is Keating. I knew she had an ex, but she never told me anything about him. Not even his last name. Now you're telling me it's Burdell?" Beads of sweat coalesced into little mini-streams on his forehead. "Oh, god. This looks really bad."

"How long did the two of you date? Was it before or after Graham's death? The first fake one that is."

"About ten months. But it didn't start until last year. I swear it."

"That will be easy to verify. I actually spoke with her yesterday."

"You did?" A small smile crept over Sable's lips. "Then maybe I owe you some thanks. She called me last night, and we met up for coffee at Northside Social. It was amazing to see her again."

"Sounds promising."

"We made plans to meet up again tonight. For a proper dinner this time." Sable shook his head. "But maybe it's more bad timing on my part. This whole Graham-coming-back-from-the-dead was bad enough. Now I find out the police will think I killed Burdell."

"If you're innocent, as you say, this will all fade into a bad memory soon."

Sarg piped up, "Too bad it's no longer Halloween. A man coming back from the dead—sounds like great fodder for a horror movie."

Sable gave a small laugh. "You should have seen my neighbor kid. I used some metal scraps from the shop to create a homemade robot costume." He looked over at Sarg. "Still interested in those other materials I mentioned? The 14 gauge milled steel?"

When Sarg said he was, Sable ushered him to a store section with shelves of steel for the planters. After Sarg had taken down prices and made some measurements, he thanked Sable and promised to call in an order when he returned home.

As Drayco and Sarg walked outside, Sarg said, "If Sable's relationship with Burdell's ex started four years *after* the whole arson thing, it'd be less likely she was involved in it."

"But they could still be partners in the treasure hunt. Especially if their break-up is a sham."

"I haven't met Vivianna, so I'll have to rely on your judgment. Does she seem like a homicidal maniac?"

"How many homicidal maniacs have we ever met who did?"

"I don't know. Maybe a third?"

"One thing's for sure. Sable was in a much better mood. Not sure if it's because he's hooked up with Vivianna again or because you were along."

"Am I the comic relief?"

"You give people that guy-next-door vibe. Very effective at luring them into a false sense of security."

"You're saying I'm a harmless pushover?"

"You're pretty lethal when you need to be."

Sarg just grinned and replied, "My wife made that very same comment the other day as I was chopping up a deer a hunter friend brought us."

"Bambi steaks again?"

"Get thee behind me, hypocrite. You seemed to enjoy them last time."

Okay, he had a point, but Sarg hadn't told him the source of the meat beforehand. Would that have made a difference? Probably not. Sarg could cook up a cute little toy teddy bear, and it would still taste amazing.

They hopped in Drayco's GSC and headed toward his townhome, where Sarg had parked his pickup truck. Drayco started up the recording of the "Variations on a Nursery Tune" once more. During his piano-touring days as a youth, he'd hoped he would play that with an orchestra one day.

Sarg glanced over at him. "The way you're obsessively listening to that tune makes me think you believe it's tied to the puzzle."

"Funny you should mention it. This morning I awoke with a glimmer of almost-insight about that puzzle. One of those 'back of your brain' things."

"All I know is I'm never going to be able to listen to 'Twinkle, Twinkle' in the same way."

That made two of them. Drayco was relieved he and Sarg had found Drayco's little "prison" from the kidnapping, even though it hadn't brought any new answers. Seeing it in the light of day had helped somehow. With what, Drayco wasn't sure.

There were all kinds of prisons. The physical kind Ezra Layton and Graham Tibbs both swore they'd never end up in again. The emotional prison of looking over your shoulder, wondering if you were targeted for death next, like Johnny Burdell. Even a forced career change—one that put an end to your dreams—was a type of prison.

But there was no sense of getting all maudlin. You couldn't smell, eat, or touch fate, and it didn't make a soft bed to lie on. Best to toss it to the curb with the rest of the trash and move on.

34

Once back at Drayco's townhome and with Sarg's new glass bowl buckled and tie-wrapped into the agent's car, Drayco waved him off and headed toward an unfamiliar address on his own. Sarg had offered to go with him on this trek, too, but Drayco knew it would take an hour on I-95 for Sarg to arrive at his Fredericksburg home. Even longer if the usual tie-ups and accidents were part of the equation.

Besides, this was a more delicate and personal errand, and Drayco wasn't sure he wanted Sarg as a witness. He surveyed his target and the grounds, noting the ordinary white clapboard house. But it was the building in the rear that interested him more, an oversized garage large enough to hangar a plane—make that a Learjet.

He headed straight for the larger building, where he heard voices and faint banging. The door was open, and he didn't bother to knock.

An ostrich-sized copper and silver bird with silverware fanning out as wing feathers greeted him as he stepped inside. In a far corner of the cavernous space, he also spied a metal horse crafted out of hundreds—thousands?—of metal scrap parts. From a distance, it looked real enough to gallop out of the building.

The voices hadn't stopped when he entered. He looked around for the source, spying two blonde heads. As he got closer, one of the two women saw him and said, "You're a few minutes early." But when he turned to her companion half-hidden behind an easel, there was just stunned silence.

Nelia Tyler sat perched on a tall stool, with Joyelle Babineaux seated in front of the easel, sketching Nelia's likeness onto a canvas. Drayco and Nelia looked at each other with equal parts shock and discomfort.

Drayco asked, "What are you doing here?"

Nelia started to reply when Joyelle beat her to it. "I'm having her pose for a new sculpture because I think she makes the perfect model. I'm paying her, of course."

As Drayco knew all too well, Nelia needed the money, even with her two part-time jobs. Law school wasn't free. He blurted out, "What are you going to call it? 'Tyler Tin'?"

Joyelle grinned at the pun, but Nelia had no reaction and just stared at the floor. Maybe she suspected, as Drayco did, that Joyelle was playing matchmaker? Drayco wasn't amused, and from Nelia's flushed face, he guessed she wasn't either.

Nelia checked her watch. "I've really got to get back to the books. I've got an important exam in a couple of days." She hopped off her chair and turned to Joyelle. "Do you have all the material you need?"

Joyelle put down her charcoal pencil and studied her drawing. "I think this will do. And I also have the photographs I took of you."

Nelia hesitated, then said, "I could stay a little longer if you think it's necessary." She gave Drayco a brief glance as she chewed on her lip.

"That's okay, dear. If I need you to drop by again, I'll call. We can arrange something later. *Tu es un si belle modèle.*"

Nelia grabbed her jacket. Drayco walked her to the door and into the little courtyard outside, even though he wasn't sure she'd welcome the company. When they were out of Joyelle's earshot, he said, "I hope she's paying you well."

"Oh, she is. Every little bit helps." Nelia rubbed her arm. "Tim is making new demands through his attorney. The expenses are adding up fast. I was hoping the divorce would be easy."

"It should be. He was at fault."

She grimaced. "Now he's claiming my neglect drove him to the affair. Too busy with work. And he's trying to blame you, too. He claims we had our own affair before he and I separated."

Drayco felt his fists clenching into tight balls. *Calm down, Drayco. Having a stroke would be precisely what Tim would want.* "You could have some of the money Harry Dickerman gave me for the opera house restoration."

Her face flushed even redder. "I don't need anybody's charity. Least of all yours."

"Then think of it as a loan. Without the enormous interest from a bank."

"Not financial interest, you mean."

Drayco stared at her. "You don't actually think I'd take advantage of you over a little loan?"

She sighed. "I didn't mean it that way. More emotionally. Psychically. Spiritually. Whatever."

Drayco uttered a sigh of his own. They'd never argued like this before that one intimate night they'd shared. Maybe he half-regretted that night now, but at the same time . . . no. He really didn't.

Nelia said, "I have to go," and with a wave, she added, "Guess I'll see you at Benny's office some time?"

He nodded, a little relieved by the olive branch she'd thrown him. He watched her drive away before returning to the art studio, where he sought out Joyelle.

She looked up from her sketching. "I hope Nelia got off okay."

"She did." Drayco studied the drawing Joyelle had made. "That's pretty good. And you can create a sculpture from that?"

"Of course. I mostly make things from my imagination. But this time, I felt I needed an actual human for inspiration."

"Perhaps you can help *me* with a little inspiration. I'd like to know more about your husband's death. And the hit-and-run."

She leaned against the stool where Nelia had been sitting. "*Dieu accorde la paix à son âme.*"

"I don't want to disturb his peace unnecessarily, but sometimes I have to ask unpleasant questions."

"It was long ago. Happened at night, but you probably know about the dingy European headlights on those cars they drive. Well, back then, anyway. They didn't illuminate much. Not roads, animals, or people."

"You were estranged from him at the time?"

She stared at Drayco. "You must mean the affair," and then she grimaced. "I haven't been back to France, or even Europe, since. Too painful."

"You left the intelligence service over it."

"It's true. I did."

"Were you involved with that same resistance group as your husband, the Liberty Legion?"

Joyelle was serene as she studied Drayco. "Your investigative skills are impressive. Not too many people know about that."

She hopped onto the stool."My husband went deep inside the resistance. And was gone a lot. He was far more interested in the job than me, and I guess that's why I had an affair." She paused and then added with a sigh, "I think we married too young. A familiar story."

"Was the hit-and-run related to that undercover work of his?"

"No, and they later arrested a local drunk, *un ivrogne.*"

"Do you have his name?"

She shook her head. "Wouldn't matter. He died not too long afterward, himself."

"You didn't share your husband's work with the Liberty Legion?"

"My work was . . . different. I'm afraid I can't say more. NDAs and all. Look, I don't mean to belittle Gerard's work and what he accomplished. But ultimately, it was too much of a strain on a marriage."

She stared at the sketch Nelia had posed for. "We both went down the rabbit hole, as you say. But I still have the utmost respect for what my husband did, for what the resistance did, and how they stood up to forces far greater than they. It was a David and Goliath moment."

"Are you still in contact with any members?"

"I lost touch with them after the fall of the Soviet Union decades ago." She studied Drayco again with the same inscrutable expression, which made him believe she must have been very good at her intelligence job.

She added, "You're wondering if I'm up to no good and somehow involved with your current case?"

"Are you?"

"I am not. But if you'd like me to give you all the names of the surviving members, or the latitude and longitude of the hit-and-run or whatever else you seek, I'll do it. If it will set your mind at ease."

"It might be a start."

"Ah, Scott." A little peek of both amusement and sadness parted her veiled expression for a moment. "I was truly wishing we could be friends. I adore your father, and we're going to be spending more time together. All three of us. Couldn't you try?"

"I just have my father's best interests at heart."

"I really hope you do."

He left her, seething a bit as he drove away, but the more he drove, the more he calmed down. That is until something Joyelle said hit him like a bulldozer and made him angry at himself for not seeing it sooner.

The coded message, the numbers, their values—it all made sense. Latitude and longitude. Had to be! He put his foot on the gas even as the traffic cop in his brain reminded him it wouldn't do to get a speeding ticket. Or worse. But now that he thought he finally had the key to that damned puzzle, he only wished his car really was an airplane.

35

Sunday, December 5

After returning from Joyelle Babineaux's studio, Drayco spent much of the evening surrounded by print and digital maps. Map-lover Christi Allingham would be positively drooling over that. At the same time, he questioned his mental faculties. Why hadn't he seen sooner that the printed numbers from the puzzle represented latitude and longitude?

He almost made another mistake as he matched the coordinates to the maps. Initially, he was thrown off because the numbers in the solved order marked a location in the Kasan District of Uzbekistan. But that would mean the stolen treasure wasn't in the United States, so why would someone search for the treasure here?

The case's ties to Uzbekistan had blinded him to an alternative. He tried the same numbers backward and found they were the latitude and longitude for a region in southern Maryland near the Calvert County cliffs.

According to aerial survey maps, the numbers matched the site of a house formerly owned by a man named Alec Van Sandt. He'd died five years ago, and the place was now the property of a bank. Drayco's interest was further piqued when he discovered the same man had also owned the "prison" house he and Sarg investigated.

The thing that sealed the deal, and the main reason Drayco got up early to drive to Maryland, was that Van Sandt died under mysterious circumstances a couple of weeks before Graham Tibbs's arson and disappearance. Another hit-and-run.

Was that why Graham vanished? He was involved in Van Sandt's death? Ezra Layton made it quite clear Graham Tibbs never wanted to go back to prison. And Tibbs had asked his former girlfriend, Christi Allingham, if there was any room in heaven for people involved with someone else's death. Even "if they're innocent."

Drayco made it into Maryland, but when he pulled up to the site at the coordinates, his heart sank. The house he'd seen on the aerial maps was no longer there. An empty yard with a walkway leading to nowhere was all that was left. It was unlikely any treasure remained buried here, if it ever was.

Maybe that was what Alistair was referring to when he said they'd used Drayco's puzzle solution, but it turned out to be unhelpful? Well, somebody believed the treasure was located around here, or there wouldn't have been two hit-and-run deaths and now, maybe a third. Three was not a "charm" in this case.

One helpful sign perched on the otherwise vacant lot had a "Property For Sale" marker with the name of a realtor, Sherry Salton. He called the number on the sign, and Salton agreed to meet him on site.

When a car parked in front, and a tall woman with a bob haircut and red glasses strode toward him, he asked, "Ms. Salton?"

She stuck out her hand, which he shook. "And you're Scott Drayco. I have to admit you got my hopes up. I did a little happy dance when you called, thinking we were finally going to unload this place."

"Sorry to disappoint you. You're representing the bank that owns the property?"

"That's right."

"When I first saw the house was owned by a bank, I assumed it was repossessed."

"That part is true. But the house got torn down in the past year because it was derelict. The bank decided it would be easier to sell the land on its own."

"Was the property repossessed before or after the owner's death?"

"A few months afterward. The estate went to Mr. Van Sandt's daughter, but it wasn't enough to cover the mortgage. Well, two mortgages. There's his other property, too."

"Other property?" Drayco thought she was going to mention the "prison house," but she surprised him.

"An old resort over on the coast. It's been closed for years. You can't even find it on maps anymore."

"I didn't know he owned such a place."

"Probably because it was listed under an LLC before it also became bank property."

"I'd love to see it." Drayco tried not to get his hopes up.

Salton put her hands on her hips. "I don't have other client showings today. So, sure. I guess you can follow me?"

He did, and within ten minutes, they were standing in front of an imposing structure that wouldn't look out of place in a Gothic movie. It was likely a pleasant, welcoming haven in its heyday. Now, it just looked old, sad, and suicidal.

But it was the sign that hung over the entrance that fascinated Drayco the most. The faded letters spelled out *Heaven's Embrace.*

Drayco's excitement must have been evident because Salton saw him staring at it and asked, "Does that mean something?"

"In Latin, Heaven's Embrace could be translated as *caelesti amplexus*, but that's a long story." And with that, he had the last piece of the kidnapping-puzzle he'd worked on.

Salton punched in a code into the realtor lockbox, and in they went. Some of the boards covering the windows were missing, which proved beneficial since there was no electricity to the building. But the streams of sunlight through the cracks in the boards made it clear the interior was empty. No furniture whatsoever.

When he pointed that out, she said, "All sold to pay off the debt." That made his recently buoyed spirits sag. Any treasure hidden in the furniture might also be long gone.

Salton said, "This place has been broken into on more than one occasion. Another reason we want to dump the place soon." She waved her hand around the room. "But no graffiti, which is odd, like you'd expect from teen prankers."

"I witnessed that somewhere else not too long ago. When was the last break-in?"

"About six months ago. But there's nothing valuable left. Except maybe the copper wires or bathroom fixtures, and even those weren't stolen. Guess it was a lovers' tryst. Or curiosity seekers."

He asked, "How did they get in?"

"Through some of those broken windows."

"That would explain the missing boards."

"I really need to have our standby contractor come around to make sure they're all sealed up again." She sighed. "In fact, we've got an inspector who's supposed to look at it again soon. He keeps getting delayed by more important projects."

"An inspector to appraise current resale value?"

"For safety purposes. In all honesty, you may be one of the last people I show this place. Mother nature may take it off the bank's hands soon. Storms and climate change have conspired to take down several homes along the cliffs. This one could be next."

Now Drayco wanted to search the resort more than ever. "Surely it could be renovated. It still has good bones."

"Personally, I think the place should be torn down. Just like the house. I'm pretty sure I could sell the property for a ton of money, but not with this eyesore on it. Condos or several high-end homes, now those would bring in a lot more."

"I hate to see historic buildings left to rot." He felt even more unhappy to think of a wrecking ball hammering away at the building when she took him on a tour. Whoever the puzzle-writer was surely loved this place. The labyrinthine layout of the resort was dizzying.

Not a single straight hallway crisscrossed throughout the interior, nor was it laid out like the spokes of a wheel. Entrances to the larger rooms on the main floor had doors offset from any other, which must have confounded former patrons. Maybe that was the point? Part of its unique charm?

The decor, what was left of it, was different in every room. One sported wallpaper with a yellow-and-gray paisley design, and another was painted with various shades of blue in a wavelike pattern. Yet another had a tiled-fresco chair rail like something out of an ancient Roman villa.

The architectural eccentricities were particularly evident in the great hall area, where Drayco noted carvings and scrollwork on the darkish wooden panels. Oak? Ebony? Cherry? With all the different colors, it was probably a mix.

Many panels were plain, but others had symbols, a few with numbers from zero to nine. Some were carved with letters of the alphabet, and some with elaborate characters such as a dragon, a unicorn, a Greek cross, and a wizard.

Still others bore astronomical—or were they astrological?—symbols. Earth was represented, along with the moon, then the sun, and then a larger planet that could be Jupiter, plus clouds and a rainbow. Another cross lay below the sun. More of Van Sandt's whimsy?

But if the treasure was hidden here at one time, why not use the latitude and longitude of the resort instead of Van Sandt's former home? Whatever the reason, it might not matter. Whether in the house or the resort, anything the man hid must surely be gone by now.

And yet why the two mysterious hit-and-runs that killed Graham Tibbs and Johnny Burdell? It had to mean someone believed the treasure was around here. Even Alistair believed it.

But as Drayco peered out the rear of the building and saw how the house lay perched on the edge of the cliffs, he had a feeling the realtor was right. Mother Nature might have the last laugh at the expense of just about everybody—Van Sandt, the realtor, the bank, Drayco, the young lovers or whoever had broken in here, and potential treasure hunters.

Salton was eager to get back to her office and didn't seem inclined to indulge his desire to poke around a bit more. He even hinted there might be a secret safe somewhere on the premises, but she shrugged.

"Didn't see any signs of such. I got a peek at the original blueprints to help draw the layout for our website."

He waved at Salton as she drove off, but he didn't leave right away. Out of curiosity, he decided to look around the back of the property. It was easy to understand why the resort developers chose this spot since the views were pretty spectacular. But they couldn't foresee time and the terror of mother nature's wrath carving out a chunk of the cliff, leaving the building perched on the edge.

Not that it would matter to Drayco since he doubted he'd be allowed inside again without a search warrant. What magistrate in their right mind would grant him one based on an inscription via a puzzle-from-beyond-the-grave? Or the ghosts of the hit-and-run victims, whose deaths could be argued away as mere accidents?

Disappointed he might have found his pot at the end of the rainbow only to find it empty, Drayco headed back to his car. After all of this—his kidnapping, his pursuit of the case, two, or possibly even three, murders—and this was how it ended?

36

Monday, December 6

Rather than drive the couple of hours down to his District townhome and then back up To Calvert again the next day, Drayco opted for a local B&B, which reminded him of the Lazy Crab in Cape Unity. He had a sudden longing for Maida Jepson's cooking and one of her famous—and potent—hot toddies.

The B&B's owners only bought the inn a couple of years before, so they hadn't known Van Sandt. But Drayco did find a town newspaper editor who knew the former resort owner. After a breakfast of a crab omelet that was good, but not quite as tasty as Maida's, Drayco drove to the office of the *Bay Weekly*. The newspaper's office lay in the middle of the very quaint town with its very quaint postcard main street in a very quaint brick building with a sign that said, "Bay Weekly, Est. 1926."

Drayco headed through the blue door into the reception area, where a woman silently pointed toward the back when Drayco asked for Wade Cassone. Drayco found the man inside an office not much bigger than six by six, crammed next to what must be the "newsroom," with one chair and one computer.

The man himself was also quaint and looked like he might have been original to the building. He sported round wire-rim glasses and a white walrus mustache, with a bowler hat perched on his desk. Was he trying to look like he'd stepped out of an old newsreel?

Cassone peered at him over his glasses, "You're the one interested in our eccentric local celebrity, Alec Van Sandt?"

"And his various properties."

"Ah, yes, the eyesores. Too bad, really. That resort of his was a beauty once. My sister even had her wedding there. Guess it's been forty years now." Cassone chuckled. "Sounds like a long time, but it seems like yesterday. Probably before you were born, though."

Drayco smiled. "Did you know Van Sandt well?"

"Reasonably well, in so much as you get to know many people in a small town."

"Did anything odd happen to him five years ago, right before his death? Anything that might have seemed uncharacteristic? Or any unusual changes? Or threats?"

"Threats, you say? Well, now, I wouldn't know about that." Cassone swiveled in his chair from side to side. "But there was this one thing. Perhaps it's not important."

"Still, I'd like to hear it."

"Alec took a trip abroad not too long before he passed away. Came back a different person."

"How so?"

"We went out drinking upon his return. He was an alcoholic, something I never knew until later, sadly. He sure hid it well. Stereotypical closet drunk. But anyway, Alec made some reference to a treasure he'd come across that he didn't know how to handle."

"He didn't say what?"

"He was killed before I could learn what it was. Or whether he'd just gone nutso."

"Did he leave behind any clues or notes? Maybe numbers and letters, like the Latin phrase, *caelesti amplexus*?"

"I took some Latin in school back in the Dark Ages. That's sky or heaven and embrace, I think." Cassone chuckled again. "Heaven's Embrace. Of course, I see now. His resort. But no, I don't know of any such clues or notes. Though Alec was a big puzzle fan. Loved adventure and mystery stories."

"You say this overseas trip took place five years ago. Do you remember the exact month and date or the destination?"

"Let's see now. It was about this time of year. Cold, windy. Middle of November, I reckon. As for the itinerary . . . central Asia or eastern

Europe somewhere. I recall the city name, Samarkand. It's in one of those 'stan' countries. Alas, I don't recall which one. I used to be pretty good at geography, don't you know. But, names are the first thing to go."

"Uzbekistan?"

"Possibly. Or Kazakhstan. Or Kyrgyzstan. Or Tajikistan. Pretty sure it wasn't Afghanistan." Cassone grabbed a pencil that he tapped on the desk. "Alec talked about his 'multi-faceted treasure problem' and then laughed as if it were some big joke."

"I don't suppose you recall Van Sandt mentioning the name Graham Tibbs?"

"Doesn't ring a bell. Sorry." He raised an eyebrow. "You said this was about an investigation on the phone. Seems like it's a lot more serious than a petty misdemeanor."

"Murder, possibly."

"Hmm. Well, now, I always wondered about that hit-and-run that killed Alec. Happened in his driveway. The police thought it was someone who got lost and panicked when they saw Alec coming out of the house. Maybe even believed he was going to attack them."

"Did Alec own guns or other weapons?"

"Nope. So unless he was brandishing a tire iron or kitchen knife, I can't imagine what he would have attacked anybody with. Or why. It's not like him."

"You did say he was an alcoholic."

"That's true, that's true. But he wasn't a mean drunk. More the morose kind who just fell into a stupor."

"What about the name Johnny Burdell? Did Alec mention him, by any chance?"

"Why, yes, I do recall that name coming up in conversation. I remember because I thought how appropriate it was since part of Burdell's name is the same as a famous crossword puzzle company."

"Were Alec and Burdell friends?"

"They'd known each other a while, I believe. Not sure I'd call them friends, but who knows? Burdell had this ex-wife and sister he ragged on all the time. Or so Alec said."

"Do you know if Alec told Burdell about this treasure of his? Or about creating a puzzle that might show where he'd hidden such a thing?"

"I don't know for sure, no. But since the two shared the love of puzzles, I wouldn't be surprised. Especially if Alec was drunk, like when he talked to me about it. Pretty crocked at the time."

"I understand Alec had a daughter. Was she the sole beneficiary of his estate?"

"Near as I know. But she sure didn't inherit much. Her father owed everything to the bank that took possession of his properties."

Cassone tsked and said, "Poor fellow. He really could be a barrel of fun. A lively sense of humor. Keen intellect. Loved big band music."

Drayco's ears perked up at that. "Like Bob Bordelon's Bayou Band?"

Cassone grinned. "Don't meet too many young folks today who know big band groups. Sure, that was one of his favorites. The arrangements they made of children's songs. You know, like 'Twinkle, Twinkle Little Star.' "

Drayco thanked Cassone for his time and promised to stay in touch if he had any additional information and to give the editor a "scoop." As Drayco stared at the *Bay Weekly* sign, he heard the strains of the "Twinkle, Twinkle" song in his head again. But who had played it during Drayco's confinement? Alistair? Iago? Graham Tibbs? Or did Alec Van Sandt fake his death like Tibbs did, and he was the one behind the two murders?

Drayco ducked back inside to ask Cassone about Van Sandt's funeral. "Sorry to bother you again, but was the funeral an open casket viewing?"

Cassone gave him a quizzical look. "Why yes, it was. The local mortician, Zeke Taylor, is a magician when it comes to patching bodies up after less-than-gentle deaths."

After bidding Cassone farewell for the second time, Drayco headed toward his car, bemused. An open casket made it less likely Van Sandt had faked his own death unless he had a secret twin. Or unless another homeless man had taken his place in that grave.

The "secret twin" notion made Drayco shake his head. All this talk of puzzles and fake deaths was getting to him. That must be why he had the sudden urge for Maida's potions with extra shots. Or maybe the shots straight out of the bottle.

At least the picture he was forming of the events of the case was coming into focus. He'd found a link from the mysterious "treasure" to Alistair to Uzbekistan. Then from there, on to Alec Van Sandt, and then Johnny Burdell—who was linked to Graham Tibbs, who was involved with Drayco's kidnapping and quite likely murder.

They were all links in a deadly chain that ultimately led to the mastermind of it all. Or as Joyelle might call it, *le cerveau*.

37

Drayco stopped by his office on the return trip, recalling Sarg's earlier comments about the covert listening bugs. He couldn't have missed any, could he? Nah, he'd been over the place with an RF detector and even a hidden camera detector. Not that he'd put it past Alistair to get a little payback for the island "jaunt" and install some spy gear.

He sat down at his computer and called up a database of international news reports, focusing on four or five years ago in mid-November. But when Drayco checked the countries Cassone first mentioned, nothing interesting turned up. Then he found a story from Samarkand, Uzbekistan. The date was from early December from five years ago.

A treasured heirloom, a diamond, from the Mikhail Artykov family had disappeared around that time. No suspect was named, and Drayco couldn't find any later articles about arrests or the return of the diamond. But he also recalled Cassone's comments that Van Sandt joked about his "multi-faceted" treasure problem. Facets, diamond.

The gem in question was a yellow diamond, so Drayco looked those up next. The Diavik mine in Canada's Northwest Territories had produced some of the most valuable yellow diamonds ever. Unlike other reports of children used in diamond mining, Drayco was relieved to find these mines didn't, using state-of-the-art technology and partnering with Indigenous people to protect the environment.

It was this mine that had produced the Firefox, a 187-carat rough diamond, as well as the Diavik Helios, a 74-carat yellow gem, and the massive 552-carat yellow diamond boasting a rare, uniform "rich color and clarity" worth millions.

Drayco dug deeper into the family who owned the missing treasure. After the fall of the Berlin Wall, it became known that members of the Artykov family had ties to the same Liberty Legion resistance group that Joyelle Babineaux's former husband had. Was it only a coincidence? Or maybe it was just part of his friend Reece Wable's "kismet" beliefs.

Drayco ran through the possible timeline in his head. Five years ago, the puzzle fan and resort owner, Alec Van Sandt, made the mistake—possibly while drunk—of telling his friend, Johnny Burdell, about a mysterious treasure and the puzzle code, both of which he'd hidden somewhere safe. It likely got back to Graham Tibbs, who may have blabbed it to others. Or perhaps Burdell himself was the information leak.

Drayco started to make coffee, when he noticed Sarg had rearranged all his ingredients in the cabinet when he was there recently. In addition to being a master chef, the man was also a neat freak. Oh well. Maybe it would be faster for Drayco to get coffee on the way home.

Good thing he didn't because when he returned to his townhome, he found Brock there making some stew. "Thought you might need more fattening up," his father explained.

"Very funny." Drayco eyed the stove. "Is that your famous beer-clam stew?"

"You know it is. One of only three recipes I know how to make."

Drayco wandered over to the pot to take a whiff. "Smells pretty good."

"But of course. When you can cook only three things, you tend to master them."

"That's three more recipes than I can make. Guess I got my lack of cooking prowess from your side."

"Ouch. I resemble that remark." Brock took a taste. "Damn. That is pretty good, if I do say so, myself. So how was your day? Solved the case yet?"

"I finally solved the puzzle. And it looks like the mysterious treasure is a yellow diamond stolen from the Mikhail Artykov family in

Samarkand, Uzbekistan. A family that also belonged to the Liberty Legion resistance movement during the Cold War."

Brock leaned against the counter. "And you think Joyelle had something to do with it since her husband was part of that same group?"

"I didn't say that."

"But you're thinking it. When did this theft happen?"

"Five years ago. December."

Brock turned around to stir the stew again. "Would have been pretty hard for Joyelle to traipse over to Uzbekistan at that time. Seeing as how she was undergoing chemotherapy for breast cancer."

Drayco gaped at him. "She didn't tell me anything about that."

"Why should she? It's a painful topic. And it's now in the past. Full remission." Brock held out the spoon for Drayco to take a taste. "You think it needs more paprika?"

"That would be overkill. It's fine as is."

Brock went over to grab a couple of bowls from the cabinet. "Who are your main suspects, then?"

Drayco sighed. "Possibly Ezra Layton or Leon Sable, or even Connie Burdell or Vivianna Keating. I can't even entirely rule out Christi Allingham. I haven't talked with the alleged diamond thief's daughter yet, Ellie Van Sandt. Of course, since we're dealing with dead-not-dead suspects, who knows? Maybe Graham Tibbs didn't really die—again. Or Burdell, himself. Or Van Sandt, who allegedly died five years ago in yet another hit-and-run."

"With all the hit-and-run cases piling up, makes me think twice about crossing the street."

Drayco sighed again. "And of course, Uncle Alistair might be behind it all anyway."

Brock pointed his finger at Drayco. "That's where I'm putting my money."

38

After Brock and Drayco finished dinner and Brock left to attend to some work on a case, Drayco dialed a number he'd only recently programmed into his cellphone. When the familiar male voice answered, Drayco said, "I think it's time we met in person. Tonight."

Drayco showed up at the suggested meeting place and wasn't terribly surprised to find it was in the basement of an old building in the warehouse district north of the National Arboretum. He'd brought a flashlight just in case, but there was still enough light from the full moon to see his way down the grimy staircase into the bowels of the derelict space.

He eased himself through a crumbling arch that hadn't seen a doorway in years. Using the flashlight, he crept over the dust and around broken bricks. With any luck, the ragged ceiling wouldn't fall down on top of him like the wall at the burned-out hardware store.

A figure stood at the end of the room, with the moonlight from the high-up window flickering down on the man's face. Drayco may not have spoken with this man in person before, but he knew him by appearance. He tried to find glimpses of his mother's likeness in that face, which had the features of a Kennedy. Even down here, the man was wearing a suit and tie.

As he always did when he spoke to his uncle, Drayco wanted to ask about his mother, but something stopped him. He came within several feet away of Alistair and studied him. No weapons that he could see.

Alistair held out his arms to his sides. "You wanted to meet in person. Here I am."

Drayco walked closer to his uncle so he could hear him better. "I have a thousand questions. And you have the answers."

"As in?"

"That yellow diamond stolen from your friends in Uzbekistan. I only just learned about it, so how did you make the connection between Alec Van Sandt and the theft? That is, I assume you made that connection from what you said to me earlier about a dead end."

"The diamond was stolen during a big soiree the Artykov family was having. For the Christmas holidays. They gave a list of attendees to the police to investigate, but nothing was ever found."

"You got your hands on that list."

"Naturally. The only American there was Alec Van Sandt. Since I have my feelers out everywhere, I would have heard if such a rare gem turned up on the black market. It did not."

"No other suspects?"

"The Artykov family believed former Soviet Union spies were behind the diamond theft as punishment for their politics. At the time, the family was just grateful it was only a theft since they were marked for assassination at one time."

"How did you get possession of Van Sandt's puzzle, then?"

"Graham Tibbs. I won't go into all the details right now. But Graham was eager to help me help my friends. Payback for my generosity."

"You helped him disappear because he had a hand in the hit-and-run death of Alec Van Sandt?"

"It's complicated."

"You know, some would say you wanted the diamond for yourself."

Alistair smiled briefly. "I assure you I only want to return it to its rightful owners. The family and I go way back. As for the money, I have plenty. It's like that line from *Citizen Kane*, 'It's no trick to make a lot of money . . . if all you want is to make a lot of money.' "

"And the Artykov family? What about their financial status?"

"The family has come upon some wealth themselves. They were planning on donating the diamond to a state museum to help bring in more funds and keep it afloat. The museum had a rather unfortunate fire."

"A fire as in arson? Like Graham Tibbs and his disappearance?"

"Not arson in this case. A careless employee put up a defective light fixture in a recently installed elevator."

"The Artykov family was part of the same anti-Soviet resistance group as the former husband of Brock's new girlfriend, Joyelle Babineaux."

Alistair nodded. "I'm truly impressed by your investigative skills. Perhaps I'll tell you more about that topic one day."

Drayco rubbed a hand over his face. "If you'd only told me the whole story about why Graham Tibbs needed 'disappearing,' then maybe Johnny Burdell's death could have been prevented."

"Such an event is regrettable. But I doubt it would have mattered. I look out for my own interests, and the rest of the world has to do the same. I'm not a magician nor a god."

Drayco stepped to one side as a small chunk of ceiling crashed to the ground, missing him by inches. "There's something else I wanted to ask. Did you find out who went behind my back to the UMD committee with a change of concert repertoire?

"It was your client, Ms. Aria D'Angelo. I'm sure she meant well. She's a lonely older woman who has adopted you as her new pet project. Do you want me to tell the scholarship committee you aren't going to perform?"

Drayco had to bite his tongue not to mention what had happened at his audition, although he was a little surprised the committee hadn't already told Alistair. He replied, "I'm a little tired of family butting into my affairs. In all honesty, I thought it was Joyelle who was the culprit."

"So you're already thinking of Ms. Babineaux as family?"

"Brock seems to like her." When he saw the look on Alistair's face and said, "You've investigated her, haven't you?"

Alistair smiled and reached out to pat him on the shoulder. "All right then, I'll tell you. As far as I know, there is no relationship between Ms. Babineaux's former husband and the Artykov family. When I looked into her background, I asked the family directly, and they said they'd heard of her husband but not had any contact. They were grateful for his efforts and saddened by his death."

Alistair put his hands in his pockets, making Drayco worry about a gun. But Alistair just continued, "The Liberty Legion resistance was part of a larger group of such outfits fighting Soviet and communist rule, so it's not that surprising to find such connections. There are probably more around than you know."

Once again, Drayco thought of his mother and her shady past. Part of him desperately wanted to ask Alistair about her. He'd been waiting for this very opportunity, yet now that the time seemed right, he couldn't bring himself to pose the question. But why? Too many feelings of anger and abandonment still? Couldn't face the truth? Or, as Nelia had asked him, "Are you afraid to find out?"

Alistair studied his nephew. "Speaking of family, how is the lovely Nelia Tyler doing?"

"That's none of your business."

"On the contrary. If she becomes part of your life, she becomes part of my business." Then he pulled something out of his pocket and handed over a DVD.

Drayco looked at the unlabeled disc. "What is that?"

"Something I came across. I thought you might enjoy it."

"Does this have to do with Nelia?"

Alistair shook his head. "Something else entirely. It was a little difficult to come by, but I have my sources." He gazed briefly at the slivers of moonlight streaming in from cracks in tiny, dirty windows near the ceiling. "It's getting late. I have other business to attend to."

"At this hour?"

Alistair smiled, his perfectly matched white teeth outshining the tiny slivers of moonlight. "My business affairs are global. It's nine in the morning in Beijing."

He waved at Drayco and headed up the stairs back into his shadowy world, which stayed shadowy no matter the time of day. Drayco turned over the little DVD in his hand. What could it be? Leave it to his mysterious uncle to leave with yet another mystery.

Had Alistair cleared up some of the other mysteries in Drayco's case? Would Johnny Burdell still be alive if Alistair were more forthcoming earlier? Was Joyelle Babineaux genuinely innocent of any involvement?

A scratching sound caught his attention, and he spied a couple of pairs of beady eyes staring back at him from under some pieces of broken old wooden chairs. Rats. And from their size, probably Gambian pouched rats some pet owner grew tired of and released.

He *would* just let them be since he'd read they were smart and could even be trained to sniff out landmines or tuberculosis. But they were also blamed for a monkeypox outbreak that sickened a hundred people several years ago.

He felt a little sorry for the critters. They were just being and doing what nature told them to be and do. That was quite unlike the human monsters he encountered, the type who'd think nothing about taking a life over money.

He sighed and made a note to report the rats to the health department. At least they would be taken care of humanely, not mowed down by a two-ton vehicle of death.

39

Drayco approached the oversized white garage structure behind the house, dodging puddles from the heavy rains overnight. He hadn't made an appointment and half-expected her not to be here, but when he tried the door, it opened.

Joyelle didn't look up from a metal fish-looking thing she was working on as he walked in. Not that he expected her to, since she wore a yellow welder's head protective hood and had a loud blow torch in one hand. He approached with caution, taking pains to avoid any sparks from the torch.

She was so involved in her work that she almost fell backward when she looked up briefly, making him feel a little guilty. He immediately apologized as she turned off the torch and removed her hood. "Sorry. Didn't mean to startle you."

"Oh? Then why not call first?"

"I suppose that's fair. Maybe I did want to catch my prey in her natural setting without tipping her off in advance."

"Prey? Am I your number one suspect now?"

"I always have more questions. The never-ending investigator's pursuit."

"Such as?"

"Did you know the Burdells? Johnny, his sister Connie, or his ex-wife, Vivianna Keating?"

She looked genuinely puzzled. "Brock has filled me in a little bit on your case. But why would I have known them?"

"Just curious. The main question is your ties to the Artykov family years ago in Uzbekistan."

She stared at him. "I did know of them. I think my husband did, too. But to my knowledge, the Artykovs never met Gerard."

"They were in the same resistance organization as your husband."

"As I learned later, yes."

"And the puzzle I was kidnapped to solve involves a treasure—a yellow diamond stolen from that same family five years ago by the late owner of a resort up in Maryland. Known as Heaven's Embrace."

Her eyes widened. "No wonder people are getting killed over this. Yellow diamonds can be worth a fortune."

"I wish I could say I've found the diamond, but the deceased thief hasn't left much of a trail."

"But, I thought you said . . . that puzzle . . . "

"I pinned down the coordinates of his properties. But one was torn down and the other stripped of all furnishings."

"Ah." She leaned against a workbench. "I'm beginning to understand why you suspected me in all of this. I would have, too."

"You have to admit the resistance angle is—"

"Striking. Intriguing. And somewhat mysterious. Who knows? Maybe my husband's spirit has a hand in all of this somehow. Trying to help out yet again."

"By the way, I have a source who said the Liberty Legion members appreciated your former husband's work protecting them. Nor were his efforts in vain since the Soviet Union fell. Death by a thousand cuts."

She gazed up at the ceiling. "Gerard was a good man. Truly. So passionate about his beliefs and so fervently dedicated to the cause of freedom in his own way. There are those who still think I'm a monster for having an affair." She rubbed her eyes. "Maybe I deserve that."

"Before I came over this morning, I looked up the fellow agent involved, Nash Wakely. His career soared after your departure, but he retired suddenly. And he was later overheard telling a colleague something to the effect of 'It was all my fault. She took the blame, but I wasn't man enough to take the high road.' "

Joyelle chewed on her lip and looked down this time without replying.

"You left the intelligence service to save his reputation, didn't you?"

She nodded. "With my husband's death, it all felt so pointless, so meaningless anymore. I believed Nash still had something to offer the Agency, while I was all tapped out. Nash did well for himself. Even reached a high-ranking assistant director position."

Drayco noted the air of pride in her voice. She also had a dreamy look whenever she mentioned his name. Relationships were like a carnival ring-toss game. A little give, a little take, and every now and then, you stick your target and win a giant purple stuffed animal. You may not recall the game, but you'll never forget the prize.

Joyelle added, "He married another woman later. They divorced after ten years." Then, as if echoing Drayco's thoughts, she said, "Relationships are hard. I'm going into this whatever-it-is with your father with my eyes wide open, and so is he. We know there are no certainties, and there isn't always a happy ending. But I really enjoy being with him. And I hope I have something to give him in return."

Drayco reached over to touch the metal fishlike sculpture. It felt cool, hard, and a little rough around the edges. "I'm sorry if I've been hard on you about the affair. I realize now how much your husband's death still affects you. How much you cared for him."

"Oh, I understand, believe me. And I have to apologize to you, too."

"Why?"

"For my ham-fisted matchmaking attempts between you and Nelia. In my defense, I really did think Nelia would make a good model. I still think you and she belong together, but who am I to say? The universe will have to sort it all out."

Drayco sighed. "Kind of like it's sorting out my difficult relationship with Brock."

She studied his face. "I've been talking to Brock about that. About you, about him, about your past. There's more than one type of resistance, you know."

"Meaning what, exactly?"

"He's resisted owning up to his failings as a parent, and you've resisted his overtures to make amends."

"And I've also resisted supporting your relationship with Brock?"

She gave a little half-smile. "*À cœur vaillant rien d'impossible.*"

"Nothing is impossible for a willing heart." And then he felt a smile forming on his lips, too. "You haven't been talking to Detective Halabi, have you?"

She tilted her head. "Halabi? I don't know that name."

"It's no matter." He owed Halabi some more French sayings, but perhaps that one was too sugar-coated for the policeman. Might be better if he instead chose "*À vaincre sans péril, on triomphe sans gloire.*" No guts, no glory. He and Halabi didn't always see eye to eye, but that's one thing they could likely agree on.

Drayco just hoped the risks he was taking on this case, the "guts" of it all, would result in success. Not some hidden disaster, like an obstacle in the road you never see coming until you hit it and find yourself in a skid, then upside down. But he was close to an end, he was certain of that. And he was starting to have a pretty good idea of how to get there.

40

After getting a call from Sarg, whose pickup truck was perpetually cycling in and out of the repair shop, Drayco offered to pick him up in the District. Sarg had spent the day at the FBI's HQ and needed a ride to Fredericksburg, but wasn't looking forward to the train.

As they entered the 3rd Street tunnel, Drayco glanced back in the rearview mirror. "Don't look now, but I think we're being followed."

Sarg pulled down the passenger side visor and studied the mirror. "Recognize it?"

"Same dark car with tinted windows and temp tag I suspect I've seen tailing me. They're experts. As if they know when I've spied them, and off they disappear."

"Did you run the temp tag?"

"Yeah. Wasn't in the system."

"Oho, so they're trying to stay untraceable."

Drayco looked for an opening, and when the traffic slowed just as they were exiting the tunnel, he veered over into the next lane, leaving the black car off to their right. The car sped up, and Drayco said, "Hold tight," as he revved up in pursuit.

Sarg called out a "Yahoo! Get 'em, tiger. Been a long time since I've gone on a pursuit like this. Any idea who it is?"

"Another one of the kidnappers, perhaps. Or an intelligence friend of Joyelle's, who knows? I can't think of a reason for them to tail me."

"Correction. Now you're tailing them."

Drayco zigzagged through the slow traffic as best he could, but it was tough going on the roads in the nation's capital, even on a light day. Too many high-powered people racing around to get to their executive meetings.

As if emphasizing that fact, he pumped his foot on the brakes with a loud screech as a police car-escorted motorcade paraded in from the right. Drayco's target made it through the intersection mere moments before. It would be long gone before the motorcade ended.

Sarg groaned. "Damn."

Drayco agreed. "This is where we need hover cars."

"Bring 'em on. I might even be able to fly one of those if they're automatic."

Drayco took his hands off the steering wheel. This was an unusually long motorcade. "Sorry I lost him. But you need to get home."

"Would have been faster to take the train with this VIP crap."

"I can drop you off at the next station . . . "

"The cellphone-free car would be full by now. And I hate sharing space with a bunch of yakking bigwigs. Scalability this, synergy that, or some frictionless paradigm shift the other." Sarg shuddered.

"You're telling me you're not a scalability type of guy?"

"After all these years, you should know, junior."

"You're more the scaloppini type." Drayco grinned as Sarg groaned.

The motorcade kept on coming, making Drayco shake his head. Life in Big-Wig Land, indeed. Something this big had to be a head of state.

He said, "I went to see Joyelle Babineaux at her studio this morning."

"Oh? And how did that go?"

"She's a sharp one. Doesn't miss much. And maybe under different circumstances . . . "

"You still don't trust her."

"I wish I could. But I have to keep an open mind since I'm a little too close to the subject." Drayco filled Sarg in on the other case developments, including the diamond angle.

"Then you're thinking this Johnny Burdell fellow found out about the diamond from that dead resort owner, Van Sandt?"

"Maybe they had a deal, maybe they didn't. But Burdell made the fatal mistake of telling someone else about it."

Sarg frowned. "I think I'd stay far away from that diamond if I were you. Misery and mayhem follow it around."

"Like the Hope diamond and all the tragedy it brought to its owners, you mean?"

"Or the Koh-i-Noor diamond." Sarg thought for a moment. "And there was that Delphi purple sapphire thing. And the Black Orlov diamond. Lots of suicides associated with that one."

"All those gems had ties to Central Asia and the Near East. Stolen, then allegedly cursed."

Sarg shook his head. "You don't believe that, right? What kind of treasure would do that for real?"

"There may not even be a treasure. I have zero proof one ended up in Alec Van Sandt's possession. It may be a big hoax. Van Sandt was known for his love of games."

"True, but Van Sandt told someone about it, and he was killed. Then Tibbs told Burdell about it, and he's killed. Then Burdell tells someone about it, and he's killed. Seems like lots of killing for a mere hoax."

Just then, the motorcade finally ended, and Drayco hurried through the intersection, half-hoping he'd spot the black car again. No joy. As he navigated over to I-95, he could at least be grateful on one level for the usual heavy afternoon traffic between Washington and Freddyburg. It gave him and Sarg plenty of time to hash through various scenarios.

But on the ride back, Drayco was alone with his thoughts as he obsessed over all the disjointed pieces of the case. They didn't fit together. It was the like the problem he'd had with the latitude-longitude puzzle. So what was he missing this time?

When he returned home, the first thing he did was ring up Aria D'Angelo to give her updates as promised. Her voice was unusually chirpy over the phone. Had she been drinking some of her extra-spiced cider again?

"Oh, Scott, that's amazing news. Does this mean you're close to finding the killer and this mysterious treasure, whatever it is?"

"As to the killer, I have some theories. Regarding the treasure, that's a little murkier. I may have located where it was once hidden, but it could be long gone."

"What a shame." Her tone took on a softer lilac color. "I'd hoped after talking with Johnny Burdell's ex-wife, she would have been arrested. After that note I found and all."

"She's still on the suspect list. I give you my word neither the police nor I have given up on solving Graham's death."

"I wondered about the police. Especially since I haven't heard boo from them lately. I was afraid they'd concluded it was an accident."

"I'm familiar with the police department involved. They're very good at their jobs. I very much doubt they've dropped the ball on this. I'll check in with them to determine the status of Graham's case."

"Thank you, truly. I'd much rather deal with you than them. I'll have to take your word they're competent. They just make me nervous."

"Not all cops are like the evil Chief of Police in *Tosca*, Baron Scarpia."

That made her laugh. "Oh, I do feel so much better after chatting with you. But I'm eager to hear what else you find out. You must promise me you'll let me be the first to know."

He took a deep breath. He wanted to ask why she'd gone behind his back to talk with the UMD staff about his recital repertoire, but he hesitated. That was a topic he'd rather discuss in person. As Alistair said, she'd likely meant well. Her new career was scheming to arrange scholarships, dedications, and patronages. It was all part of the process.

Maybe the other reason he didn't want to talk to her about it was how the audition ended. Not that it was her fault. No, that was the young punk who'd coveted his car one night two decades ago and mangled Drayco's arm during the carjacking.

Some might say the supernatural had a part in all of this. Like Joyelle believing the spirit of her late husband was guiding the investigation. And now maybe Johnny Burdell's? Drayco wasn't the superstitious type, but discordant elements were coming together rather harmoniously in this puzzle-of-a-case. Somehow, that seemed like a game even Burdell himself would have loved.

41

Drayco awoke from one of his hypnopompic dreams, half-paralyzed while trying to arouse himself out of sleep. In the dream, he had a replay of the car tailing him and Sarg yesterday. But that car morphed into a different vehicle, the one that hit and killed Johnny Burdell and injured Drayco.

In his dream, he thought he recalled bits of the plate and more of the make and model of the hit-and-run car. Was it a dream, or was his subconscious trying to send him a message? If so, he'd seen that car before in real life.

Still groggy, he stumbled out of bed and glanced at the time. Five-thirty. Early enough to squeeze in a quick run followed by some Bach fugues. True to his word to Aria D'Angelo, he also made an appointment to talk to Johnny Burdell's ex-wife again.

He'd tried to set up another interview with Burdell's sister, but the sister was now playing hard to get. She'd told him on the phone, "I talked to a lawyer friend, and he said I should only speak with the police. I watch TV. I see innocent people get wrongfully arrested all the time." And then she'd hung up on him.

He drove out to Vivianna Keating's animal rescue instead, noting as he got closer how isolated it was out in the boonies. Surrounded by acres of vegetation and a small marshy area, it reminded him of the Eastern Shore without the fishy smell.

He remarked on the isolation when she opened the door. She replied, "I chose this place to keep down insurance costs. Liability, mostly. In case one of the dogs gets loose and bites someone."

"Does that happen often?"

She laughed. "In my experience, it's the people who bite. Honestly, though, I like being away from humans. I had enough of the crazy ones in my law practice to last a lifetime."

"Speaking of 'crazy,' I tried to chat with Connie Burdell Spanton again, but she's pulling her own lawyer card."

"That sounds like her. Flighty and paranoid. However … " Vivianna rubbed her chin. "She used to have a weekly salon appointment as regular as clockwork on Wednesdays, which happens to be today. You might catch her there. It's Chez Curl. In McLean."

"Thanks for the tip. So this is your animal rescue facility." Drayco noted the kennels off to the side and pointed. "Lots of dogs?"

"And cats, rabbits, gerbils, guinea pigs, birds. Occasionally snakes and even raccoons."

Drayco walked over to peer into the fenced-off area where one dog was snapping and snarling. But when it looked directly at Drayco, its ears popped up, and its tail started wagging. It even looked a bit like the "Demon Hound" from the carillon.

As Vivianna laughed, her high-pitched squeak filled Drayco's head with teal corkscrews. When she caught her breath, she said, "Dogs know good people. Do you have one?"

"My father does, but my schedule's too irregular for a dog. Although I do sort of have a cat."

"Sort of?"

"She's mostly feral. I put out food and water and made a little shelter. Sometimes she comes inside briefly."

"Ah, cats know good people, too. They just don't often make it known. If she's been outside most of her life, it may take a while. She'll come around."

"I could bring her here, I guess. That is, if I can catch her."

"Would you want to? It's a no-kill shelter if that helps."

"I'll have to get back to you on that."

She laughed again. "You'd better watch out. My rescue house started with one little stray cat."

"It was a big leap from a high-powered attorney to rescue proprietor, wasn't it?"

"I loved that job, and I was damned good at it. But one of my cases involved an older woman who took in a bunch of animals but couldn't handle them all. So she was charged with neglect and animal abuse. I got a first-hand look at all the neglected and abandoned animals, and I knew I had to do something. Since I'd socked away some of that 'high-powered attorney' money," she winked at him, "I used some of it here."

"I'm hoping you can help me right now with some information. Did you know a man named Alec Van Sandt? Your ex-husband knew him."

"Why, yes, I do recall meeting him once. He was an odd little fellow, kind of shifty. Not well versed in the art of niceties. Or civilized manners. Now that I think about it, that makes him and my ex a lot alike. Van Sandt drank. A lot. He and Johnny got to know each other since they shared a love of puzzles and games. I believe Van Sandt frequented Johnny's store."

"Did Johnny's sister know him, too, then?"

Vivianna leaned over the fence as a different dog, a huskie, came up for a quick head scratch. "Maybe. It was at a cocktail party where I first met the guy. Connie was there, too. So she must have at least chatted with him briefly."

"Just briefly?"

Vivianna grabbed a nearby ball and tossed it over to the dog to chase. "Johnny was pretty chatty with Van Sandt and spent a lot of time at the party with him, so maybe Connie did, too. I didn't like that man, so I kept away from him. Some of that dog-personality radar has rubbed off on me."

"When you were dating Graham Tibbs's former business partner, Leon Sable, did you ever meet Graham's sister, the opera singer?"

"No, but Leon mentioned her. She'd be a fascinating person to meet one day. Not that I'm into celebrities. They end up disappointing you. Like toys and kids, you know? The toys seem shiny and alluring, but the reality is far less than the fantasy."

"Aria D'Angelo is retired, so there's a lot less of the shiny these days."

"I could say the same about me. But I like the grime and dirt that goes with this job."

He grinned. "The best kind of grime."

She pushed a strand of hair behind her ear. "I hope you catch up with Connie, and good luck if you do. I never liked my sister-in-law. I tried, but she was so scheming and manipulative. Always in debt up to her eyeballs, too. I got the impression even Johnny didn't like her much and was a little afraid of her."

"Why is that?"

"She was an adrenaline junkie. You know, sky jumping, bungee dives, driving fast cars." Vivianna paused. "Hell, I wouldn't put it past her to have been the one to mow down her own brother. That would be so like her. Empathy isn't her strong suit."

The dog proudly fetched the ball back to Vivianna, who threw it into the far corner of the enclosure. Vivianna said, "You know she's dating Ezra Layton, right? Despite the age difference. He likes to drive fast cars, too, so I guess that's how they met."

Drayco stared at her. Neither Ezra nor Connie had hinted at it whatsoever. But Layton had mentioned something to Drayco about trusting the wrong people, especially older women.

He said, "There's one other thing I wanted to ask. I don't suppose Johnny mentioned Graham Tibbs coming to him about a treasure and a coded message?"

"It's funny, but I do remember Johnny saying Van Sandt told him about a treasure of some kind. But it was while Van Sandt was drunk, so neither one of us put much stock in it. Pink elephants, treasure—not much difference."

The dog bounded back again and up went the ball one more time. "Do you know how and why my ex-husband died, Mr. Drayco? Since I'm getting the impression you don't think it was an ordinary accident."

"That treasure of Van Sandt's might be very much real. Johnny likely got in over his head because of it and paid the ultimate price."

Vivianna shook her head. "I can't believe Johnny was involved in something shady. Yes, we got divorced. But I never suspected him of being a common criminal."

"Perhaps he wasn't. It's possible he was an innocent victim and confided in the wrong people. Greed is a powerful motivator."

"I'm a former attorney, remember? I know all about greed from my various cases."

The dog bounded over again, and Drayco reached over the fence to scratch his ears so Vivianna wouldn't have to throw the ball again. "By the way, I chatted with Leon Sable the other day. He said the two of you scheduled a real date."

She smiled. "That makes it sound official. A 'date.' But by any definition, that's exactly what it is."

When her phone rang, she pulled it out of her pocket with an apologetic expression. He mouthed "Thank you" to her and headed out.

He'd been angry with Joyelle for her matchmaking attempts, and here he'd just done a little of that on his own. Maybe Leon Sable and Vivianna would get back together, or perhaps they wouldn't, but he wished them better luck than he was having.

He had a far different mission in mind next—from matchmaker to stalker. The setting might be a spa instead of a safari, but not all lionesses were found in the wild.

42

Drayco indeed felt every bit the stalker as he parked near Chez Curl, taking stock of his surroundings. The salon lay toward the end of the block, with a small park between it and the next group of stores. He tried to look busy checking his cellphone and even ducked into a wine shop across the street with big picture windows where he could keep an eye on the salon.

His patience was rewarded when a familiar auburn-haired woman rushed into Chez Curl. He hoped this was just a quickie trim and not a full-color job. How long did those take, anyway? An hour? Two?

When Drayco noted the same parking enforcement car had passed by his location twice—slowly—he ducked back into the wine shop for another bottle. Right as he was exiting, he spied Connie Burdell leaving Chez Curl.

He strolled over as nonchalantly as possible and approached her. "Hello, Connie. Vivianna Keating said I might find you here."

The woman's eyes narrowed. "Oh, she did, did she?"

"She wanted to be helpful, seeing as how I'm trying to get to the bottom of your late brother's death. I have a few more questions about Johnny I'd like to ask you. Shouldn't take long."

When she looked like she'd make a run for it, he said, "Just a few questions. I'm sure you wouldn't want a scene in front of your friends in the salon, right? So why don't we walk over to this nice park over here? It's a lovely, brisk day."

He held out the bag. "I've even bought a bottle of Chardonnay for your troubles."

She looked into the bag and got a big smile on her face. "That's top-notch. Well, if it's only a few questions. About Johnny. Just a little tête-à-tête, right?" She pronounced it tate-ee-tate.

They walked to the park and sat on a bench not far from a cracked stone fountain. Connie clutched the bag with the wine to her chest. "Guess I'm not surprised Vivianna would set this up."

"She did nothing of the kind. She merely suggested where I might be able to find you."

"Yeah? Well, she's always been so greedy and demanding. And manipulative. The more I think about Johnny's will, the more I believe Vivianna tricked him into leaving everything to her. She's a former attorney, you know."

"Yes, she told me that. She also told me about a cocktail party she once attended with you and Johnny and a man named Alec Van Sandt."

"Who?"

"He's the former owner of a resort up in Maryland called Heaven's Embrace. He and Johnny shared a love of puzzles."

"You said former owner. Did he sell that place?"

"It's owned by a bank now."

"Oh. Well, I guess I do recall meeting him. Odd little fellow. I really wanted to stay at that resort of his someday. Too bad he sold it."

"He didn't sell it. He's deceased. Another hit-and-run, the same type of death as your brother's."

She sat very still for a moment. "Another hit-and-run? Do they think it's the same person who killed Johnny? I hope they find the monster and throw the book at him. Or better yet, tie him to the road and run *him* down over and over. Maybe the Bible had it right with the 'eye for an eye' thing."

"There's a chance Van Sandt mentioned a stolen treasure to your brother at one point. And Johnny might have been involved in something less than legal because of it."

She stared over at the fountain. "I could totally see that. Even though I hate to speak ill of my late brother. But he wasn't all that savvy, you know?"

"I understand you're dating Ezra Layton, a good friend of Graham Tibbs. Vivianna said you're quite the adrenaline junkie. And since Ezra loves racing cars, you might love driving fast cars together, right?"

She narrowed her eyes. "Vivianna shouldn't be making up stories to attack my reputation. If you must know, Ezra's a lot of fun. He's never boring. And if there's one thing I hate, it's being bored. But I'm beginning to understand why my attorney friend said not to talk to you, so I think I'm going to leave now."

She grabbed the bag. "Thanks for the wine."

Drayco watched her scurry away around the corner and waited a little longer on the bench, watching the fountain. All the players in this drama were pointing fingers at each other. Which of them was telling the truth? All of them? Or none of them?

When he made his way back to his townhome, he first made sure Cat had her crunchies. As she munched away, he muttered, "I don't think you'd be happy in that animal shelter, Cat. For one thing, there's no piano."

The piano. Now there was an idea. Drayco headed toward his Steinway for some therapy, not so much physical as mental. But first, he made sure to soak his arm in warm water. Even without an audience, he hated that feeling when the muscles and tendons warped into a tight, painful clutch of useless flesh. When he was satisfied his arm was in playing condition, he eased into some Bach, simpler two-part inventions at first to warm up.

As he'd told his father, Drayco refused the hypnosis his former therapist wanted to use on him. All he needed was the piano and Bach to induce a type of self-hypnosis. There was nothing better to help his brain untangle dissonant information and tease out the harmony of hidden details to the fore.

He switched to the Prelude and Fugue No. 4 in C-sharp minor from BWV 873 as he mused that if Graham Tibbs was killed over that treasure, then Johnny Burdell must be connected. But if Van Sandt buried the diamond on his property, even the densest criminal could see it was long gone. So why the continued interest?

In reviewing all the primary suspects and possible motives—Connie Burdell, Vivianna Keating, Ezra Layton, Leon Sable, Christi Allingham, and yes, Joyelle—he couldn't see any of them being the sole mastermind. Unless the puppet master was Uncle Alistair, perhaps?

As Drayco's fingers started the fugue, with its subject in the bass in c-sharp minor followed by a switch to the treble in g-sharp minor, he wondered, who else would have the connections to sell the diamond if it were ever discovered?

Graham Tibbs and Ezra Layton were only small-time crooks in their day. Alistair was the only one among them with such connections. Drayco knew his uncle led a shadowy existence but hadn't seriously entertained the idea Alistair had killed before—or had someone else do it.

Drayco made it all the through the fugue, but without any new insights into the case. With a sigh, he hopped up from the piano, disappointed that Bach seemed to have let him down. He sank down on his sofa, grabbed a copy of Graham Tibbs's obituary he'd printed out, and read through it again. He'd never lost a case yet, and he wasn't ready to have this be the first time.

Strains of the "Twinkle, Twinkle" song popped up in his mind again, only this time, it was arranged in the style of Bach's counterpoint. As he let it play in his head, a thought struck him. There was another way of rearranging the possibilities of the case, something far more monstrous and twisted. And yet, it made perfect sense in a Machiavellian sort of way.

43

It was a little late in the season for mid-Atlantic morning fog. Still, traces of this one lingered as Drayco made his way south of town again, this time to Lake Anna in Spotsylvania. His target was another Van Sandt, the resort owner's daughter and sole beneficiary of the man's estate.

The realtor he'd conferred with at Heaven's Embrace had speculated that the daughter, Ellie, received little from the will after the bank repossessed her father's properties. But the house he found himself in front of wasn't a shack. A modern take on the more traditional cabin, the two-story A-frame lay partially hidden by a thick mini-forest on either side. He could just catch a glimpse of the lake behind.

Ellie Van Sandt had a very musical, high-ish soprano voice, and Drayco asked her if she was a singer. She replied, "Maybe in the shower and the occasional karaoke when I'm drunk."

She ushered him to a den, and as he looked around, it was immediately evident she'd inherited her father's belongings. Stacks of puzzles and books lay crammed into built-in shelving, a metal replica of the Tin Man leaned in one corner, and the throw rug had a giant crossword puzzle pattern.

He pointed to the rug. "Did that belong to your father?"

She laughed. "You'd think so, wouldn't you? But after I moved some of his effects here, I decided to add a few whimsical touches of my own. Might as well keep the theme going. Plus, it reminds me of my dad, which makes me feel close to him again."

Her eyes glistened a little more brightly as she sat down on an uncomfortable-looking club chair and waved toward a green velvet sofa for him to use. He said, "I'm sorry to bring up such a painful topic."

"It's painful, yes. But not in the way you'd think. Before his passing, I hadn't seen him in a few years. I blamed him for my parents' divorce. But there were a lot more layers to that relationship than I knew. My mother was so distraught over his death that she passed away not long after him of a heart attack. It literally broke her heart."

"But he left everything to you and nothing to her?"

"I guess there were still some hard feelings about Mom."

"I don't suppose he also left behind any papers? Notes, diaries, journals, ledgers?"

She pursed her lips. "You said you thought the same person involved in a couple of recent deaths might also be behind my father's hit-and-run?"

He nodded. "I'm hoping to figure it all out. And nail the culprit."

"Then feel free to go through whatever you wish. Hope you're not disappointed—all the papers fit into one medium-sized box."

She stood up, but when he moved to join her, she said, "You can stay comfy there. Enjoy the scenery." She waved toward the lake outside the sliding glass door. "I'll go get the files and bring them to you."

As she'd suggested, Drayco took the time to look out the door. Lake Anna was one of the largest reservoirs in Virginia, with a popular beach and campground. It was soothing as he stared at the clear, non-polluted cerulean blue water. He was way overdue for a scuba vacation.

After a couple of minutes, she returned with the box and set it on the table next to Drayco, adding, "I'll go make us some tea. Ginseng, horseradish, garlic, and honey. Sounds horrible, but it's better than you'd think. Good for what ails you."

Most of the papers in the folders were receipts, legal documents related to the bank and mortgages, plus some old stock certificates and health records. Her father might have been a poor businessman, as evidenced by his money woes, but it hadn't taken a toll on the man's health because his tests were good. The man could have lived a long time if he wasn't struck down by the car.

Things got more interesting at the back of the assortment of folders. Drayco found a file with only one piece of paper. On it, Van Sandt had written a brief, cryptic reference to a yellow diamond and his plans to make a puzzle that would lead to its location.

He hinted he'd hidden the diamond in plain sight, but didn't spell out where. Since the house was bulldozed into history, that only left the resort—an assumption likely verified by the last line of the note, which only had two words, *Caelesti Amplexus.*

Alistair had said Graham Tibbs was the one who found the puzzle, but Alistair refused to say where he'd acquired it. Drayco had a pretty good idea where now. When Ellie returned with the tea and set it beside him on the end table, he thanked her and asked, "Have there been any break-ins recently?"

"You mean this house? Why, yes, there was one about six months ago. Funny thing, though. I couldn't find anything stolen." She frowned and added, "But now that I think of it, those papers weren't as messy when I finished looking through them after probate. Was the thief interested in them?"

"It's possible." He recited the puzzle note to her from memory. "Do you recall seeing something like that among these papers?"

"You know, I think I do. It's been a few years now. At the time, I discounted it since my father loved puzzles so much. I believe it was in the back folder."

He held up the folder with the cryptic note. "This one?"

She set her tea down, took the folder from him, and opened it. "Yes, this was the one. I remember this note. Again, I just thought it was a joke. But the paper with the little puzzle is gone. Who would take it?"

"I think I know the answer to that. But the thief is one of the other hit-and-run victims."

She paled a little. "This all sounds very dangerous. I added one of those door cameras after the break-in. Now I'm wondering if I should add more security." She stuffed the folder back into the box.

"You're probably fine. I think the thief got what they were after. But I'll never advise someone not to add more security, if it will make you feel safer."

Ellie flopped into her chair and grabbed her glass of tea to take some quick sips. "You know, so many things make more sense now. After Dad died, I had to go through his things at his house, and it was much more of a mess than usual."

"Like someone had gone through his belongings there, too?"

"Exactly. Even when he died, I wondered if he'd caught some burglars in the act, and they ran him over as they were escaping. He was coming home that night from the store. He'd just got out of his car."

Drayco pushed the file box aside. "I'm curious. Did you know about a property your father owned in Fauquier County? A somewhat isolated house. It's empty and unoccupied now."

"Oh, that one." She wrinkled her nose. "The house and resort in Maryland now belong to the bank. But that shack in Virginia nobody wants. I've tried to sell it, but no luck. Thank God the property taxes are low."

"A few weeks ago, I was kidnapped and taken to a remote location. I'm certain it was that exact property."

She stared at him. "But I don't understand. Who? How? Why? The electricity's been shut off for years."

"It's related to that puzzle of your father's." He didn't mention her father's possible theft of the diamond. Time enough for that if and when it was found.

"Maybe I should just have that house bulldozed to the ground. Like the other one." Ellie got up from her chair to stare out at the lake. As she stood there, she started humming softly, and Drayco immediately recognized the tune.

"Is that 'Twinkle, Twinkle, Little Star?' "

"What?" She turned around, startled, and then gave a small smile. "I hum little tunes sometimes when I don't even realize it. Yes, it was my father's favorite song. Well, this big band arrangement of it." Then she got a stricken look on her face. "The LP. Oh my God."

"What's the matter?"

"The LP with the arrangement of the song. It was in that box. But it's gone. The thief must have taken it, too, but whatever for?"

So that's where Graham had come by the big band version of the nursery song. Drayco asked, "Did your father ever mention a Graham Tibbs?"

"As I say, I hadn't talked to Dad in a few years. But that name's familiar." Her eyes widened. "I remember now. I read about him in the news. He'd supposedly been dead and then turns up alive again—only to be killed in a hit-and-run."

"That's the one."

"You know, I thought at the time the man's photo looked familiar. And I think it just triggered something. I'll be back in a moment."

She disappeared again but quickly returned with a photograph album. She flipped through the pages, stopped on one, and handed the book to Drayco. The photo was from a charity ball where Van Sandt and Graham Tibbs were standing close together, along with Graham's sister, Aria D'Angelo.

Ellie said, "I'm not sure if they knew each other well, but from the looks of those smiles, they had a good time at this charity thing."

"Does the name Alistair Brisbane ring a bell?"

"I never heard Dad talking about him. Hard to forget a name like that, because that's one of the Australian cities I'm dying to visit."

Drayco held back a smile since that's how people always remembered his uncle's name. He asked if he could make a copy of Van Sandt's note, and she made him one off her combo printer-copy machine. He thanked her for the tea and her time, promising to fill her in should he learn who was behind her father's death.

After he left, he sat in his car outside her house, fiddling with the rearview mirror, musing about his visit with Van Sandt's daughter. Why did Graham Tibbs choose Van Sandt's house in the boonies? Because he knew it was unoccupied and hidden away? Or did Tibbs think the treasure might be hidden there?

He and Alistair's goons had likely gone over it with a fine-toothed comb, and Sarg and Drayco had also searched it. But maybe it wouldn't hurt to go back and have another crack at it, especially if Ellie followed through on her threat to have it razed to the ground.

Then again, the nearby carillon to Drayco's prison shared similarities in notes with the "Twinkle, Twinkle" song, so maybe that had inspired Graham Tibbs's choice of location. Or perhaps the "gang" used it as a planning or staging area at another time.

Another one of many such questions for which he might never get answers. Unless you believed in séances with the dead.

§ § §

On his return trip to the District, Drayco made a detour to a home address he'd looked up for Ezra Layton. He drove slowly by the house and was in luck—the garage door was open, and he could see the car parked inside. It was the same "ordinary" car Layton claimed to own when Drayco visited him at the racetrack.

The car was backed into the space, and Drayco could see that the front licence plate matched the partial he recalled during his dream. There was some fender damage in front, too—from a hit-and-run, perhaps?

Drayco pulled over and parked a few houses up the street. Confronting Layton wouldn't do much good since Drayco had no actual proof. He'd pass along the dented fender info to Detective Halabi for further investigation, but the car looked like it was recently washed. Unless there were traces of Johnny Burdell's blood on that fender, it likely wouldn't pass the court-proof test.

Just as Drayco decided to leave since there wasn't anything further he could do right then, Connie Burdell drove up, scrambled out of her car, and banged on the house's front door. Drayco watched as she and Layton got into a heated exchange while she paced back and forth. After several minutes of that, she finally got back in her car, slammed the door, and peeled away.

That was intriguing. Certainly didn't look like a lover's tiff. It wouldn't have anything to do with Drayco's little chat with Connie outside the hair salon, now, would it? He'd hoped his questioning of

Connie might shake loose a few threads of the case, and it appeared to have worked.

Maybe Connie was involved with her brother's death, or perhaps she was just covering up for her lover, Layton. Judging from the panicked look on Layton's face, it seemed a sure bet he was in pretty deep and likely in well over his head. And the tide was rising fast.

44

This time, Drayco didn't have far to go to find Leon Sable. The man stood at the entrance to LS Metals, adding paint to a window sign. When he saw Drayco, he gave a little wave of his hand, making a few splatters of paint drop onto the sidewalk.

Drayco stood beside him to admire the man's handiwork. Sable said, "Early Christmas sale. Not that Santa tends to bring people metal pipes or sheets of aluminum and put it under the tree."

"Better than lumps of coal."

That elicited a rare grin from Sable. "Or socks. Those argyle monstrosities most of all."

Drayco pulled his pants leg up an inch to make sure he hadn't put some on today. Nope. Basic black. "I think I'm making progress on Graham's case."

Sable said, "You said Aria D'Angelo was the one who hired you?"

"That's right."

"She and Graham may have had some disagreements, but I'd like to think he'd be happy with the way Ezra Layton stepped up to help Aria after Graham's death. Layton talked of Ms. D'Angelo in such glowing terms. She really made an impression on him. I guess she became a surrogate sister."

Sable chewed on his lip. "Or something else." Isn't that close to what Alistair had told Drayco? That Aria had adopted Drayco as her new pet project? Drayco asked, "I actually stopped by today to ask you about a man named Alec Van Sandt."

"Van Sandt? I met him once. Had to deliver some metal supplies to a property of his up in Maryland at this big resort. Haven't heard from him since. Guess I didn't make much of an impression."

"You may have. But you haven't heard from him because he died five years ago."

"That's a shame. Seemed like a nice guy."

"Did he or Graham ever mention a hidden treasure? A gem of some sort?"

Sable's eyes widened. "What's that? A treasure? No, never. Hell, if Graham had something like that, he could have helped save our business."

"I'm not sure he was ever in possession of it per se."

Sable shrugged. "Oh well. If it's out there somewhere, some rich guy will end up with it. Or else it will disappear into some other rich guy's private museum. Who knows? I doubt any of us will ever see it. That's the way the universe works."

"When you and Ezra were partners, did he ever mention Van Sandt? Or this treasure?"

"Nope. But we didn't have much to do with each other aside from business. That is, nothing personal. Though I've heard a rumor Ezra is involved in a relationship with someone you'd never expect."

"Who might that be?"

"I never pass along rumors, so I'm afraid I can't help you with this, but I will say the age difference is weird."

Drayco didn't tell him he already knew about Ezra Layton hooking up with Johnny Burdell's ten-year-older sister, Connie.

Sable put his paintbrush into a tray. "I owe you, you know. Thanks to you, Vi and I are back together. I'm even toying with selling my business and making that move to Australia."

"Is Vi okay with that?"

"She wants to come along. Says the Aussies need animal rescues Down Under, too."

§ § §

Benny Baskin was out-of-town doing some lawyering, but he'd left some materials with Nelia Tyler to deliver to Drayco. They both agreed Drayco's townhome wasn't the best choice, so they met outside a skateboard park not too far from Nelia's apartment in the District. It was her choice—public, open, and no chance for temptations. Despite that and the tension between them, he still felt more at ease with her at the skateboard facility than with Christi Allingham at the ice rink.

As they sat on a bench watching the helmeted skateboarders doing their kick turns and rail stands, Nelia handed over a manila envelope. "If anyone's watching us right now, they'll think they're witnessing an espionage exchange."

Drayco lifted his sunglasses to peer at her directly. "Who says we aren't?"

"I'm not exactly dressed as a secret agent."

Drayco surveyed her clothing, trying not to look like he was ogling her. "Oh, I don't know. There was the husband-and-wife spy team, Amy and Marco Gattaway. They were arrested wearing T-shirts and sweatpants."

The hint of a smile that crossed her lips was good to see. He'd witnessed too few Nelia smiles lately.

She asked, "Since we're on the topic of spies, still considering Joyelle Babineaux, the ex-spook, as a suspect?"

Drayco watched a young girl, rare among the testosterone-heavy skateboarders, execute a perfect backside flip. "If Joyelle decided to jump into the murder business, I have no doubt she'd excel at it."

Drayco shook his head. "Funny thing. I think she and maybe Alistair are the only players in this whole affair who didn't seem to know the resort owner, Alec Van Sandt. But since Alistair is so secretive, who's to say? He may have known the guy all along."

"But what would be his angle? Use you to find the diamond for him and bump off anyone who gets in his way? Sounds messy. And not at all his style."

"Feels that way to me, too. And I have my sights on someone else."

"Who?"

"If I'm right, it shows I've been blind and manipulated all along." He filled her in on his latest theory, and she thought about it for a few moments. "I hope you can prove it. After all, three murders . . . "

"Yeah." Drayco shifted his body on the cold, hard seat, trying not to edge too close to Nelia. He thought again of his chat earlier with Leon Sable and how the guy was in a much better mood than the past two times Drayco saw him. Love can do that to you, so they say. He gave Nelia a quick glance. Hopefully, she wouldn't see the regret reflected on his face.

But her following words were unexpected. "I'm thinking of quitting law school. It's too much to handle while pulling down two jobs."

"As I said, I'd be happy to float you a loan—"

"No," she answered, then tucked a strand of hair behind her ear before adding, "But thanks. I know you're sincere. I just don't want to be in debt to anyone."

Drayco was sympathetic to her plight on the one hand, but on the other, he didn't want her to give up on her dream. He said gently, "Have you mentioned this to Benny? Perhaps he could help."

She sighed. "I haven't wanted to burden him since he's got a big caseload. But maybe if the time is right."

She straightened up against the bench and peeked over at him with the ghost of another smile. Two for two, sort of. "This conversation has taken a turn for the serious. I think I need to change that."

"How so?"

"Why don't I host the Christmas dinner this time? And I promise I won't make you perform."

She batted her eyelashes at him, making him do a double-take and almost choke. But when he saw she was kidding, he relaxed at the double entendre. It was nice to be back on surer footing with her, joking around more with the recent tensions lifting.

He replied, "How could I refuse such an offer?"

"There's something else I've been meaning to ask you. Did you ever look up piano porn on the internet?"

That made him laugh so hard that some of the skateboarders looked over at them for the first time. Drayco finally squeaked out, "I think we should go before they call the cops on us."

As they parted to go their separate ways, Drayco walked toward his car, shaking his head. What in the world was she trying to do, kill him?

45

Drayco parked at his townhome and checked the voice mail on his office number. There were two new messages, and he started up the first one.

Ezra Layton's voice was unusually agitated as he said, "Scott Drayco? Are you there? I have to talk to you." Then the message broke off.

When Drayco played the second message, it was Layton again, even more upset than before. "Look, I really need to talk to you. I just . . . I don't know how it got out of control. One thing led to another and then . . . Oh my god, if I could just go back in time."

There was a slight pause before he continued, half-laughing, half-crying. "I don't know what to do. I need someone to tell me what to do. Graham, oh Graham. I'm so sorry." And the call ended there. Drayco looked at the time stamp. Two hours ago.

Drayco didn't know whether to call the police or check on Layton first. He opted to drive by the man's house and see if he was there. But as he arrived, he had a sinking feeling when he spied a fire engine and ambulance along with EMTs. Detective Halabi stood off to one side, observing.

Drayco hopped out of his car and approached Halabi. "What happened?"

Halabi gave him a funny look. "Suicide or accident, hard to tell yet. I'm leaning toward suicide."

"Are you sure?"

"That's the preliminary call. We found an empty vodka bottle and two empty bottles of antidepressants near the body. The crime scene techs are in there now. We'll check into all the aspects as we *always* do. These guys are pros. The very best."

"I'm sure of that. But how did you find out about Layton's death so quickly?"

"A neighbor saw the guy's dog wandering outside without a chain. Noticed the backdoor was open. Since she takes care of the dog when Layton is gone, she went in and found the body. She's pretty upset, as you might imagine."

"I'll bet."

Halabi tilted his head. "So ... how did you get here so fast yourself, Drayco?"

Drayco told him about the two messages on his machine that were odd and disturbing.

Halabi nodded. "Maybe it's about this," and he showed Drayco a hand-written note wrapped in a clear plastic bag. "It's another reason I'm leaning toward the suicide theory."

As Drayco scanned it, Ezra Layton admitted he was behind the hit-and-runs. The note went on to say Layton was sorry for what he'd done and that he was a fool to trust the wrong people. He hoped Graham Tibbs, Johnny Burdell, and Alec Van Sandt would forgive him if he encountered them in the afterlife, "Most of all Graham, who was my best friend."

Drayco shook his head at that and finished reading the rest of the note, which continued with, "I should never have listened to Burdell's crazy sister. It was Connie's idea to run Van Sandt down when we surprised him and later Burdell. She was even the one driving."

Halabi pointed to that last bit and asked, "What do you know about that? Connie Burdell Spanton sure put up a good show when she came to the station for questioning after Johnny Burdell's death. Sobbing, shaking, the works. Her own brother, no less. She's quite the actress."

Drayco wrote down Connie's address and handed it over. "This might save you some time. But be careful. I think she bites."

"So were they lovers or something?"

"Seems so."

"A regular Bonnie and Clyde, eh? See, I told you so, didn't I?" Halabi looked rather pleased with himself.

When Drayco didn't reply, Halabi said, "You don't look surprised by any of this."

Drayco held out his hand for the bagged note, and Halabi handed it over so Drayco could read the very last part. "Death and despair blaze about me. But I forgive her. She is far greater than I will ever be."

Halabi grimaced. "He sure had a high opinion of this Burdell woman. We'll see how well she can keep up the act this time." He motioned to a couple of officers nearby and gave them the paper from Drayco with Connie's address. "Double check this address and bring her in. If she's not there, we'll put out a BOLO."

Drayco looked over at the officers and said, "Hope they've had their tetanus shots."

Halabi grunted. "How does it feel to wrap up the case?"

"Is it?"

"What?"

"Wrapped up. There's still the treasure."

"Treasure? What treasure?"

Drayco gave him a grim smile. "I'll have to get back to you on that. It might be something, or it might be nothing."

Halabi muttered, "*C'est le bordel.*"

"It's a mess, all right. And your French accent is getting better."

Halabi just snorted. "You know the drill. I'll be seeing you down at the precinct as soon as possible?"

"Of course. You may remember how much I love filling out reports."

"No offense, Drayco, but try not to bring us any more business. At least don't get yourself kidnapped again. We've got our hands plenty full with run-of-the-mill drug busts and assaults."

Drayco left the scene to give the police crew time and the space to do their jobs. Halabi was right that Drayco wasn't at all surprised by Layton and Burdell Spanton's roles in all of this. Though since Layton was the fast-car lover, Drayco had pegged him as being the rampaging driver in the hit-and-run cases, not Connie.

But maybe that was reverse sexism at work? After all, Vi Keating had told Drayco that Connie Burdell was an adrenaline junkie, too. Vi even said she wouldn't put it past Connie to have mowed down her own brother since "empathy wasn't her strong suit."

Empathy. Something that was in short supply in this case, all around. But it was all about greed when you got right down to it. Wasn't it always? As the Bureau was fond of saying, "You have to follow the money."

Johnny Burdell and now Ezra Layton ... two people Drayco might have been able to save if he hadn't had lousy timing. His friend Reece Wable's kismet philosophy about life and death wasn't helping much. But Drayco couldn't think of anything else that would help, either. Just two more tragedies to stuff inside his mental lockbox.

What was it his early FBI mentor told him? *Stay safe to stay sane.* At first, Drayco thought he meant to watch your back, but when the man later suffered a nervous breakdown, Drayco realized it went deeper than that. Keep your emotions in check and don't let the darkness eat away at your soul. And thus, Drayco's mental lockbox was born.

46

The weather forecast called for stormy weather, but when the morning dawned leaden but dry, Drayco hoped for the best. Those hopes were soon shattered when a cold, driving rain began to fall and grew heavier with each passing hour.

He had second thoughts about his upcoming trek back in time. Still, he'd somehow managed to get two other people to goad him into letting them come along. He wasn't sure why, but when Brock learned Drayco was planning on heading to Heaven's Embrace, he insisted on coming along. Then, when Joyelle Babineaux found out about the plan, she'd invited herself.

Drayco warned them, "This visit isn't sanctioned by the bank or the realtor."

"You mean breaking in?" Brock had appeared intrigued.

"Sort of."

"Count me in."

The trio now stood under umbrellas in front of the resort's lockbox, and it was Brock who said, "What's the code? I don't think anyone's going to arrest *me* for breaking and entering."

Joyelle Babineaux patted him on the shoulder. "No, dear, I should be the one to enter the code. Neither one of you can afford to bring the police down on your heads."

Drayco stepped in front of his companions. "Seeing as this is my case, and I'm the guy who remembers what the realtor punched into this thing, I'll do the honors."

After he'd successfully opened the creaking front door to the abandoned resort and they headed in, Joyelle studied the cracks in the ceilings and walls and the uneven floorboards. "So this is *Heaven's* Embrace? Because the other place is starting to look a lot nicer."

"It's a hell of a disgrace to let such a historic building go to seed." Drayco led the way inside, noting the other two were as grateful to get out of the cold and the pouring rain as he was.

Brock eyed the interior skeptically. "You really think the diamond is still hidden inside here somewhere?"

"I have no idea. But I had to give it one last shot."

"For your client, for Alistair, or for you?"

Drayco sighed. "Maybe all, maybe none. Maybe out of a sense of fairness. And history."

Brock looked around the main hall they were standing in. "This doesn't look too promising. Should we split up?"

Joyelle said, "Divide and conquer sounds like a good plan. I'll start on the second floor."

Brock headed over to the windows in the rear that overlooked the Chesapeake Bay. As he peered outside, he said, "Huh. Looks like we're perched on a waterfall out there. You sure this place is safe?"

"The realtor thought so. She admitted she was secretly disappointed it hadn't fallen down the cliffs so they could be done with it."

"Okay, then," and Brock headed toward the north wing, adding over his shoulder, "This leads to a former stage and movie theater. Might be a good dramatic choice for hiding something."

As Brock and Joyelle departed toward their chosen sections, Drayco made his way to the south wing, where the kitchen and bar had once served Dom Pérignon and *pâté de foie gras* to the wealthy guests. As the realtor said, just about everything that could be sold off had been stripped out of the place. That left only a few cabinets and some empty built-in racks in the large walk-in pantry.

But the pantry also had little else besides thick layers of dust and old stains from spilled goods on the wooden shelving. He looked around for vermin, but there wasn't even one little mouse in sight.

That was odd. Mice were always on the lookout for warm, dry places to access, and they didn't know for certain there was no longer food here. Was this place too depressing even for them?

He re-entered the main kitchen area, which also had tall windows facing the Chesapeake Bay, and the wind was whipping the rain in all directions. He could barely see outside to look for Brock's "waterfall." But he could hear the rain patter, which ordinarily had a puffy emerald pyramidal shape.

He'd always liked the sound of rain with its usual soothing effect, but this was different. Angrier, as if the Norse rain god Freyr was having a really bad day.

With a sigh, he began to question his sanity about coming to this place on a far-fetched quest. And on such a day as this, to boot. If Van Sandt ever had the diamond in his possession, it was likely already sold and in someone's private collection.

But he took pains to open each cabinet and drawer, tapping on all sides to see if there might be a hidden storage space. One cabinet was stuck shut, and it took a large amount of elbow grease to force it open. That effort resulted in a loud creaking that echoed around the live space, bouncing off the tile floors and high ceilings.

But the creaking didn't die down. In fact, the creaking seemed to be getting louder. And it wasn't coming from the cabinets. The creaking soon morphed into more of a groaning and then into a full-throated roar as the floor began to shake like an earthquake.

When Drayco heard a shout from the other end of the building, he raced down the hall and back into the great room just as Joyelle came bounding down the stairs, her eyes wide in shock. "What the hell's going on?"

The shouting originated from the north wing, and as Drayco charged into the old entertainment section, the world started moving in slow motion. Glass shattered, and the cracks in the walls and ceilings started to rip apart into extensive fractures as the back wall of the space buckled and crumbled. Right as Drayco was getting ready to tell his father to run, the floor beneath Brock caved in and sloped down toward the cliffs below.

As Drayco watched in horror, Brock lost his footing and slid down with the floor, heading toward the now-gaping hole where the walls once stood. Somehow, one of his arms managed to grab onto a piece of floorboard. But the rest of him was now dangling over the precipice.

Drayco yelled over at Joyelle, "Go outside and call 911." Then he eased himself closer to his father and looked around for anything he could hold on to to brace himself as he tried to reach Brock.

Half of the room had disappeared over the cliff, making the rows of bolted-down theater seats now at the edge of the gaping hole. Drayco lay down on his stomach, wrapped his legs around one of the seats, and reached his hand out toward Brock.

Brock yelled to be heard over the surf, the rain, and the groaning of the collapsing building. "No! Save yourself."

"Not on your life. And I mean that literally." Drayco clasped his hand around Brock's wrist and yelled, "Do not let go."

"I absolutely, positively will not let go!"

Ignoring the renewed screaming pain in his shoulder, Drayco managed to wrap his other hand around Brock's arm and began pulling with all of his might. The groaning and shuddering hadn't let up, and Drayco offered a prayer to whoever might be listening to let the floor under the seats stay in place just a little longer.

With one last yank, he hauled his father halfway over the opening, enough that he could grab his belt and pull him the rest of the way onto slightly firmer ground. They were both winded, but they didn't have time to catch their breath. He half-pushed, half-pulled Brock toward the hallway leading into the main room and then out of the house and onto the front lawn.

Emergency vehicles pulled up with the lights and sirens still flashing. Two firefighters hopped out and ran over to Drayco and Brock as Drayco told them, "I'm fine, but please check out my father. He came close to going over the edge." The firefighters helped Brock limp over to their truck, with Drayco and Joelle following behind.

As Drayco turned to look back at the house one last time, the "Twinkle, Twinkle" song started playing in his head. That's when the last piece of the puzzle fell into place—the great hall, the bizarre carved panels, the astronomical signs. Once again, he was questioning his sanity, but he knew what he had to do.

He turned and ran back inside as he heard a "Scott, don't!" call from his father and Joyelle. It felt like the earthquake Drayco experienced one summer in San Francisco. That one had registered a magnitude of 4.4, but this was much worse.

He raced over to the wall with the astronomical carvings, specifically the sun symbol with the cross beneath. He pressed on the sun, the "little star," and a small door popped open somewhat to his amazement. As he reached inside, his fingers touched an even smaller box he thrust into his pocket before dashing outside again.

He sprinted toward a newly arrived ambulance parked near the firetruck where EMTs checked Brock for injuries. As Drayco approached, Joyelle said, "Oh, thank God. Brock was going to head right back in there if you didn't reappear soon. Why did you do that?"

"I had a hunch. Sometimes they work out. Sometimes they don't."

Brock studied him as Drayco kept his expression neutral. His father was alive and mostly uninjured, and that was all that mattered right then.

Joyelle replied, "I'm just thrilled and relieved everyone is safe. But that realtor sure got her wish for the building to fall over the cliff."

As if hearing her words, an even louder groaning and shuddering emanated from the old resort, as the rest of it, room by room, tumbled like dominoes over the cliffs. First the north wing, then the south wing, and finally even the great hall began to slip over the edge, pausing for a moment as if saying its last goodbyes. And then it, too, was gone.

With everyone's attention on the building, Drayco slid the little box out of his pocket. Inside, on a plain black velvet cloth, lay a clear, multi-faceted gem with hints of yellow. He closed the lid and slid the box back into his pocket. Time enough to deal with that later.

47

"Are you sure you're up to this?" Drayco looked over at his father with his arm wrapped in a sling. Even though it was two days since the incident at the old resort, he could tell Brock's pain level was still pretty high.

"It's only a bad sprain. Could have been a lot worse." Brock gave Drayco a sideways glance. "Your shoulder any better?"

"I'm fine. Let's go have you meet my diva client, shall we?"

Drayco had called ahead, and the driveway gate buzzed open as they arrived. Aria D'Angelo welcomed them inside her house with a big smile as Drayco introduced his father.

She said, "So, you've solved it all. I'm dying to hear the details." She paused before adding, "And I guess you found the yellow diamond."

Drayco and Aria took seats opposite one another. But Brock started walking around the room, looking at all the opera paraphernalia and concentrating on the photos. He picked one up. "Is this the Queen of the Night from *The Magic Flute*?"

"Why, yes, it is. I suppose it's what I was best known for. Most sopranos have a signature role, of course." She sighed. "Thank you for coming today, by the way. My poor, dear, sweet Ezra. I just can't believe he's gone. And I was shocked to hear that he of all people was behind Graham's death."

Drayco replied, "Yes. Although he had help."

"Oh?" Aria rearranged herself among the pillows that surrounded her on the sofa.

"The sister of one of the other men killed was involved."

"That's horrible. To kill your own brother that way."

Brock said, "Isn't it, though? Like an operatic plot."

She seemed unable to get comfortable. She hopped up, grabbed Drayco's arm, and pulled him toward her Bösendorfer piano. "This should be a celebration of sorts, shouldn't it? I have the sheet music for 'Porgi, Amor' on the piano. You must play while I sing."

Drayco half-fell onto the piano bench as he looked over at Brock, who gave him a knowing smile. Drayco asked Aria, "I'm curious why you called the University of Maryland to change the repertoire for my audition."

"I know a few people over there, and I merely believed it would help. Playing some of the greatest hits is a great way to wow the audience. When you only have one chance to make an impression, you must make it count."

Maybe she did "know a few people" over there, but she still wasn't admitting she'd made the call anonymously. Hubris, perhaps? He said, "It came as a bit of a shock."

She waved her hand in the air. "You are more than up to the challenge. Now, let's try this Mozart aria, shall we? I haven't had an audience of my own in some time. One goes through withdrawal without it."

Drayco sat down at the piano and accommodated her whim, grateful the piano reduction for the piece was simple and wouldn't tax his arm or shoulder too much. For her part, Aria sang with clarity and hints of the beautiful bel canto lines that had once been the talk of the opera world.

When they finished, Brock attempted to applaud as best he could with his arm in the sling. She bowed to him.

Still sitting on the bench, Drayco said, "I've read many of your reviews. You were billed as one of the best actresses in opera."

She bowed again. "And I was thrilled to hear it since that's what they said about Maria Callas, no less."

"I'm curious. When I first met you, and you cried for Graham, was that genuine emotion? Or were you playing another role?"

"What?" She put a hand to her throat. "I . . . don't understand what you're asking."

"I guess it was our mutual love of music, how both our careers were cut short, and our shared situation of an opera house legacy that clouded my judgment. I should have been more objective from the start."

"I'm sorry, I just . . . What?"

"The whole obsession with your legacy should have been a clue. The constant scraping for money to fund scholarships and opera houses and grants that will be named after you. My sympathy toward you kept me from seeing this obsession was so great, you were willing to allow people to get killed over it. As long as it meant getting funds for your grandiose plans."

She stood ramrod straight and hauled herself up to her full five feet four. "That's absurd. Are you accusing me of killing my own brother?"

"Ezra once told me it was women who'd ruined his life. Especially older women. At first, I thought he meant Connie Burdell Spanton since she's ten years older, and perhaps he was. But Connie wasn't the only one. Leon Sable also mentioned he'd heard a rumor Ezra was involved with someone I'd never expect. He wouldn't say who but did indicate the age difference was shocking."

Aria laughed and waved her hand in the air again. "But my dear boy, there are hundreds of millions of older women."

Drayco closed the piano fallboard and leaned on it. "When I considered all the various players in this drama, the whole scheme felt disjointed. It didn't seem likely Ezra and Connie Burdell, or even her brother, could have planned most of this."

"Scott, I have absolutely no idea what you're talking about. But it does make for a very entertaining plot, doesn't it? As you say, quite operatic."

"In a way, it is, like the puppet master in Chinese opera. It made more sense if someone was coordinating everything. Pulling the strings."

She stared at him. "Are you saying that person is me?"

"You were the central node of connection. Alec Van Sandt told Johnny Burdell about the diamond and his coded puzzles. Burdell told his sister, who in turn told her lover, Ezra Layton. And then Layton spilled the beans to his other lover, who happens to be his childhood friend's much-older sister. You."

This time, she was the one who applauded. "Such a grand story. You might write it down in a book. But it's totally implausible, you know. As if I'd be involved with a deadly treasure hunt."

Drayco gave her a small smile. "Funny thing, that. I never told you what the treasure was. But when we arrived, you asked me if I'd found the diamond. Even more specifically, a rare yellow diamond."

"I just guessed, that's all. What else would it be?"

"Something else funny, too. Ezra taped some of your phone conversations with him. I'm guessing it was a type of potential blackmail. Or safety net. Connie Burdell found those files and kept them, and they're now safely in the hands of the police."

Brock piped up from where he was still holding the Queen of the Night photo and parroted her own words. "That's horrible. To kill your own brother that way."

"The police have tapes?" Aria walked over to the sofa and sank onto the pillows. She grabbed one of them and picked at the fringe, twisting it around her fingers. "Then you should know that killing Graham wasn't my idea. I didn't know they were going to do it. It's something Ezra and Connie planned together."

Drayco asked, "Made easier because they'd already done it once? To Alec Van Sandt?"

She stopped playing with the pillow fringe and tossed the pillow aside. With her chin jutting out, she looked him directly in the eye. "I think I told you Graham and I always had a fractious relationship. He could be scary and threatening. But even so, his death was ... regrettable."

"And was Johnny Burdell's death regrettable, too?"

She sucked in air between her teeth. "He was going to go to the police—to you—and blab about everything."

"How did you get Ezra Layton to agree to your plans to have him find the diamond and steal it for you? Didn't you worry he'd take the treasure for himself?"

"I told him I'd pay him good money for it. I could sell it under the table due to my connections, but he couldn't. You can't simply go out and shop those around. You have to know the right people who will do it behind the scenes."

"A lot of blood's been spilled over that diamond."

At the mention of the diamond, her eyes took on shimmering glints of their own. "Did you bring it? I'd love to see it. Just once."

The sound of car doors slamming in the front driveway caught their attention, and Brock looked out the window. "Looks like the police are here. And so is Sarg. Did you ask him to come along?"

Drayco shook his head. "But this case has international implications. Maybe the police decided they had to drag in the Bureau."

Brock let the officers through the door and nodded over at Aria, who stood up and meekly allowed them to escort her to a waiting squad car. But right before she disappeared, she turned around with a wistful look toward Drayco. "I suppose this means you won't be naming your opera house after me."

Drayco replied, "I haven't decided on a name yet."

Her face bloomed into a smile, and she left with the officers. Brock said, "You aren't really going to . . . ."

"Who knows? Right now, I'm thinking of just calling the thing Generic Opera House."

Sarg bounded into the room, taking a moment to appraise Brock. "You look pretty good for an almost-dead man."

Brock grinned and pointed with his good arm at Drayco. "Helps to have a quick-thinking son."

Sarg barked out some commands to a couple of agents about combing through the house, and what to look for, then he turned back to Drayco. "An opera singer as a killer. Didn't see that one coming."

Drayco grimaced. "Technically, not a killer, since she just oversaw the whole thing. The irony is she did all of this to get her hands on a bunch of money so she could be remembered as she thought she deserved."

Sarg chuckled. "She'll be remembered, all right. For something else entirely."

"'Der Hölle Rache kocht in meinem Herzen.'" Drayco hopped up from the piano bench.

"What's that?"

Brock explained, "It's the 'Queen of the Night' aria for which our diva Aria was well known. 'Hell's vengeance boils in my heart.'"

Drayco added, "That was another clue. Ezra Layton wrote in his suicide note the words, 'Death and despair blaze about me.' That's the second line from that same song. Why would he have included that particular reference? It didn't make any sense, especially after he told me he hated opera. Unless he couldn't bring himself to point the finger at Aria directly."

Sarg said, "A sort of subconscious confession?"

"Perhaps. He knew police would find a money trail from Aria to him, his so-called inheritance. The walls were closing in, and he was adamant about not wanting to go back to prison."

"That's really mucked up, from every angle." Sarg tilted his head at Drayco. "But speaking of music and confessionals, you didn't tell me how your audition went, junior."

Drayco sighed. "Not well."

Brock finally put down the photos of Aria and patted Drayco's arm. "You can try again."

"I don't think so. We worked out a compromise instead."

"What kind of compromise?"

"To have students in the music school play some of my compositions."

Brock and Sarg said in unison, "You're a composer?"

Drayco winced. "I've been dabbling."

Brock brightened. "Well, I'll be. You gotta let me know the dates, and I'll clear my calendar."

Drayco could only stare at him. All those years of Brock being AWOL during Drayco's concerts, and all the times Drayco peered out into the audience hoping to see Brock or Drayco's mother—but all he saw were empty front-row seats reserved for family. Yet Brock wanted to come now?

Sarg said, "Let me know, too." And then he tugged on his ear. "So, what's the final story about that diamond?"

Drayco chewed on his lip and stayed silent. Brock gave him a sideways glance and said, "It's too bad the diamond probably fell into the ocean along with a chunk of the house, right?"

Drayco just uttered, "Hmm." He looked around the room again, taking in the collected memorabilia of a lifetime of performing. "I'm not sure Aria planned on this being her final act."

Sarg asked, "Insanity, perhaps? Dementia?"

"More like she lives in a fantasyland of her past. She wanted to cement her legacy out of jealousy over how others got more love and accolades than she did."

Sarg tugged on his earlobe. "I've got my money on psychopathy. There's heaps of that going around in this case of yours. She kills her brother, and that Burdell woman does the same to her brother. And the second-rate Bonnie and Clyde mow down that resort owner just because he caught them breaking into his house."

Drayco replied, "After Detective Halabi questioned Connie Burdell, he called her one of the coldest, most calculating criminals he'd ever seen—no sense of morals or ethics whatsoever."

Sarg grimaced. "Like I said, psychopathy." He looked from Brock to Drayco and added, "Guess it's good that cursed diamond was lost. It's caused enough bloodshed."

48

Tuesday, December 14

Sometimes, having darkness fall earlier in the day wasn't such a bad thing. Due to the encroaching dark and the thermometer dipping down below the freezing point, there were few people around the East Potomac Park at Hains Point. Drayco leaned against his car, looking out over the grayish-green water of the Potomac River.

Soon, another car pulled up near his, the only two cars at the little park. Even in the dim light from the crescent moon, Alistair Brisbane looked very much the part of a gentleman kingpin as he exited the car to stand beside Drayco.

He said, "I was a little surprised to get your call. As I understand it, your case has reached a resolution."

"You could call it that."

"Yet, you don't sound pleased."

"Why should I be? Three senseless murders over a shiny little rock. And a woman who was once a leading figure in the music world will spend the rest of her life in a dingy little cell."

"Oh, I don't know about the latter part. A good attorney could get her committed to an institution. An incompetency defense."

Drayco uttered a humorless chuckle. "And five years from now, she'll be rehabilitating her career by going on the chat circuit."

Alistair looked up at the moon, shining brightly with no obscuring clouds. "Nice night."

"A good night for a few answers."

"From me, I take it. I suppose I owe you that."

"Did you help Graham Tibbs disappear when he learned about Alec Van Sandt's murder and the treasure?"

"He wasn't involved in Van Sandt's death. But when he found out his friend was, he felt he'd get sucked into the heist plot. He told me he'd rather die than go to prison again."

"I guess he got his wish, in a way."

"And I am beyond furious that Graham's friend was the one who killed him. It's probably a good thing the man is dead."

Drayco glanced over at Alistair, noting his tight jaw. Maybe Ezra Layton's demise was going to happen one way or another, all things being equal. Drayco asked, "Since you knew Layton was involved in Van Sandt's death and the treasure hunt, why didn't you do anything about him then?"

"I investigated Layton. But after searches of Van Sandt's properties by my associates, there were no signs of the diamond. Still, I kept an eye on Layton. And also on you, when you got close to him."

"Have you done a little tailing recently? In a black car with tinted windows and an untraceable temp tag?"

"I like to protect my investments."

"And I'm one of your investments, now, am I?"

Alistair chuckled. "You definitely have a great deal of worth. I knew I was kidnapping the right person."

"It was Graham who broke into the home of Van Sandt's daughter and stole the treasure puzzle and a recording with 'Twinkle, Twinkle' on it, wasn't it?"

"Yes, and I am sick to death of that damn song. Graham played it all the time. And I'm a fan of big band music, too." He paused and then added, "I've still got that LP of his. Want it?"

Drayco surprised himself by saying, "Yes. Yes, I would." If nothing else, he could return it to Van Sandt's daughter.

The fact Alistair liked big band music was one of the first personal details Drayco ever got out of his uncle. It humanized him a little bit. Drayco reached into his pocket and pulled out a tiny box he handed over.

Alistair stared at him for a moment and then took the box. He flipped it open and raised an eyebrow as he noted what was inside. "I'm surprised you didn't take this to the police. Or the FBI."

"I learned my lesson with the rare Chopin manuscript and its jewel-encrusted case found inside my opera house. Both are still tied up in legal maneuvering."

Alistair nodded. "You're correct it would be a long time before this was returned to my friend. That is, if you'd gone through normal channels. And my friend is elderly and could die before he ever sees it again."

"If any law enforcement types find out about this, I can kiss my career goodbye."

"You haven't told anyone else about this? Not even your father or Agent Sargosian?"

Drayco shook his head. "You're the first. I didn't want to implicate them as accessories if it comes to that."

"This means you trust me to return the diamond to its rightful owner. And ultimately the museum where it's headed?"

"I don't know about the trust part. But let's just say I'll be watching to read about the diamond's sudden discovery and the announcement of the museum's new exhibition."

That elicited a full-blown chuckle from the other man. "I would expect no less."

"One thing's been bothering me. Did you already know the solution to the puzzle, with the latitude and longitude coordinates, when you had me kidnapped?"

"I did not."

"But you searched Van Sandt's house and resort."

"My associates checked into those properties, yes. But it was years ago right after the man's death. They found nothing, of course. Except for Graham's theft of the puzzle from Van Sandt's daughter's house."

"Well, someone broke into the resort recently, so that must have been Ezra Layton and Connie Burdell."

"That seems logical."

"So, you kidnapped me not only to decipher the puzzle but because you knew I wouldn't let the whole thing go—and would help you find the diamond?"

"Of course. You are obsessive, loyal, smart, and talented. Speaking of which, I never heard how the scholarship recital audition went. I called them, but they said to speak to you first."

Drayco rubbed his arm. "Let's just say it didn't go according to plan. The committee and I have arranged for scholarship students to play a few of my compositions instead."

Alistair's eyes widened at Drayco's words. "Your compositions? I had no idea. I'm doubly impressed. I'd be more than happy to provide the funds to have them published."

"Thanks, but I'll hold off on that. For now."

Alistair pocketed the diamond with a small sigh. "The roads we choose. How differently things could have been for you, for me, for us, if only . . . " He paused for a moment, looking at the Potomac. "I have a feeling I know why you picked this spot for our meeting. This is where you dove into the water to save your mother. I can imagine her pride at learning you're a composer now."

As he turned to walk back to his car, Alistair patted Drayco on the shoulder and said quietly, "She loves you, you know."

As Alistair cranked up his car engine and pulled away, the man's wording hit Drayco with full force. He'd used the present tense, not the past. So was Drayco's mother still alive, after all?

He barely had time to contemplate that when another, more familiar car slid into the same parking space Alistair had vacated. Brock motioned to his son, who climbed into the passenger seat and said, "This is a huge coincidence. Not."

"I had an inkling you might pull something like this. After what Alistair did to you with the kidnapping, I don't trust him as far as I can throw him. So I admit it. I followed you."

For some reason, Drayco didn't feel irritated this time. In fact, he was touched by the gesture. "Well, I doubt I'll be seeing Alistair again. For a long while."

"It's just a good thing I got stopped by a couple of red lights and an ambulance, or I would have got here in time to punch Alistair's smug face."

"If you lost my trail, how did you know where I was headed?"

"I had a hunch."

Drayco retrieved an object out of the pocket of his coat and handed it over to Brock. His father took the unlabeled DVD as Drayco explained, "Alistair gave it to me."

Brock asked, "Related to the case?"

"At first, I thought it might be. He said he pulled some strings to get it. Take a look."

Brock manipulated the overhead flip-down video system and put the DVD into the player. A tall young man walked out onto a wide stage in front of an orchestra and bowed as the audience began applauding, then sat down at the waiting piano and began to play.

Brock watched, mesmerized. When the piece ended, he paused the DVD. "When was that taken? You can't be more than sixteen."

"Fifteen, actually. It was with the Philadelphia Orchestra. A pirated video someone made."

Brock's voice had a slight hitch as he replied, "God, I'm sorry I never made it to most of those. You were a damned fine pianist."

Not wanting to talk about it further, Drayco changed the subject. "One little gemstone started this whole case. One little rock associated with so many failed legacies and dreams."

"Too bad about that diamond. Guess we'll never know what happened to it," Brock looked over at his son out of the corner of his eye.

"Oh, I don't know. These things have a funny way of turning up."

"Well, if it's ever found and magically appears in that Uzbekistan museum, we'll see if it can finally break the cycle of curses."

"*Magically* appears?"

"If you can call airplane travel and intermediaries magical, then yes."

Drayco stuck his fingers in his ears. "La la la la la." He removed them to add, "I didn't hear any of that."

Brock laughed. "How old are you, seven?"

"Going on eight, I think." Drayco looked up at the night sky through the car window. "Twinkle, twinkle, little star, how I wonder what you are . . ."

"Up above the world so high, like a diamond in the sky?"

"Graham Tibbs isn't around for me to ask, but I suppose we can guess the story behind his obsession with the nursery tune."

"And maybe yours?"

Drayco smiled briefly. "Maybe." But was it the diamond connection that made Graham obsessed with the song? Or the fact the song was tied to his dead mother?

Drayco popped out the DVD and pocketed it again. "I have to wonder if Aria D'Angelo broke that glass piece from Ezra Layton on purpose. In retrospect, the octahedron inside looked an awful lot like a diamond. Perhaps a little joke between them."

"Could be, could be. What a pair."

Drayco turned to look at the back seat of Brock's car. "No Joyelle?"

"She was busy tonight. The gallery opening is tomorrow evening."

"Oh, lord, I'd forgotten about that."

"You are coming, aren't you?"

"I don't know. Has she—and you—forgiven me for doubting her integrity?"

"She was in the business. She understands what it means to have to question everything and everyone. Even if you love them."

"Guess I could give it a try."

"Several people you know will be there. Benny and Lailani Baskin, Mark and Elaine Sargosian, Nelia Tyler."

Drayco sighed inwardly. Sarg had phoned him earlier to relay that Nelia had once again called *him* to see how Drayco and his father were doing. At least she still cared to some degree.

Brock reached down to pick up a small rock from the cup holder, explaining, "Found this in the driveway as I was leaving," and he turned it over in his hand. "It's funny what humans consider valuable. Not this rock, of course. But another rock, made of clear carbon."

"And even stranger what lengths humans will go to possess those little rocks."

Brock opened his window and tossed the rock outside. "All I know is I have something very valuable right here," and he pointed at Drayco. "Who else can I count on to be crazy enough to throw himself over a cliff to save my sorry ass?"

Drayco grinned. "Guess this means you're buying dinner."

"I could buy you dinner every night for the rest of our lives, and it wouldn't be payment enough. But sure, let's go get some nice, juicy steak. With a heaping order of humble pie for dessert."

Brock pointed over at Drayco's car. "You'll follow me?"

Drayco paused, then said, "I always have, Dad. I always have."

Lightning Source UK Ltd.
Milton Keynes UK
UKHW011843180722
406042UK00009B/395/J

9 781951 752118